# The Trident and the Book

Vic Broquard

Broquard eBooks

# The Trident Series Volume 1 The Trident and the Book

Vic Broquard

For Morgan and L. Ron Hubbard

# Table of Contents

Maps
Chapter 1 The Gift
Chapter 2 Stilmar Pond
Chapter 3 Hail, The Savior
Chapter 4 Mandy Blackthorn
Chapter 5 Alison d'Ambrose
Chapter 6 Rothwood Castle
Chapter 7 The Rescue
Chapter 8 Lady Ursla of HollybineWood
Chapter 9 Trapped
Chapter 10 Darless
Chapter 11 Zaire
Chapter 12 Caleb Durward and Dispater
Chapter 13 Lady Ursla's Challenge
Chapter 14 The Theos Tree
Chapter 15 Such a Deal
Chapter 16 Morrigan
Chapter 17 Farewells

# Maps

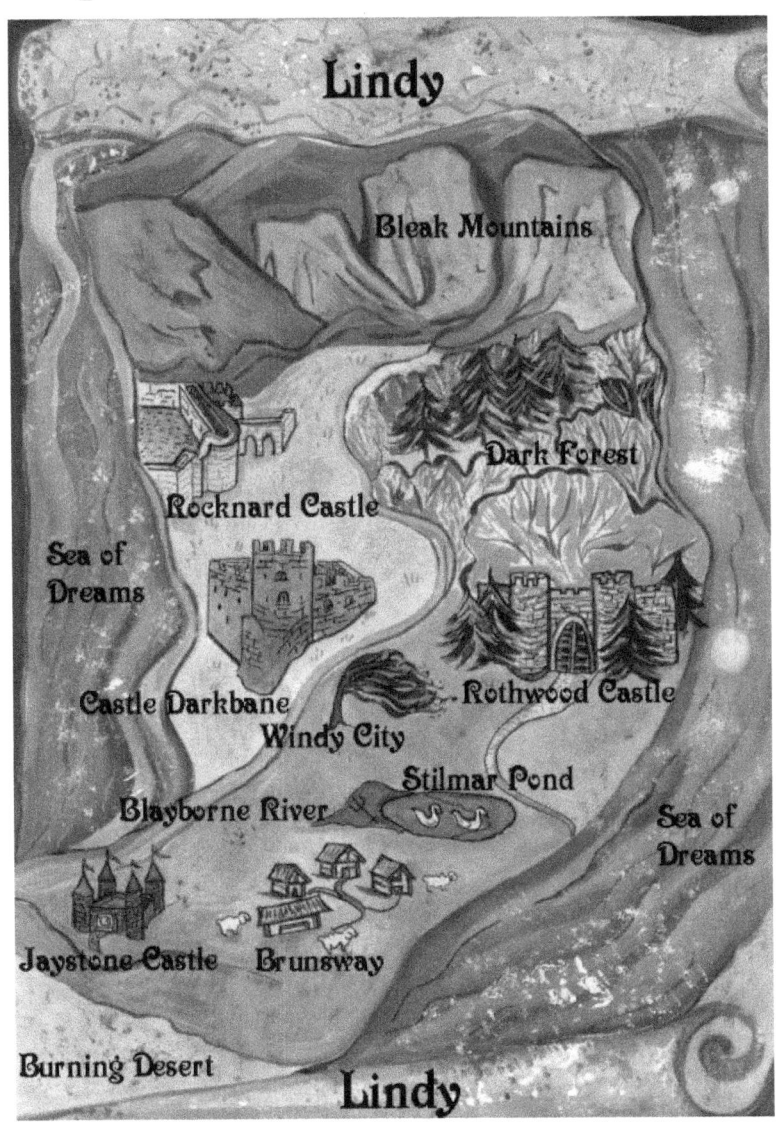

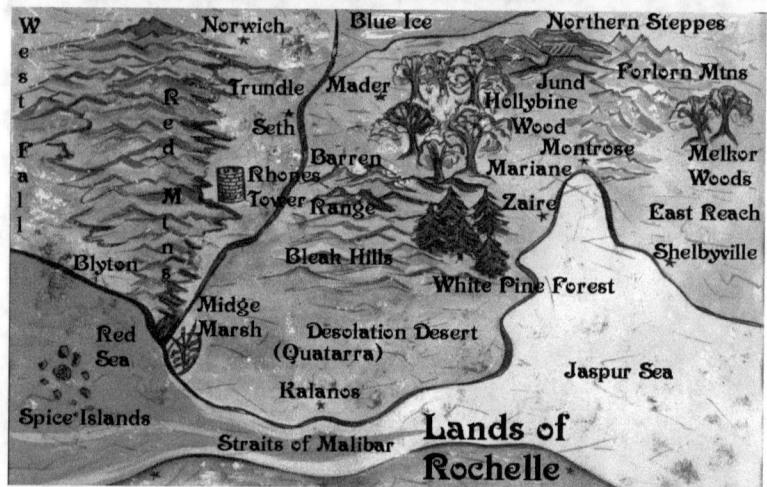

# Chapter 1 The Gift

It was midnight. Jon dragged his tired body up the creaking, wooden steps beside the "hot house" on Green Street. His apartment was directly above the student Laundromat, a noisy place that never failed to add to the humid heat when summer came. The steady drone of the dryers rumbled in his ears as he unlocked the door, stumbled inside, and plopped wearily onto his bed. The semester was almost over. It was early May. Soon now he would graduate and then face tense rounds of auditions for a position as a symphonic flutist. Jon knew he could not begin his career as a soloist because it would not pay his bills. "

Jon had just returned from his third job of the day. After his morning music classes, he washed dishes at Mel's Place for his meals. Afternoons, he was a mail sorter at the college dorms, and nights, he worked as a janitor at Uni-High. The last two jobs were university sanctioned; the first, illegal for a full-time student. "What the Administration doesn't know, they're not likely to find out," was his view. Grandpa was always saying that he would be a better person by working his way through school. Yet the old man had always helped Jon out. However, during these last two years Grandpa's aid had slowly dwindled along with his health. Now he was gone.

Nearly numb, Jon rolled over and carefully removed the telegram from his pocket and read it for the fourth time.

Jon.

Your Grandfather passed away yesterday. The Home

has made the arrangements. Funeral at 10:00 on Thursday. Johnnas Brown was loved by us all. He was such a kindly man.

Mabel Bronx.

And the suppressed tears came.

At ten o'clock the next morning, the Swallow Lines bus pulled into Peoria. Jon took a deep breath, shouldered his rucksack, and stepped off and hailed a taxi to the funeral parlor. Services had already begun; he entered inconspicuously. Though the room was nearly empty, Jon recognized Mabel and a half dozen others from the old folk's home. He took a seat and stared at the black coffin. The lid was still open and Jon saw the pale pallor of his grandfather. Somewhere an organ played while the minister's monotone voice talked of heaven's gate. Jon was not really listening.

Grandpa! Oh Grandpa. Why didn't you tell me — call or something? I knew you were not doing so well. The cough was getting worse. But as bad as this? I love you. Can you hear me? No. Get it together, man. He's dead. But I didn't know he was that ill! Maybe I should have visited him more. No. Remember — he said "Do your school work first that's the truly important thing. Visit me only when you can. Send me a tape of your big recital." Yes, he wanted it this way. As soon as the service was over, Jon went up to the coffin.

"Goodbye Grandpa. Thank you for all you have done. I hope you have found happiness." He turned away, restraining tears.

Mabel hailed him. "Jon — I'm so sorry. He was such a nice man!"

"Mabel, thanks for telling me. How did he —" Jon faltered.

"In his sleep, we think. He was found in his easy chair with *that* book in his lap. His last view must have been of the swans on the lake."

*Yes, that figures. It was his favorite.* "Yes, Mabel, he always loved those birds."

"You are all alone, now, aren't you, Jon?"

He mumbled a yes.

"Well, when it's all over, why don't you come by the home? We can talk — if you like."

Several hours later, Jon left the attorney's office. Since there was no next of kin, save Jon, the will was simple. Jon got everything. Five hundred dollars remained after the burial fees, along with a few meager possessions at the home and whatever was in the safe deposit box at the Commercial Bank. So with a sigh, Jon headed to the Brethren's Old Folks Home, where his sole relative had lived for the last four years. His young parents just starting out in life had died somewhat mysteriously in a car crash when he was just barely old enough to remember them — or so he was told by his Grandpa. From that ill-fated day onward, his Grandpa raised him. He had no sisters or brothers or, now, any other relatives that he knew of. He was a "loner." However, he was used to this — especially since he'd gone off to the university at the same time that Grandpa had moved into the home.

Perhaps the most miserable time of the entire rotten day was spent cleaning out his grandfather's possessions from the room in the home. Jon donated his grandfather's clothes to several elderly men there at the home. Mechanically, he went through the other odds and ends, discarding almost everything except a family scrapbook, the bank safe deposit key, and the picture book. The smell of the home's sterile air combined with the stench of decaying flesh was more than he could bear at this time. He hurried as fast as he could. In less than a half hour, Jon was saying good byes to Mabel and the others, promising to come for a visit later when he had recovered. It was a promise he would never keep.

At last with fresh air in his lungs, he headed downtown to retrieve whatever was in the bank vault. *I wonder what's in the locker. The picture book was his most prized possession. He had no money.* His curiosity grew as he was led to the vault, he did not hear the mumbled condolences. When he was left alone, he hastily inserted the key. *A shoe box and a letter — hum — to me. He sure has that box tied shut. Boy, it's heavy! I'll stick it in the sack, before anyone gets curious.* He sighed and looked about the tiny room. Steel walls enclosed him just like Grandpa's coffin. Shivering, he suppressed any further actions. He hastily left, muttering a "thanks" to the attendant.

Pale and shaking slightly, Jon went back to the bus station to catch the last bus for Champaign. The short wait for the bus went quickly as Jon sat staring into space, numb and feeling very much alone. Once on the bus, he took his usual seat in the very rear. Just as soon as the bus rolled out of the station, Jon opened the letter. It was the strangest message he had ever had from Grandpa!

*Dear Jon,*

*I am gone. But not gone really . . . Remember the yellow fields, pond, and the swans. Come here first, if you are able. The box will help or the box will hinder — I know not which. I love you, but the body is just too old.*

*Grandpa*

I had better ignore the box until I get home. Sounds like he went a bit senile or something. Like he knew he was going to die — but he writes like he isn't — or wouldn't be — if he were. Oh Grandpa! Why didn't you call? Suppressed tears began to flow. He let them come as the bus rolled the weary miles.

It was dark and midnight, when Jon finally stumbled up the stairs — home at last! He collapsed onto the bed. No thoughts came; no thoughts were wanted. At last he jerked. *What was that?* He listened and realized the world was now silent. The laundry below his room was closed. It was 2:00 a.m. He rose and fixed some tea and a snack. Then he examined the shoebox. He untied it carefully. *Good God!* It contained twenty thousand dollars in bills along with about a hundred thousand in stocks and ten pounds of strange gold coins! *Oh, Grandpa!* And he cried.

Friday morning he spent playing some mournful scales, pondering his loss. He cut classes. He couldn't face anyone yet. Later that day, he began to worry about being robbed. Wiping his eyes, he resolved to face the banks. He opened accounts and safety deposit boxes in three different banks. At noon, he cut work as well, no appetite. In the early afternoon, it began to rain, but he went home satisfied.

Now, he had time to study that weird letter. He reread Grandpa's cryptic letter several times. Next, he examined the leather bound picture book.

Jon knew that this book was his Grandpa's most prized possession. But it was a strange book. *Grandpa never showed it to anyone but me. He always said it was his special secret. Let's see — it was on my tenth birthday that he actually let me look at it. "My special book. None like it anywhere!" he'd said then. I could only glance at it at the time.* The cover was just as he'd remembered — a plain brown leather cover with no writing on it — except for the huge embossed trident that seemed burned into the leather. The trident looked like a three-pronged pitchfork. However, the middle prong was slightly longer than the outer two. Near the long staff's bottom was a crossbar, rather like an upside-down cross. His fingers traced the engraved pattern. *Yes, it is real leather. Strange book.*

The book had no title. Grandpa had always referred to it as the "book" and had kept it hidden from curious eyes. Jon remembered that he had seldom actually seen Grandpa looking through it. On the other hand, he recalled that he had often found his grandfather sitting in his rocking chair staring off into space with the closed book in his lap. That his grandfather had spent much time with the book, Jon was certain. Carefully, he opened the leather book. All those special times when his grandfather had permitted him to look through the book flooded into his mind. Those were such happy times. But now, Grandpa was gone forever. Tears came again.

Later, Jon began to study the book once more. It had no title page and no writing of any kind in it anywhere. Perhaps it was just a picture book after all. The pages were ordinary, except they seemed very thick. On one side only, there was a color picture. Each was unique. *Perhaps they're watercolors. No, they do not look quite like that. Maybe oil paintings? No, not exactly that either. They are just so REAL looking to be a painting. More like color photos. But not quite that either.* He leafed through the pages. There were maybe fifty pages. *I never noticed that before! The last quarter of the book is blank! Curious.*

*Ah. Here is my favorite.* He stared at the rustic setting of a castle. A beautiful yellow flowered meadow with tall pines growing on either side greeted his eyes. Hills of yellow buttercups rolled higher and higher. Perched on the highest hill in the background was an old, gray stone castle. Two towers were connected by a wall with a battlement. Some taller stone buildings were just barely visible inside. *Rothwood Castle* — he suddenly remembered Grandpa telling him. For a while, Jon was lost in memories of the times his grandfather had told him great stories about Rothwood Castle.

A large flash of lightning and a resounding thunderclap brought him out of his reverie. He laid the book down and went to make some Earl Grey tea. As he came back with a steaming cup, he remembered Grandpa's cryptic letter and its message. Hastily, he flipped through the pages of the leather bound book. "There it is," he exclaimed. "This one was Grandpa's favorite." Gently rolling hills full of blooming yellow buttercups flowed down to a clear, calm, blue pond, which delicately reflected the low hills. Two swans came gliding gracefully across the pond. The smooth surface of the lake was cut by the v-shaped wake left by the swans. The sharply defined edges of the wake grew larger and larger until, at last, all traces of the birds' passing blended into the mirror surface once more. A large boulder lay on the near bank. *The picture looks so real! I think I could reach out and touch the water. I can see why he liked it so much. It is so different from our Illinois cornfields.*

With a sigh, he put the book down and stared out the window into the rain for a time. Then he picked up his flute and began to play or rather to improvise. Ever so soft and low, the melody began — sad and mournful. Slowly he picked up the tempo in an attempt to ease his grief. Louder and higher and brighter the sounds moved. It crescendoed in a flurry of fast, high notes. Then the tempo slowed and the pitch lowered. He ended in a low, melancholy mode. Grief returned. The last notes trailed into nothingness.

After buying supper at a fast food restaurant — he couldn't face Mel's Place just yet — Jon reread Grandpa's last message to him once more. What did he mean? "Come here first — to the pond of swans." Once more he studied the page in the book. *I'm here staring at it. Yes, the box will help me through school — that's for sure. Perhaps I can now afford grad school. But the "come here" means to really arrive somewhere. I don't know where this place is or what it's called. Or even what country it's in. I've got money now — so I could travel there. But where is this place? I suppose I could look through books in the library for a clue. But I'd better not show anyone the book. Wait! The swans! They have moved! I'd swear they were only half way across the pond earlier. Now they are almost to the other side! That's impossible!*

Jon, now very carefully, examined every inch of the picture. Definitely the swans had moved, but so had the shadows. It was as if some time had passed in the picture! Then, Jon noticed another peculiarity: a small trident was carved into the boulder at the pond's edge. Curious, he looked carefully at other pictures. There was a trident in each, usually on some foreground object.

The bell in Altgeld Hall struck eight p.m. Jon paced the room. "That cannot be! Pictures don't move. It's spooky — that's what it is." *Come on, Jon, get a hold of yourself. The swans didn't move. It's your imagination. Maybe I'm just tired. Stress and all. Why don't I just watch them for a while? That'll prove they don't move.* He sat down in his old stuffed armchair, opened the book to the swans, and watched. After a time with nothing happening, Jon got up and went for his flute. "I might as well practice, instead of wasting all this time," he proclaimed. So he practiced his recital pieces while keeping an eye on the swans.

After an hour or so, he stopped playing and studied the picture once more. Jon swallowed hard. The swans had definitely moved further to the shore. Their motion was very slow compared to his time, but they were moving. He stared at the picture even more. *It is just **so** real. I can almost see the grasses and flowers moving in the soft breeze. I can feel the balmy temperature of the day. The smells — ah those flowers!* He inhaled deeply as though he could smell the yellow buttercups. And he smelled them! Now he was aware of having just the four corners of the picture in his vision as if they were the only points from which his view of the universe was anchored. The picture was so real. His room melted away.

A gentle honking sound touched his ears. The fragrance became nearly overpowering. The swans were really moving now. They flowed in a graceful arc toward him. Jon seemed to be sitting in the field of yellow flowers. The balmy breeze brushed his hair. His senses felt totally alive. Soon a swan came honking out of the water, up the bank toward him, water dripping from its bottom. It waddled up close and looked at the intruder. Jon reached out. He found that he could actually pet the swan. It seemed very tame. Jon thought but did not speak. *You are beautiful.* In his mind, he sensed a reply.

"Yes, I know. Did you bring any crackers for me?"

Jon jerked and thought, *Why, no. I didn't think of that. This, this cannot be! I must be dreaming. I am in my chair. I have got my flute here.* With what felt like a monumental effort, Jon struggled to make his body rise from the chair that he knew he had to be sitting in.

As he did, the realness of the scene before him diminished. His attention picked up the corners of his room instead of the corners of the picture. He saw very vividly the trident carved into the large boulder by the pond. For a brief instant, Jon seemed disorientated, but then, the room seemed to solidify. Jon found himself standing up in front of his chair with his flute in one hand.

*What happened to me? It's like I went into the picture! I'm flipping out! I got to get out of here.* He grabbed a jacket and umbrella and quickly headed out and down the steps. Outside, the sun was shining brightly. Jon did not notice it for several minutes. He just walked.

He looked at trees, cars, people, buildings, and sidewalks. He thought nothing for a few desperate minutes. Suddenly, he realized that it was now daytime! He stumbled and nearly fell! He took a deep breath and looked at his watch. It was nearly noon on Saturday! He had lost fifteen hours.

After hard pacing the next four blocks, his grasp on reality returned and he headed home. He knew something strange had happened. Of that he was absolutely certain. The significance of it eluded him. It had to be the book, and what had or was happening just could not occur. But it had — or had it?

*Enough of all this. I'm hungry — better head to Mel's and wash some dishes and eat. Why? I can buy anything I want to, now. No — I agreed to this job. Besides, if I don't show up, one of the other guys will just have to do my work.* Mel ran several rooming houses for students. He had some fifty men at one place and some twenty women at another. Jon worked at the men's place.

As Jon entered the back door into the kitchen, the heavy smell of greasy fried chicken assaulted his nose. "Hi, Jon. Where you been?" called out one of the pot washers named Red.

As usual, there was a lot of confusion around, and Jon merely gestured. He helped himself to lunch and headed downstairs to eat. Several others were just finishing up, and greeted him. "Well, long time no see. Where have you been? I got stuck doing your job yesterday."

Jon replied in as level a tone as he could muster, "My grandfather died — went to his funeral."

The ribbing stopped at once. His friend, Harry, offered condolences and said, "Why are you here now? He was your only relative wasn't he? You should ask Mel for some time off."

"No," drawled Jon, "Work is the best thing for me now."

"You're right. But if there is anything I can do, let me know. I'll stop by tonight." The others went back upstairs to work, leaving Jon alone.

Jon was nearly done when he heard the heavy footsteps of Mel coming down. "Hey, sorry about your grandfather, Jon. Harry just told me about it. I thought you were just goofing off or something. Say, if you want some time off, I think I can get someone to fill in for you?"

"Thanks, but I think I'd rather work now, Mel. I'm sorry I didn't tell you — I found out late Wednesday night — left before anyone was up. Just now, I'd like to work, but if I want some time off, I'll let you know."

As Jon got up to go, Mel laid his heavy hand on his shoulder, "Hang in there guy."

"Yeah, ok."

Mel was just trying to be friendly. As usual, he could not quite find the right words. Mel always tried hard to be "one of the guys." He always fell short. As Jon went up the steps, a thought hit him in a flash — *Mel's very insecure.* In an instant of clear seeing, Jon had a total understanding of Mel and his actions. As he washed dishes, Jon pondered his bit of newfound wisdom. It fit Mel completely. He had a wife who had married him for his money, and she made no secret of the fact. Mel just had to talk to everyone — the topic did not matter. However, after the conversation, one could never remember anything significant about it. *Mel has to be friendly. He needs others to constantly give him the right to survive.*

The afternoon drifted by as Jon did all the little things he had ignored the past few days: doing the laundry, sweeping the floor, making the bed, and so on. After supper, Harry, his philosopher-to-be friend, stopped by to visit. (Jon had only two close friends. Harry was one; the other was Nick, an engineering student.) Redheaded Harry always wore sweaters, even in the summer. He smoked a pipe nearly continuously and always had words of wisdom for Jon. At one time, they shared an apartment, and now they still met frequently to discuss recent events. On the other hand, Nick was an old high school buddy. Just now Jon felt like talking and he related the events in Peoria. Finally, Jon carefully told Harry about his newfound wealth.

Harry concurred that his banking actions were for the best. He advised, "Now that you're rich, don't stop working. It'll do no good if you are idle. The rich have money, and they're not happy. Just look at Mel! Give up that janitor job. You will have reasonable hours then."

"Probably, you are right. I thought I'd keep on working at Mel's — that way I don't have to worry about food and all. But I do not want to sort letters or clean any more toilets! The university can give someone else that janitor job, even if it's only for a few weeks."

"You are altruistic."

"What's that?"

"Forget it. Hey, can I see that book your grandfather left you?"

Jon tensed briefly, but then relaxed and brought it out. "What do you make of this?" inquired Jon, perplexed.

Harry examined it carefully and replied. "Boy, this sure is a strange one. It's not a normal publishing job. The paper is specially made, probably by hand. See how uneven the thickness is. I cannot tell how old it is. The pages are not brittle. Looks like oils. Maybe it's someone's sketchbook. There is room for expansion; one-quarter is blank."

"Yeah, I know. But what about the pictures?"

"Well, they are neat looking."

"Have you ever seen any of these places before?"

Harry looked at each and replied slowly, "No, and I don't even recognize any of the locales. I used to study geography when I was a kid. Mom took me everywhere. However, none of these is even remotely familiar."

"What's the significance of a trident anyway?" inquired Jon.

Harry launched into his philosophic mode. "The word comes from the Latin meaning three-toothed. It was the spear carried by the gods of the sea, Neptune or Poseidon. On the other hand, it is said that devils carry tridents." Harry talked on for ten minutes but Jon lost interest.

"Say Harry, can this be some kind of magical book or have some magical properties?"

"Not likely. There isn't any real magic, you know. It's all just 'hand is faster than the eye' — illusion — the appearance of reality."

"But what if it were really magic? You know, having some force fields or whatever?"

Harry pondered this one for a moment and replied, "Well, you could test it for electric fields or magnetic fields — that sort of thing. Nick's an engineer. I'll bet he could test it for you."

"Now that's an idea," mused Jon thoughtfully.

"Hey, let's go get a beer," proposed Harry.

"Yeah, my treat," exclaimed Jon.

"You're on, millionaire." The two left and headed for the Thunderbird.

It was Sunday afternoon before Jon found himself preparing for what he knew he had to do. He put a box of crackers in his lap along with his flute. As an afterthought, he decided to take along a picnic lunch, just in case. At last he sat down in the old easy chair, opened the book to the picture of the swans, and stared at it. Sure enough, the swans were way off to the right side of the pond where he'd always remembered them being. He waited.

# Chapter 2 Stilmar Pond

*How does this magic work? Nothing happens if I just stare at it. Patience.* Jon waited. Soon he became engrossed in the picture of the yellow flowers, the pond, and the swans. They seemed so graceful, just floating on the still waters. Now he paid no attention to the room or chair he was in. His full attention was on the swans. The corners of the picture became the points that anchored his point of view. *So graceful. So beautiful. I can almost feel their motion.*

"Did you bring the crackers?" appeared in his mind.

Somewhat startled by the suddenness of the thought that was not his, he blurted, "Yes. Yes, they're right here." To his amazement, he found himself sitting in the field of buttercups, near the bank, crackers and flute in his lap. At once, one of the swans floated toward him.

"I didn't think you'd come." Another thought appeared in his mind.

*Why? Why not?* He thought.

"Some come; few talk; fewer still feed; all go," came the mental reply.

*Are you a male? Is that your mate?* He thought.

"Of course. Cannot you see the difference?" This time, the mental thought seemed to come from the other swan. She stayed back as her mate waddled onto the shore toward Jon.

Eagerly Jon began to crumble some crackers. The majestic swan just as eagerly pecked them up. *See. It's safe. Why don't you come ashore too?* Jon thought to the other swan. Then he felt her insecurity and understood at once. She was more timid and preferred to stay back until all was verified safe. Cautiously, she joined her mate pecking the crackers. Jon beamed and felt radiant.

After they ate their fill, Jon stretched out to bask in the sun. He felt the golden warmth of the rays. *This sun is definitely much more yellow than ours. Somehow the fragrances are more real here. How can that be? Maybe I am just more aware of smells here.*

"Probably. They all say that," came an unbidden reply.

*Who are they? Do many come here?*

"Not too many like you — just fading in as you do. Most walk here."

"Some ride big horses," the other added.

Jon rolled onto his side to look at the swans. *It seems strange talking to swans.*

"Why? Don't you talk to swans where you come from?"

*Why no! I never thought I could. Or more honestly, I never tried.* He felt a little ashamed about this, but he was not sure why. At home, no one ever talked to birds, unless they were crazy. Jon did not think of himself in that way.

A bit of brown movement caught his eye. Jon spotted a squirrel sneaking up on them. *Hi, little fellow. Come on over. Have some crackers.* Jon sensed a wave of extreme timidness and then the movement of strange muscles as the creature ventured forward. The squirrel cautiously came closer. Carefully, Jon spread out some more crackers a little distance from him.

"Thank you," came a meek reply, full of curiosity. "I never met a two legger that could talk to me before."

As that image passed through his mind, Jon smiled at the novel view point — a two legger. *Where do you live, little squirrel?*

At once Jon perceived a sharp withdrawal by the squirrel. In a flash, he realized his error. *I'm sorry — that really is privileged information. You cannot just go around telling strangers where you live. They might decide to have you for dinner!* In his mind he sensed a surge of revulsion at that last, and realized he committed another breach of manners. *Sorry. I won't harm you. I am not too skilled in talking to squirrels.* The squirrel seemed not to mind and proceeded to eat the offering.

Jon laid back enjoying the powerful sensations of the world flowing through him. Then, he took up his flute and began to improvise a melody for the occasion. He tried to blend his sounds to the universe he was in. The swans listened, enjoying his playing. He felt really inspired and played with all his heart and mind.

"That was very good," the swan replied.

Then a new voice appeared in his mind. *Yes, Jon, that was good. I'm glad you came.*

"Grandpa!" cried Jon, "Oh Grandpa. Where are you? I thought you died!" Conflicting emotions swelled through Jon. *He died. I saw him buried. That's his voice — or rather what I think he sounds like.*

"Yes, I am here, Jon. Over by the boulder."

Jon stared at the weathered granite, but saw no one.

"I'm sorry to frighten and startle you so. You probably can't see me, but I'm here. My body just got too old. The cough did it in, you see, and I knew I was about to go. Not much fun sitting in a rocker all day long. It was time for me to move on. However, I wanted this one last opportunity to talk to you."

For a minute, Jon just hugged the rock and let the tears flow. "You're dead. Your soul has gone to heaven. I'm cracking up."

"No. It's all right grandson. This is a shock to you. However, it is time that you learn a bit of the truth. You see, we are not just bodies. Each of us is really a spirit who occupies and runs a body. Oh, I know that we've been taught that we are a body and that we have a nebulous soul somewhere, although preachers are not quite sure where it is. If you've been good, then your soul goes to heaven — if not, it goes to hell. But that is only modern perversion. Nearly two thousand years ago, they had it correct. Your soul is you — all that there ever is or will be. "

"Man is a composite, Jon, a composite of a body, mind and spiritual being or soul. Some spiritual beings are more powerful than others. I'm certain we've only tapped a small part of our true mental abilities! I've found that some's got it, and some's not. And some's that got it don't know they've got it. Your dad was like that — good potential, but he was afraid to use it. You've got it too. You're here. Don't be afraid to use it. For most people these days, the body is all that is real."

"My body got old, boy, too old to be useful anymore. I need a new one. Soon I must leave and follow my destiny. Yet, we may meet again. Do not be too concerned for me — I am not afraid, much." There was a tone of concern in his mental voice.

With a distinct change of tone, he echoed in Jon's mind, "But first I wanted to tell you a bit about the book."

Jon wiped his eyes. He thought he could see a grayish glow near the rock now. He wondered if that was Grandpa.

"I was not sure you'd be strong enough to come through the passage, as I call it."

Jon thought instinctively, *How?*

As if in answer, his grandfather continued, "No, I do not know how or why it works. I just used it. The more you come through, the easier it becomes. At least, it was that way for me. Where these places are I do not know. I just come. I have discovered that some of these places, though primitive by our civilization, are far advanced in the respect for human life and values." He paused.

His grandfather now seemed to grow serious, as if this was what he so desperately wanted to tell Jon. "When using the book, I have found that there are two things you need to be careful of: time and the tridents. You may have noticed that time seems to run different here. You are gone for a little while; and, when you get back, it's been a lot. Don't know what to do about that one. The other — remember always to know where the trident is — it is the only way to get back that I know about. To come, as you discovered, merely look closely at the picture. Now, to get back, you have to face the trident and sort of back out the way you got into the picture. At least that's how I always did it. Don't know if there's any other way, though."

Gathering heart, Jon asked, "How often did you come here, Grandpa?"

"Oh, lots of times. Once I helped royalty out — name of Sir Wayne Gilbold — he gave me some gems as a reward. I put them in my pockets; and, sure enough, they went home with me. Turned them into cash. You got the cash and stuff?"

"Yes, Grandpa. Thank you very much. I can easily finish college now. But I'd rather have you." More tears rolled down his face.

"Yeah, I know, but it can't be helped. I need to go soon, son. I need my life — my freedom." He paused, as if reflecting. "You are wondering why I am here and not back in Peoria? Well, long ago I decided that I will acquire my next body here — not quite sure how that is done just yet. You see, I love this place and the people. Perhaps someday you can understand my viewpoint. But enough of this. Is there anything you want to know before I leave you?"

Jon thought, restraining the tears as much as possible. "Are you going to be with mom and dad now?"

After a reflectful pause, his grandfather replied, "No, I think our paths diverged many years ago. Both your father and mother just could never accept their spiritual nature. I found that I could not help either of them. And now, I do not know where they went after that car crash."

A surge of helplessness swelled in Jon, but he knew it was Grandpa's emotion, not his. Jon struggled to put up a brave face. Jon queried, "How did you get this book? Is it really magic? Where are we? Another planet? World?"

"It must be magic, but I don't know for sure what magic really is. I know this place is called Stilmar Pond, and it's in a land called Lindy. Don't know where that is, though — never needed to know, I guess. Rothwood Castle is also in Lindy — you know, it's your favorite picture. Also, that picture with the lonely, solitary, red tower is in a land called Trundle, I've been told. But I don't think they are related at all. I never have found out what or where the other pictures are. Never had any reason."

"How did you get the book? Where did it come from? Who made it?" Jon wondered aloud.

"Well, it is a strange tale, but altogether too short for you, I think. When I was thirty, I went on a trip to the Colorado mountains. One day while I was hiking, a man wearing strange clothing staggered up to me. He looked badly mauled by beasts, blood seeping from wounds about his legs and chest. So I said, 'Are you hurt, mister? Can I help you?' He looked at me and said, 'You'll do. Take this. Guard it with your life.' In an afterthought, he added, 'Use it if you like.' Something caught his attention. He turned around; some giant, gray hounds suddenly appeared. They breathed fire at him, but missed. He yelled something at them and just faded off into thin air! The hounds did too, just as I was fixing to be scared. Well, I kept the book and used it, but he never came back. So, when my time came, I passed it onto you. May it help you."

The two fell silent. Jon could think of nothing more to ask. He just felt love for his Grandpa; his grandfather, likewise for him. Finally, his grandfather, with grief building, said, "Jon, it's time you returned. Much of your time has passed. And I must go."

Jon felt the surge of grief from his grandfather. "I love you, Grandpa. I'll miss you."

"I love you too. Think kindly of me."

"I will."

Then Jon saw that gray form float off into the sky toward the west. For a moment, he wondered what would become of his grandfather. Then he sadly picked up his gear and stood in front of the boulder and tried to remember how he had entered. Soon he could see what could only be the four corners of a picture. Then there he was sitting in his chair, his flute in his lap. Someone was pounding loudly on the door.

"Jon! Jon, you in there? Come on it's time for class!"

Instantly, he recognized the voice of Tina, a fellow flutist. "Coming," yelled Jon, instinctively. The two were in the same morning master class. They were going to perform a duet for their senior recital. Hence, for several weeks now they walked to class together, planning and discussing their upcoming recital.

Jon dreaded the recital, for it meant that he had become a musician and would graduate into the working world. He had not thought that he was ready for that. Now, thanks to his grandfather, he could afford to go to grad school.

However, Jon was startled. It must be Monday. He'd lost all the rest of Sunday and the night. He did not feel particularly tired. So he grabbed his flute and music and headed out the door.

"What took you so long? I knew you were in there. Sounded like you were crying or snoring or something. Still asleep?" inquired Tina. She was rather homely and had adopted Jon as her little brother.

*Oh — yeah, that'll do nicely.* "Yes, I overslept. Thanks for waiting. Did you have to wait long?" Jon inquired curiously. At once, he realized that he did not need to ask. He knew that she had been pounding on the door for five minutes and had become quite concerned. "Yeah, thanks for waiting." Jon added again, before Tina could reply. They rushed off toward the music hall, discussing their music.

Part way across the Quad, a huge grassy area between campus buildings, Jon noticed a girl pulling and tugging a large malamute. She obviously wanted to go north, but the dog was trying to go south. Without thinking, Jon sensed the dog's mind. *She's in heat and smells a male. Boy, that odor is really strong!* Then in a flash of insight, Jon realized that the girl did not yet know her dog was in heat — hence the frustration.

Acting on impulse, Jon mentally told the girl, "Hey, she's in heat." As they passed by, Jon saw the gleam of realization in the girl's eyes, and she stopped fighting the dog. *Curious! I'm doing it here now.*

The music lesson went well. However, halfway through, Jon saw that his professor seemed tired and edgy. Then he felt the man's overwhelming sense of frustration. At once, the cause of it popped into Jon's mind. The professor had intended to have sex with his wife last night, but hadn't and now did not realize that this was still affecting him. Jon sent into the professor's mind that complete thought of the failed intention and subsequent upset. He saw the man's eyes suddenly light up; the professor smiled to himself as he recognized what it was that was still bothering him. Jon was fascinated to see his teacher's tiredness disappear at once as if it had never been.

Later, during lunch at Mel's, Jon discovered that he could very easily read minds. While running the dishwasher, he listened to the other workers' thoughts. He found that actually he had to be careful not to know what the others were thinking. The ability was now almost second nature! *What is happening to me?*

He left Mel's pondering the larger question. *I can read minds — others' thoughts, but is it ethical to do so?* To Jon, this was a vital question. *No more mind reading until I sort this out!* Was it prying? Was it an invasion of privacy? These seemed of major importance to him. "Harry would know," he muttered to himself as if in answer to an unspoken question. Thus, Jon decided to visit his philosopher friend that night.

After washing dishes at Mel's, Jon followed Harry home. "Well, let's have it," Harry began as he settled down into his easy chair, "What's this major question you're dying to ask?"

*This is not going to be easy! Where do I even begin?* Jon probed, "What would you say if I told you that I can sometimes read minds — know what people are thinking?"

"That you are pulling my leg!" Harry burst out. "A parlor trick."

Harry filled his pipe, lit it, and blew a small cloud of Amphora smoke into the room.

Amused, since he already knew that would be the response, Jon related some of his recent experiences with the swans and squirrel of Stilmar Pond, with his music partner Tina, with the girl and her dog, and with his music teacher.

"Coincidence. Obvious. By accident. That's how," replied Harry, puffing on his pipe. "None of it is truly conclusive. You need to really conduct an exhausting test. Maybe you're psychic or something."

Jon was silent for a moment. *Don't be silly. I have no interest in tests and such fooling around. If I read his mind, it will be spooky. He might get offended. I sure would be. One would have no secrets. True, self-revealed, and all that that implies. But he'll never be convinced otherwise. And I do need his opinion.* "All right, Harry. Right now you are wondering if I have been doing drugs. Answer, no."

Harry's face reddened perceptibly. His pipe nearly fell from his mouth. Jon sensed Harry's body temperature rise slightly. "Well, isn't that the obvious choice — when someone tells you he can read minds," Harry retorted as he relit his pipe.

"You think of something, and then I'll tell you what it is," sighed Jon. He knew that this was the only option that would convince Harry. Harry agreed and the game began. *Not too strong, or I'll overwhelm him. Light touch here.*

"An egg," Jon replied in nearly a monotone as devoid of emotion or insinuation as he could make it. As they continued, Harry became more and more nervous, more flustered. His anxiety rose with every word Jon said. The room filled with smoke. It was painful for Jon to put his friend through this sort of humiliation. He could feel Harry's rising emotions; they were excruciatingly real. He knew also that Harry was feeling smaller and smaller, like he was being made less of. He knew that there was a limit to what Harry could take, before he became completely upset. He also realized that he was monitoring Harry and could tell when he neared that point.

*Save face! That was the way out.* Intentionally, he missed the next one. He felt Harry's huge sigh of relief.

"You missed that one," he blurted in obvious relief. The building tensions melted.

"You see, Harry, I can do it — read others' minds. Now, is it ethical?"

Harry was now on much more comfortable ground, philosophy. Tamping his pipe, he suggested, "Suppose that the information you could pick up would save your life or some others' life?"

"But wouldn't that depend on whether the other was willing to give me the information or not," replied Jon, questioningly. "If he was refusing, then yes, I think I'd just go ahead and get it. Otherwise, shouldn't I let him just come out and say it?"

"The real question is: are a person's thoughts public domain or private?" Harry proposed. "Answer that first, the rest will follow." He relit the pipe, certain he had said something of immense significance.

"That's sticky!"

"Yeah, I know. If we lived in a society of telepaths, then thought reading would be commonplace. However, we live with the notion that our own thoughts are ours alone. On the other hand, one can argue that thoughts are made of matter, energy, space, and time — the same stuff as that chair is made of. The chair can be seen and evaluated by anyone. Are thoughts the same?"

"I don't know, Harry. This does not seem to be getting us an answer. It's what people *assume* about their thoughts that matters, at least to me," responded Jon.

"How so?" probed Harry. He got up and opened a window. The smoke was now even bothering him.

"If I think something and if in doing so believe that thought is mine, and mine alone, then if someone else picks it up without my consent, is not that thievery? However, if I give my consent or if I do not originally conceive of the thought as *my* thought, then if someone picks it up, it is of no matter. Now, suppose that there is this girl who is trying very hard to be liked by boys, but I personally do not like her. Now, I meet her and I think 'Boy, I sure do not like this girl.' That is my private thought. If in thinking that, I considered that to be *my* thought and no one else's, that is one thing. If she read my thought as if I said it out loud, then she most certainly would feel very affronted. I would have caused an upset, which certainly was not my original intention."

Jon continued, "You see, people do have things that they are withholding from others — things that they do not want widely known. Good or bad things. And you know how very uncomfortable you get when someone gets too close to one of these hidden truths. Embarrassing, to say the least."

Frustration rising, Harry interjected, "So where does this get us? That one should always get another's consent before reading his thoughts?" He furiously puffed his pipe.

"Well, that would seem to be the polite thing to do!" Jon retorted playfully.

At once, both laughed. While laughing, Harry blurted, "Pardon me miss. May I read your thoughts to see if you truly love me?" Both roared.

"Yes, reading another's thoughts is not an effect that they can easily experience. To live happily, I'll not do that. Harry, the answer that I needed I have found. If reading another's thoughts will bring more good to all concerned, then I'll do it. But if reading thoughts will not, I will not do so."

"Hell, you can't lose that way," exclaimed Harry, knocking his pipe out into the ashtray.

"Precisely," Jon triumphantly replied. "Now, how about playing that new record of Brahms you've been telling me about?" The evening went by rapidly.

On his way home, Jon felt more confident. *I have grown. Somehow that book has helped me. I can communicate with animals; I can read people's minds or thoughts at will; I can feel others emotions — empathy, I guess. Many questions are answered, but now I have even more questions than I began with. Ah, but these are not about me, but rather with that other world and that book! Big difference.* He felt truly happy.

## Chapter 3 Hail, The Savior

It was several days before Jon had another opportunity to visit the realm of Stilmar Pond. The pressures of the recital were growing. Although Tina and Jon spent many hours rehearsing, the music never seemed to go right. One reason for their difficulties lay with Jon's preoccupation with the effects of time between his world and the picture book realm. Musicians habitually work with regulated time. So it was bothersome to Jon that such a time problem could exist. Since his attention was not on the recital music, Tina finally called it quits for the day.

Jon resolved to visit the magical land once more but this time to experiment with time. It appeared that a minute of time in Stilmar Pond translated to nearly half an hour of his time. This caused problems. Jon did not like problems. Further, he had a nagging curiosity. When he visited the picture lands, did his real body go there or not? He was certain that the answer would raise even more questions. However, this was a starting point. Unlike his grandfather, Jon did not like to take things on faith alone. He preferred to know what and why. The "how" he could ignore, for that was the realm of his engineering friend, Nick.

If he could have someone watch him, then part of the answer could be found. Understandably, Jon was very hesitant about this. It most certainly would be a situation that someone else could not easily experience. His solution was more inventive. He purchased a Polaroid camera with a timer on it. The plan: set the timer; go to Stilmar Pond; wait five minutes by his watch; return. The camera would take a picture exactly one minute after the process started. The area covered by the photo should include his chair and his wall clock.

When all was ready, he started the timer, dove into the chair, grabbed the book, and headed for Stilmar Pond. All was the same as before.

"Any more crackers?" came the mental voice of the swan.

"Not just yet," Jon replied. "I am doing an experiment." "What is that? Can you eat it?"

Jon chuckled at the lack of comprehension. "No. I am trying to find out if my body comes here, and how much time passes in my world when I am here."

"Oh." Then after a pause, the swan questioned, "Is time important? I'm sure you have a body here. Can't you see it?"

"Oh, yes. But maybe I have two bodies. I don't know."

"Is it hard to have two bodies? I have enough trouble feeding just one. Life must be hard for you if you do have two."

Then the female swan asked, "Does the other body look like this one or is it different? It must be quite a strain having two."

The male replied, "Perhaps his other body is a female. That would make sense."

Jon laughed. He couldn't help himself. "Well, friends, that is what I am trying to find out. I have to go now. I'll be back shortly and bring some crackers."

"It must be strange not knowing whether you have one body or two!"

He found the trident on the rock and backed out into his chair. *First, check the time. Ah, my guess was correct. Five minutes of my time corresponds to thirty minutes in the land of the swans. What a pain! I wonder if I can control it? On the next trip, I wish the time to be the same between the worlds.* His resolve was firm.

Next, he processed the instant picture. The result was startling. There was the empty chair with the book lying open. In the photo, he could see the picture of Stilmar Pond clearly. There were the swans and his body! "Wow!" he yelled.

He gathered some crackers and his camera, put together a sack lunch including ham and Swiss cheese on rye along with a half dozen cookies, and headed for Stilmar Pond. He fed the swans, took several pictures of the area from several other angles — all of which turned out rather nicely. *I wonder if I can get here from these? I will find out.* Then he decided to take a stroll around the pond.

The area was very beautiful and the aromas, enticing. This had to be one of the most soothing, relaxing places he had ever found. It stimulated his aesthetics. Jon regretted not bringing his flute. Several brush patches about two feet tall grew about half way around the pond. His eyes caught the gleam of some blue cloth and he went to investigate. He saw a woman in a light azure, long dress sprawled on the ground, apparently lifeless.

"Hello there," he called out. Concern grew with the lack of response. He knelt beside her and touched her. "Miss, Miss," he said no more. His guts tensed in pain. His throat constricted shut suppressing a scream. *Pain! Sharp stabbing pain! She is dying. What's happening to me? I can feel it.* He reeled from the waves of chest pains coming from the unconscious form. Struggling with the foreign overwhelming emotions and pain, he carefully rolled her over. *Oh, the pain — it's hers! It's coming from* — the thought was never finished. The pretty azure dress was ripped across the front. A knife protruded from her chest just below her breasts. A pool of semi-coagulated blood soaked the remains of the torn dress and nearby ground.

He gagged uncontrollably. *Do something! Do it fast, man! She's — she's dying in my arms!* Jon knew he had to move quickly. Thoughts of first aid drifted nebulously through his mind. Jon wrestled with his out of control mind currently overwhelmed with her emotions and pain. *Damn. This empathy stuff has bad side effects! I've got to control this. I cannot think straight.* He wrestled with the sensations. *I've GOT to get in control! There,* he found that he could just barely control them. Gently, he examined the girl. *Got to get that knife out. Wait! If I pull the knife out oh, no. That blade is in an artery! If I pull it out, she'll bleed to death in seconds! What do I do?* Slowly, his awareness of the wound grew.

By sensing through her body, he knew exactly where the knife blade was. That this was a strange action in itself did not register until much later when he was recalling the event. On a hunch, he pulled it out a tiny fraction of an inch. He sensed the blood beginning to flow, while his eyes confirmed the bleeding increased. *If only the cells there would close — go back together like they were — there like that — yeah, just like that. Oh, my god! They did!*

He stared in complete disbelief. Then, curiosity roused. *I wonder if it'll do it some more?* He pulled the knife out a bit more. Again the blood began to pour out. Once again, he saw the cells in the area and commanded them to close the gap. The bleeding stopped. He pulled more of the knife out and repeated his actions on the individual cells. Sweat and tension began draining his energies. Doggedly, he kept on pulling the knife out by tiny fractions and closing the wound immediately afterwards.

In about five minutes of the most exhausting work Jon had ever known, he had the entire blade removed and the whole wound sealed. He lay back, exhausted, soaked, and panting for breath. His patient was alive! He sensed her excruciating pains had subsided now that the blade was removed. Soon her anxiety dwindled, and she began regular breathing. Jon carried the girl to the pond's edge to wash her off.

Jon sat on the ground, supported her head in his lap, and washed her forehead with cool water from the pond. Shortly, he sensed that she was regaining consciousness. He sent out thoughts of calmness and tranquility. *Everything is now all right. You are just fine.* She opened her eyes. Jon's mind filled with images of her instant recollection of the incident and the accompanying wave or flash of terror. Involuntarily, he winced from the empathic pain.

"It's ok. You are now all right. Everything is fine. You are not going to die." He tried to be as reassuring as he could. "Hello there," Jon half muttered, bashfully. *If only she had been a boy. I am just terrible with women! I don't ever know what to say.*

"How do you feel now?" He knew her reply, even before she said it. *Here I have just saved this girl's life, by means that I don't even know, and I cannot think of anything to say.*

"I — I am very weak and so tired."

"Yes, I know. Don't try to talk too much just yet." (He remembered someone had said that on a TV show sometime.) "You have had a nasty knife wound there, but you heal fast. Just rest a bit." *What **do** I say? What should I talk about?* She lay still as her mind made the slow transition from not dead, to alive, to feeling healed. It was a slow process. Jon could not think of anything to say, so kept quiet.

At last, she seemed recovered. She looked up at him and asked meekly, "Who are you?"

There was the slightest twinge of red in his face as he answered, "Jon. Jon Brown. And you?" *I guess that's what I'm supposed to say.*

"Gwendolyn Saxbury, but you can call me Gwyn. I feel so hungry and weak."

For a moment, Jon's stomach both growled in hunger and recoiled in nauseousness. Then he had it under control once more. "You need some fluids. Here, let me get you something to drink."

He fetched his picnic sack, retrieved the U of I mug, and brought her some water. Soon she was sitting up and asking for food. He found that in spite of all that had occurred, he was ravenous as well. They split the sandwiches, but Jon insisted she eat most of the cookies. The meager lunch did not satiate either's hunger, but it relaxed Jon a little and he ventured wonderingly, "Who were those two men on horseback that threw the knife at you?"

She looked at him more than a bit startled. "Did you see them?"

His face flushed with a slight burning sensation. "No, I just found you lying over there by the bush."

Gwyn seemed relieved, "Oh, I didn't think I saw you before —" she faltered as the horror of her attack flooded over her.

*Damn. Now look what I've done.* Jon let her regain her composure and then said, "I saw the images in your mind when I was pulling the dagger out."

Suddenly, Gwyn realized what had and had not occurred. Her eyes opened wider than Jon could imagine. Her mouth fell open involuntarily. She gasped. Jon felt her flow of immense awe.

"You — you healed me! You healed me! I do not even have a hurt left. It's like the knife never — never stabbed me! Are you a god?"

The awe of the girl was more than Jon could handle. That it came from a woman made it even more so. He turned beet red, and embarrassingly muttered, "No. No, I am no god. Just a normal man. Please, please don't look at me that way."

"I — I can't help it. I should have been dead. You saved me. I'm not even hurt. Only a god can do that! You must be a god." She got down on her knees and attempted to kiss his feet.

Jon's face turned even redder. "No. No, don't do that! I'm not a god. Really, I'm not. Please, Gwyn." His eyes pleaded. She instinctively straightened her dress, brushed her hair back, and tidied herself up as best she could, giving him time to compose himself.

"There now — that's better. Tell me about yourself. Where do you live? How come you are out here? How come those bad guys would want to knife such a pretty young girl?" Involuntarily, Jon blushed at that last. Now that he looked at her, she was very pretty, and probably around eighteen. (Jon was twenty-two.)

She had long brown hair that was braided back from the sides. Her eyes were brown and searching. *God, I am around a beautiful girl, too. Doubly awkward. Maybe she'll just talk.* He noticed her dress now. Even it was stunning or rather different. Generally azure in color, it was heavily embroidered tiny checkers of very bright reds, yellows, and browns. His orange, U of I tee shirt and blue jeans looked pale and drab beside her. He felt very out of place. Somehow she reminded him of a picture of a Swiss Miss that he had once seen.

"I come from Brunsway," she began, looking at him expectantly.

Jon shrugged indicating to her that he did not know where that was.

"It's a village about two miles from here. Over there," she pointed nearly due west. "It is a rural village and we raise many sheep. We make clothes and quilts to sell in Rothwood Castle." She saw that he recognized the name, "You know of Rothwood?"

"No — well sort of. I have seen a picture of it," he replied.

"A what?" she asked confused.

Jon thought for a minute and then realized he had taken some pictures of Stilmar. He showed her one, "Like this."

She stared in further wonder. "Are you a magician?" she eagerly asked, thinking that this would explain everything.

"No, no I'm not a magician. I am a musician. I play the flute."

"Oh," she seemed as confused as ever about him. "My father is one of the village elders, Lord Saxbury."

"Our village has been plagued by the slavers," she went on, but Jon could sense a deep emotional loss. "For nearly a year, they have been raiding our village. They take strong men to work in Trundle's mines it is said. Sometimes they even take women as domestic slaves, but only the pretty ones. Two weeks ago, they took Hank." Tears swelled, and Jon knew at once that they were close. He let her lean on his shoulder for a moment. "He we were going to be married this fall. Now I'll never see him again." Now, she sobbed, all her stifled emotions flowed over Jon.

He let them pass, and he comforted the girl. When she felt better, Jon asked, "Now, how did you get here?"

"Oh, I went for a walk. I was sad and the day was beautiful. I had to get away. So I came here to Stilmar. Then they found me. There must have been another raid. Someone must have seen me coming here and told them where I was. 'Come with us,' the big one snarled. They were on horses. 'Never,' I cried and I tried to run away. They chased me around here and cornered me. The big one tried to grab me. That's when I threw my knife. I got him too." She had a satisfied smile on her face as she related this. "He fell off his horse. The others fetched him up and the small one cursed me and threw his dagger." She cringed in remembrance.

Presently, Jon inquired, "Where do these slavers come from? Don't you have a sheriff or something to stop them?" He sensed her frustrations grow.

"They just fade in! They usually arrive near the eastern edge of the village. One minute there is no one there, and then they sort of fade in and come riding into town on horseback or on foot."

Jon suddenly knew the full impact of her words. *Other travelers — like myself — but with evil designs. Where do they come from? Grandpa said something about Trundle. Is it a bad place?*

"They killed our sheriff on the first trip. No one wants the job now. Rothwood Castle is too far away for immediate aid."

"Can't all of you villagers band together, or something, offer mass resistance?"

"We tried that once. We drove the slavers off, but they came back and dropped some gooey stuff on the edge of the village. The houses disintegrated!" She recoiled in revulsion. Jon did likewise, as he watched the vivid images in her mind.

"It was some evil wizardry. We have no magics against that."

"Boy, what a mess you are in!" declared Jon. After talking a little longer, Jon suggested, "We should be getting you home soon. You will need food and rest. Are you able to walk?"

She replied stoically, "I think so."

Jon helped her up, but she needed to lean on him heavily. Being this close to a beautiful woman caused Jon to redden once more. *What do I say? Think man!* Yet, he said nothing, and they started walking toward her village, Brunsway.

He felt her breasts leaning upon him. He grew more embarrassed. Finally, he blurted out, "Will your parents send out a search party to look for you?" He dreaded anyone finding him like this.

"No, I don't think so," she wearily replied.

Monitoring her strength, Jon set a slow pace. He did not want to have to carry her, if he could avoid it. They took frequent rests. Twice, Jon saw a herd of sheep on the horizon and finally, the village. Jon was surprised in two ways. First, it was in his picture book! Second, it looked much like a village of Swiss chalets — only there were no mountains in the background. As they drew nearer, the gay colors of the native clothes blended with the chalets. It was very picturesque. Soon aid arrived.

They were surrounded by helping hands and plied with questions. By the time they reached the center of town, the whole village was in the street all talking at once. Jon felt very out of place. His clothes marked him as different, very different. Gwyn kept telling her story and the miracles that Jon had done.

With each telling, the truth seemed more and more stretched and more so the awe of the villagers. Jon became engulfed in the emotions of the people and became more and more embarrassed.

Soon shouts of "The Savior has arrived!" "Hail, the long awaited Savior!" "The Savior comes!" were everywhere.

Frantically, Jon looked for a place in the crowd through which he could escape or a place to hide. Meanwhile, the folks crowded in closer, trying to catch a glimpse of their Savior. Some wanted to touch the Redeemer. Pawing, pleading hands seemed everywhere. Jon began to panic. He had visions of being mauled to death from unrestrained love.

"Let me through. Stand aside!" boomed a deep voice full of command. A burly, robust man shoved his way to Jon and Gwyn. Jon knew instinctively that he was her father and council elder. The crowd parted somewhat. "Come with me," he commanded to the two. He led them through the noisy throng.

Presently, Jon found himself inside the Saxbury home. Her mother was fretting over her, insisting that she change out of the ruined dress and clean up. And so order finally came.

Lord Saxbury thanked Jon repeatedly for saving his only daughter. His gratitude was second only to his awe at what Jon had done. He offered Jon a reward, but Jon refused. *I wonder if this is how Grandpa got his money. I have more than enough with what Grandpa left me.* On the other hand, it took considerable denials for Jon to convince Lord Saxbury that Jon was not a wizard or a god. In the end, Jon finally felt that he had convinced him.

Jon managed to divert the conversation to the defenses of the village. He learned that realistically the village had none. At last, he convinced the Lord to try once more to get some aid from Rothwood Castle and the Lord there, Sir Giles Grescham. The argument rested upon the loss of valuable cloth and wool and food. The Lord agreed to try again. Finally, Jon knew that he had to go — or rather return home. He had spent many hours here, and he was alarmed to think how much time had passed in his own world. He took his leave and was escorted to the edge of the village.

Acting on a hunch, Jon trotted around the village before heading back to Stilmar Pond. Sure enough, on the western edge, he found a trident carved onto a wall just like it was in his picture book. More importantly, he found another trident on the eastern side of the village where the slavers had always arrived. It was carved onto a large boulder that marked a passage into the village. This angle was also in the book. However, from this side, the village did not look quite the same. He had the beginning of an idea.

Pondering his thoughts of how to stop the slavers, he jogged back to Stilmar Pond. He bid a goodbye to his friends, who had by now eaten all the crackers. Then he backed out into his easy chair. He was expecting the worst — days had passed. Quickly, he called time and temperature and was shocked to find that he had been gone exactly the same number of hours that he had been in Lindy! It was only early evening. Then, he realized that as he had gone to Stilmar Pond, he had stated that he had wanted the time elapsed to be the same. His decision had held! He wondered why.

Mentally, Jon was racing. So much had happened, yet he was still trying to grasp their significance. His body was physically drained and very hungry, so he hastily started supper. After eating three hamburgers, a can of corn, and a mound of instant potatoes, he fell asleep almost at once. His thoughts would have to await the morning.

# Chapter 4 Mandy Blackthorn

When Jon awoke the next day, he knew that he had many events to consider. The book jarred his tidy package of notions about life and livingness. As he dressed, he noticed the book lying open, as he had left it. Impulsively, he went over to it to close it and put it on his bookshelf.

*What's this? The picture — it's raining on the pond!* Jon stared in disbelief. The beautiful picture of the swans, pond, and yellow buttercups was now dark and grey. He could see raindrops suspended in their downward fall. Others had plunked onto the surface of Stilmar Pond, creating a myriad of time—frozen bubbles and ripples. Curiously, he flipped to the other picture of the village of Brunsway. It was raining there as well. Same for Rothwood Castle.

*Amazing. I get even more questions, and no answers. Now it seems weather is reflected in these pictures.* Pondering this and his many other questions, Jon headed to Mel's for breakfast and dishes.

Classes, homework, and practice for his senior recital occupied most of his day. It was after supper before he had the time to give serious thought to yesterday's events. He brewed a pot of Darjeeling tea, opened the book, collected his snapshots, and began to reflect.

*Yes, it's still raining there. Ah, just as I thought. Several of the pictures are now dark or moonlit. But my snapshots are just as they were — sunny.* In a flash, understanding came. *This is **not** a picture book! These are **not** pictures. Each of these is somehow a reflection* *of an area of some other worlds, rather like a portal. Time appears to run much slower in these images. Now if time ran at the same rate as here, then I'd be seeing motion pictures, not stills. I've seen that I can control the time by having it be parallel to my time when I go. I bet I can slow it down and have little actual time pass while I am gone. That would be useful. So, Jon, you have here a book of portals, windows to other worlds.*

He mused upon this for some time. *Evidently, the book of portals was meant to include more actual portals than are currently in it — the blank pages. I wonder how they are made. No, for now I will leave that one for the engineers. All right, so what have I got? A book of portals — portals with tridents. That's an important point. Each one has a trident in it somewhere. Apparently, the trident is the key to entry.*

Jon leafed through the pages. There were two pictures of the village, Brunsway, taken from two different angles — from the east and from the west. *Brunsway looks like two **different** villages!* A curious thought struck Jon. *What would happen if a trident was removed? Would it prevent passage? I'll take odds that it does! And if it does prevent passage, then I could remove the trident on the eastern side of the village that the slavers use. Presto. No more slavers — unless they try the other side. But I would surely like to try it first, before I depended on it.* Jon paused. He did not want to test his theory on any trident in his portal book. They were too precious to waste. In the end, he decided to try it on the slaver's trident, untested.

Next, he examined some of his photographs taken around Stilmar Pond. The rustic beauty again drew forth Jon's admiration. He carefully studied each. Just as he was about to pin them up on his wall alongside of his poster—sized movie photo of Raquel, he let out a whoop. "Well, I'll be. There is another trident in this one photo!" Surrounded by a small clump of brush was an unmistakable white trident carved into the ground. *Chalk, I'll wager. This means that someone else has access to the pond.* Quickly, he leafed through the book to find the corresponding picture. *There it is — a view looking away from the pond — it's of open hills.*

He mused upon this new aspect for a moment. Then an idea formed. *Can I get there from this photograph that I took including the white chalk?* "I'll try it," he cried out loud.

He put on a rain poncho. Then he opened his book to the usual Stilmar Pond page. It was raining on the lake. After sitting in his easy chair, he placed his photograph in his lap. It was a sunny picture, just as it was when he had taken it yesterday. Jon concentrated, making mental allowances for the rain. Presently, he was sitting in the rain in front of the bushes with the white trident.

Jon examined the form carved into the ground. Sure enough, it was chalk. Someone had carved the trident in the soil and filled it with chalk. Nothing grew in the chalk patch. Carefully, Jon covered the chalk with mud. In a few minutes, there was no trace of the trident. Now Jon rushed over to the other side of the pond where his boulder was. He backed out into his room, waving to the swans as he did. To his utter amazement, his photograph of the other side of Stilmar Pond had gone black — completely black! Jon let out a war hoop. He also discovered that he now had the book in his lap along with the "black" photograph. The book was open to the correct page — the other side of Stilmar Pond! "Simply amazing!" All other photos were unaffected.

"Since I do not know who may be using this particular trident, I had best restore it." Soon he was back beside the pond. He removed the mud covering the chalk. However, he found that it was easier to cover the chalky patches than to clear the mud off of the chalk. It took him nearly a half hour to make the trident "white" once more. Quite muddy himself, he backed out into his room again. At once he looked at the picture. There it was, fully restored, looking like the bright sunny day it mirrored, when the Polaroid was taken. The picture in the book was there once more, and it was raining. *A black page means the portal is now closed!* He felt some relief at that observation. Only about ten pictures were black, but there were even more that were just blank pages.

He still had one nagging thought. Could he enter by way of one of the other photographs that did not have a trident? Could he enter without one of the photos at all, just a mental image of the pond? However, trying either seemed entirely too risky. *Sometime when I am desperate, I will try it.*

He knew that he could get to Lindy in one of six ways: to Stilmar Pond by two ways, to the village of Brunsway by two ways, to Rothwood Castle, and to Stilmar Pond via his secret photograph.

Jon also knew that he had a viable way to prevent the slavers from easily getting into the village — as long as they did not know that the Swiss chalet view was also Brunsway. Perhaps he could provide some protection for Gwyn and her people. A feeling that HE was somehow important came over him. *No! I can't go around with a big ego.* The emotion fade away, but he knew that he had made the right choice.

*Well, now I really must look at the major event. I have been putting it off. But I must come to some understanding of just what I really did do with Gwyn. She sure is pretty.* His face once more reddened noticeably.

It was several minutes before he could concentrate on his actions of yesterday. *Somehow I did heal her. No, actually I did not really heal but rather I controlled the cells in her body. If I can do it to her, I should be able to do it to me.* It took him five minutes to get up the courage or foolishness to try it on himself. Carefully, he nicked himself in the cheek with a razor blade. Now instead of applying the shaving cure, he felt for the cells in his cheek. A few minutes later, the bleeding stopped and all trace of the scratch was gone. *Amazing!* Jon pondered his newfound awareness for some time.

Later, Jon's attention drifted to the significance of Gwyn's remarks about his being a magician or wizard and the attack on the village that had disintegrated homes. Evidently, in this realm there were magicians that really did do magic. It was a safe presumption that they were not merely parlor tricks. Nope. *In no way can I be considered a magician, nor a fighter, for that matter.* He was what he had said that he was, simply a musician — a flutist, albeit an intelligent, bright one.

Lastly, Jon reflected on the culture that he'd seen in Lindy. By his standards — twentieth century American — the village was very primitive. They were basically unmechanized. They had no electricity and no running water. Jon imagined that Lindy was similar to our Dark Ages, but with perhaps less oppression. Brunsway was a village of several hundred people. The main industry was raising sheep. The rolling grasslands were perfect for it. Thus, everything in the village revolved around the sheep. The young tended the flocks. The older women made clothing from the wool.

The smithy forged implements to support the economy. It all fit into a nice, tidy, ideal package. *Ah ha! Idealistic **only** as long as what you wanted to do in life fitted into an occupation that was present in the village! I wonder what happens to those with other ideas? I wonder if they have any actual choice.* He had vague recollections that in our Dark Ages, people were more or less cast into fixed roles in life without individual choice. He formulated some questions to ask Gwyn the next time he saw her.

Since he was getting tired and had no intention of going to Lindy in the rain, he went to bed early. In the course of the next two days, he had little opportunity to go to Lindy. The end of the semester was rapidly arriving, with all that last minute, maddening rush of frantic study. His senior recital practices took much of his afternoons now. It was only a week away. He and Tina practiced diligently. Afterward, would come finals and graduation. Finally, Thursday noon he was able to once more visit Lindy.

"This trip I'll look nicer," he told himself as he made his preparations. He blushed once more as his thoughts turned to Gwyn. He wondered how she had been and if the slavers had given her and her village any more trouble. *If they have and my plan would have prevented it — well, I'd rather not think of that eventuality.* He put together a rucksack containing a large lunch — several salami and cheese sandwiches, chips, and butter cookies — water, his camera, his flute, a generous supply of crackers, and some miscellaneous gear he thought might come in handy. The weather looked promising so he stepped forward onto the banks of Stilmar Pond. There were the two swans.

"Hello, there," Jon called out. "Here are some crackers!" he projected to them. He beamed as they floated over to him.

"Glad you came," honked the male, as he waddled up to Jon. His mate was, as usual, slightly behind him.

"Yes, we missed you," she added.

"Didn't stay because of the rain," Jon explained.

"Oh." The male replied wonderingly, "Afraid of a little rain?"

"No, he doesn't want to get wet," she answered for Jon. "The two leggers don't like to get wet. Have you forgotten already?"

Jon laughed and said she was a "right proper judge of two leggers." He gave them a box of crackers. "Now save some for the squirrel, will you?" Jon implored, thinking of the little one.

"He'll be back," replied the male between nibbles, "He ran off when she came."

Startled, Jon asked, "Who came, Gwyn?"

"No, another girl — two legger. Different. Talked to us. Asked about you."

Jon was suddenly very cautious. Who in this land knew that he frequented Stilmar Pond? Someone was after him and it wasn't Gwyn. "How long ago?" Jon asked.

"Oh about three quid."

Jon frowned in non-comprehension.

"He doesn't know what a quid is silly," pronounced his mate.

He merely honked, "How could anybody not know what a quid is."

Jon changed his tack, "When did she leave?"

"Hasn't, as far as I know."

47

Jon became nervous at once. Someone was near, probably spying on him. He looked around and saw no one. "Where is she?"

"Last we saw of her, she went behind those bushes over there — said she could see the boulder better."

"You mean she could talk to you?" Jon inquired, rather shocked at the notion that someone else could talk to his special friends. He realized that he had rather taken a strong liking to these two swans. Somehow he felt invaded, almost violated. "You had better stay here and finish the crackers. I'll go see what she wants."

Two honks was the reply. Senses alert, Jon slowly walked around the pond toward the bushes. Suddenly, he felt that someone was probing or sensing his mind, attempting to read his thoughts. He felt annoyed, until he remembered what he had done to Harry that time he tried to convince him that he could read another's thoughts.

*If you read my thoughts, here's one for you. What's the big idea and who are you?* He felt a slight emotion of startledness that he knew came from his watcher. *Serves you right for probing. Please note that I am not doing the same. I have not been asked to do so.* Immediately, he regretted his thought, for it would have been useful, perhaps, to know what lay hidden before him behind the bushes.

Suddenly he felt a strong thought. *Just try it bud!*

Now he felt sure that he had made the right choice. *A bit testy aren't you. Come on out.* The bushes rustled slightly, and she stepped boldly out to face Jon.

Out stepped the most beautiful woman Jon had ever seen. She was about his size — five feet nine inches. She had beautiful, dark brown eyes that seemed radiant, accented by long lashes and well-formed brows. She had light brown hair that was rather long and slightly wavy, with bangs just down to her eyebrows. Her face was accentuated by high cheeks, a slightly pointed chin, and what Jon thought were a perfect set of lips. Under her bangs, a leather headband could be seen with several eagle feathers dangling from the right side. She wore a skimpy leather top and leather shorts that almost could not be any shorter. The top revealed about all that was possible and yet remain modest. From the curved bust line dangled many beads. Her arms and legs were very well formed and muscled. Yet she was slim. On each forearm, she wore a leather band that served as a bowstring guard. Her matching, high leather boots came up to her knees and had numerous feathers dangling from them. An expensive looking white sable cloak was tied around her neck was tied; it looked as soft and precious as she. Slung over her back was a quiver of white feathered arrows, and she carried a short bow in her right hand. Strapped to her waist was an ornate and jeweled scabbard holding a sword. All her gear seemed matched in color, a pure, light brown. Her skin was tanned and soft looking. She looked stunning! And she knew it.

Jon was speechless. Actually, he was completely overwhelmed by her beauty. He just stood gasping, his mouth open, yet utterly unable to move. She saw a young man in blue jeans, leather hiking boots with wool socks protruding. He had on a white sports shirt that had vertical bands of bright colors zigzagging upwards. He had fairly short hair, and a fair face. He carried a red, French-make rucksack over one shoulder. He was not ugly, but he did have his mouth open with a silly expression on his face. She took this in stride, for she knew that she had this effect on most men: on some, she wished she didn't; and on others, she was glad that she did.

She looked him over from head to toe twice, before speaking. "So, this is the famous 'Savior of Brunsway'?" she taunted. "You do not look like a god, and you are better looking than your statue."

*Statue? I do look like a statue. My god! She's the most beautiful woman I have ever seen! Here I stand gawking like an idiot! Jon, get hold of yourself man! Relax. There.* He relaxed a bit and shut his mouth. He tried not to stare too much. "I — I am Jon, Jon Brown." He stumbled out trying to regain some self-control, and he held out his hand.

For an instant, she hesitated and then said, "I am Mandy." And she shook his hand.

*My god. What a hand! What a body! What a person!*

"You're very free with your name," she probed. "Do you always give your full name to strangers?"

Momentarily confused by her unexpected challenge, Jon replied, "Why not? It's who I am."

"There is much power in a name, if it is in the wrong hands." She saw at once that he did not understand. "What kind of god are you?" she countered, looking him over once more, from head to foot. "You do not look like a fighter-type at all."

She sensed his mental "No."

"You do not look nor act like a magician or illusionist. You do not have the dexterity or the quick wits for a thief. You are not evil, so no assassin. You heal, yet claim no god, so not a cleric or minister. You have a way with animals, perhaps a Druid, nature wise. Yet no, I do not sense such a mind. What are you Savior Jon?" She did look puzzled.

He said, "I am not really sure what you ask, but no to all of those you mentioned. I am a musician, that's all."

She cocked one eye in complete disbelief.

Jon had regained some of his faculties, and suddenly knew that she was trying to compare a huge gray statue that resembled him to the real person before her.

"That's me? They really didn't listen to me. Oh my god. They did build a statue of me!" Jon was shocked at the image that he had glimpsed in her mind.

Likewise, she was just as shocked that he had seen it, in spite of her mental defense. She threw up an even more solid wall to prevent his further observation of her thoughts. She readily perceived his thoughts and emotions. In a flash, Mandy realized that his shock was real, that he truly had tried to prevent the folks from thinking that he was godlike.

She grew less cocky and confident. "Then, you are telling the truth," she replied no longer so haughty.

*Damn, Jon. Now you've gone and done it! You have a whole village thinking that you are their savior. That you are going to make everything all right — stop slavers single-handedly, like Superman. Now you really are responsible for the well-being of that village, whether, Jon Brown, you like it or not! I will have to do something.*

Mandy picked all his thoughts up at once, including his sudden panicked thought: *Have the slavers returned yet?*

*No, not yet.* She sent to quell his rising emotions and fears. Jon eyed her as he realized that she had sent him that thought.

Now that the shock of the initial encounter has passed, Jon said, "I am truly sorry that Gwyn and the others believe that I am a god, but I did save her life, I do talk to animals, I do read people's minds, and I do come at will from another world, Mandy Blackthorn."

She knew that he was telling the truth and was totally sincere, but she was shocked — he had discovered her name. *Damn! How did you get through that mental barrier? All right, Jon, let's see you get through this one?* She challenged him.

Jon was a bit confused by her sudden challenge. "I don't know what you mean; do you want me to read your mind?"

"Yes. I am Mandy Blackthorn. Please do not tell others my last name; I guard it. Names have power in the wrong hands. But now Jon, I mean it. Let's see you get through this barrier. Tell me what I am? Go ahead. Probe."

Jon said at once, "You are called 'The Ranger of Reylona,' but I do not know what either is."

It was Mandy's turn to look shocked. He had picked up her thought immediately, right through the strongest mental barrier she could create. Only her god, Reylona, had been able to do that. A degree of awe spread over her. *Who is this man? Is he really a god after all?*

"No," Jon protested, "I am just an ordinary man."

Now that she seemed on the defensive and no longer thrusting the questions, Jon began to fidget. He knew, as Harry often said, "The ball was in his court — do something." Of course, Harry was a lady's man, and he always knew just the right thing to say. Jon was the opposite, and now his embarrassment began to grow. There was an awkward silence. Jon's face grew redder and redder, while Mandy struggled for comprehension of how he had been able to get through all of her barriers as if they were not even there.

Mentally, Jon was near tears, fighting his personal problem. He really wanted to say, "Mandy, you are the most exciting woman that I have ever met. I would really like to get to know you!" However, he could not get the words out, and with a great effort, managed to ask feebly, "So, do you live around here?"

She looked at his red face and heard both the said and the unsaid. She felt his conflicting emotions. "Boy, you sure are shy!" Mandy replied, more to herself than Jon. "No, I do not live nearby at all and thank you for the compliment." She thought, *This is not at all how I figured this meeting would go. If I do not help him over his own hurdle, I will get very little useful information from him.*

So she suggested, "Come, Jon, let us walk to the village of Brunsway together. We can talk as we walk."

Action was just what Jon so desperately needed. With each step, more and more of his embarrassment left him. For a while, neither spoke. Mandy dropped her mental defenses, but Jon did not pry. When she sensed that Jon was more comfortable, she said, "You are honest and truthful, Jon Brown. You wanted to know what a ranger was, I believe."

He nodded, "Yes, I would."

"Well, a ranger is a special kind of fighter, in the cause of good. We often travel alone. Rangers are skilled at wood crafting, tracking, and scouting. We are very fond of nature, but I am especially fond of forests and the creatures that dwell in them. I can talk to animals nearly as easily as you do. We protect the woodland creatures as we can. All rangers are basically good, as opposed to evil in nature. It is rare for one of us to be taken by surprise or unaware. You see, just by looking at the ground here beneath our feet, I can tell you what manner of creatures have passed this way. Because of our love of nature, we rangers can learn some nature oriented magical spells. I know quite a few."

"How did you get those feathers? They are most becoming, Mandy." Jon asked quietly.

"Thank you. I think so too. These I got many years ago. As a young girl, I would roam the woods near my father's castle. A few I found, but most were given to me by an eagle whom I rescued from a hunter's forgotten trap."

"Was he all right?" Jon asked, mentally picturing a huge eagle soaring high above.

"Well, I cured him up a bit and he was fine. Rather like what you did for Gwendolyn."

"So you can adjust cells too. I thought that I was the only one who could. In my world, I think that I probably am the only one."

"What a strange world you must live in! In mine, curing is a rather common ability."

"You said that you were — no, I saw that you were the Ranger of Reylona. Who is Reylona?" Jon inquired attempting to be as honest about his choice of words as possible while not disguising his curiosity about Mandy.

"Reylona is my goddess. She is the goddess of our forests, meadows, animals, flowers, and fertility. She is worshiped by good folk who live in forests and woodlands. She is very beautiful and very powerful."

*No one could be more beautiful than you are, Mandy.*

"Thank you for the compliment, Jon. However, she really is much more attractive than I, really Jon."

"I find that hard to believe. Is Reylona real? I mean, can anyone actually meet a god? In my world, people pray and worship God, but there is no real body. Many think that there is no god at all."

"Strange place you come from, Jon! Yes, she is real. There are many lesser gods, and indeed there is a hierarchy of these. Yet above all of them, I feel, is one supreme God."

"Oh, I see, rather like our historical gods of Mount Olympus." Jon saw a rather blank look on her face and said, "Never mind, two thousand years ago my world may have been similar to yours. But you say you have met Reylona and that you are her special ranger?"

"Yes, but that is a very long story. I sometimes go on special assignments for her."

"You must be a very special person, Mandy!" Jon's admiration was heartfelt. She understood. They walked in silence for a while.

Then Jon inquired, "Mandy, you said to be careful of giving your name to just anyone. That it could be dangerous. What did you mean?"

"There is evil in the world. There are powerful magic spells that can imprison a person, but the caster of the spells must know the true name of the one he wants to entrap."

"Then, Gwyn was right in saying that there are magicians about. I thought that was preposterous."

"I am afraid that there are both good and bad magicians. So be careful to whom you divulge secrets."

"I will be more careful." Jon's head bobbed slightly as he made his mental resolve to do so. After a while, Jon asked, "What's your world like? How do you travel here to Lindy?"

"I live in my castle — Blackthorn Castle in the middle of The Gnarled Oaks Wood. It is much like this world. As for how I get here, I'd rather not say, just yet. Although it would seem that I have no way to stop you from finding out."

Jon reddened, but said, "No Mandy, I will not pry without your consent. For me, such an act would not be ethical. I will not."

"That's one of the reasons I like you, Jon." He turned red as a beet. *She said that she just might, maybe, sort of **like** me. Incredible fortune.* "You certainly are insecure, Jon."

"It's not you, Mandy. I — I am just no good around beautiful women. I get tongue—tied. I never know what to say. I am inexperienced at — at courting another." Suddenly he blurted, "I just do not know what the real problem really is. If I did, perhaps I could do something about it."

"I understand," she said softly. "Come tell me about your world."

Jon welcomed the opportunity to just talk and not have to be thinking carefully of what to say next. He told her about the university, his flute playing, his jobs. He told her about his Grandpa, the last of his relatives. He told her of his life. Mandy was an excellent listener. Soon Jon found himself telling her about the death of his grandfather, and that led to the book. He talked about his adventures in Lindy and of the facts that he has uncovered regarding the use of the portals. By the time he had told his entire life story, the edge of Brunsway was before them.

"Well, I have got to face that statue!" Jon said resolutely. "Show me where it is." He could not miss it. Squarely in the middle of the village rose a grey statue nearly six feet tall formed in a crude likeness of Jon. Soon the villagers spied the pair. Word of the coming of the Savior had spread like a prairie fire. Crowds gathered quickly, but out of deference to Mandy, they did not press close to Jon. Rather, this time they stood back in awe, waiting for their Savior to speak. Gwendolyn came out, but she reacted much like the other villagers. Suddenly, Jon had an idea.

When everyone had gathered around, Jon began to speak, using as commanding a voice as he could muster. "People of Brunsway, last time I asked you not to build statues of me or to worship me as a god. Still, you have done so anyway."

Cries of "Forgive us!" "Save us!" "Help us!" besieged his ears. Jon raised his arms to silence the shouts.

"Hear me, people of Brunsway. This is one god that does not like to be openly worshiped. I detest statues. If you want me to help your village, then you must remove the statue and stop public worship of me. If you do this, I will aid you."

A hush fell over the crowd. Then slowly a man moved toward the statue, then another, then more followed. Shortly the statue crashed to the ground and crumbled into pieces. Then, as if in challenge, an eerie wailing cry came from behind the crowd, to Jon's left.

Cries of dismay came from everywhere. People fled in panic to their homes, as if the very devil had descended upon their village. Jon faced the challenger, somewhat dumfounded. One he recognized immediately as a fighter, clad in some form of black chain mail like something out of the Middle Ages. He had a huge two-handed sword raised above his head. He looked like an impossible opponent. However, the cry came from the other creature. Jon knew instinctively that it was the more dangerous opponent of the two.

"Zagroot Zounds! It's a shadow demon!" Mandy whispered.

Jon flinched. *Damn! What have I gotten myself into this time? I am not a fighter, but fight I must. Somehow.* The creature appeared to be an ill-defined shadow, nearly manlike, except that it was black — entirely black. Strong black wings kept it aloft, hovering menacingly. Long, clawing hands groped for action.

In a creepy, high-pitched voice, it commanded, "Jon Brown! Come with me. The Master wishes to talk to you. Come now and I will not harm you."

The rough voice of the fighter added, "Yeah, and you little lady, you come with me. Maybe I'll only take you to bed with me!" His boasting laugh accosted their ears.

Mandy moved with a sudden quickness. With the ease of a continuous, well-practiced motion, Mandy feathered an arrow and let it fly. The fighter saw it coming and attempted to react, but he was too slow. The arrow pierced the side of his throat. He raged, splintered the arrow and came charging toward Mandy. He held his huge weapon high intending to crush her; his neck continued to ooze blood down onto his chest.

At the same time the shadow demon lunged for Jon. The creature was fast, far faster that Jon had presumed. Its wings gave it an added impulse. Jon dove for the ground and avoided narrowly the clawing hands of death. Rolling up onto his feet, he heard the clash of swords and knew that Mandy was busy. *I've got to find a way to fight this thing, fast.* Now the shadow demon charged again, and Jon tried to punch him instead of dodging. His fists connected doing little damage. However, the claws scraped huge gashes on his back. Jon felt the surge of intense pain, and felt blood flowing down his back.

With an effort of concentration, he adjusted the cells partially, and the rush of blood subsided. In the meantime, the creature was nearly on top of him.

*Blast him with your mind!* Mandy had sent him that thought.

*I don't know how!* was Jon's first reaction. Necessity overruled him. The creature was reaching down for him. He had no time. Mentally, he formed the idea of a force field, like a pair of invisible hands. He felt the shadow demon contact his field and try to force it down upon him. More weight forced Jon down, weakening his attempt. Still, the action gave Jon a moment to think. He imagined one tiny particle like a miniature rock flying from him, smashing into the demon. Then two, then four, then more. Faster and faster he created the particles. Harder and harder he forced them at the creature that was attacking him. He sensed the creature's attack weakening. Jon took hope and created his flow harder and faster. He imagined a fire hose blasting away. Now he had fifty hoses firing, now a hundred. Jon grew more and more excited about his actions and doubled it again, then again.

Suddenly, there was a terrible cry of utter anguish, a flash of light, and sparks seemed to engulf the shadow demon. A smoke cloud appeared where the demon had been standing. A fine-textured dust slowly drifted to the ground. The sounds of the sword battle abated, as both blade wielders turned to see the end of the shadow demon. At once, all the fight left the man, and he pleaded to be let go. Jon noticed that he had not fared too well he had several deep cuts on his arms, and a nasty gash in his side was pouring blood. His throat wound trickled a crimson rivulet down inside his mail. Mandy had no mark on her. Jon felt relieved at that.

Instinctively, Jon commanded "You may go — return to your Master. Tell him that the Mind Smasher has closed this portal to him. If he ever sends anyone to this village again, I shall come to his place and disintegrate him. Go now before you bleed to death."

The man stumbled backwards, until he could see the trident. Slowly, he faded away. As he disappeared, Jon slumped to the ground, exhausted and wounded. Distinctly, he felt Mandy's mind join with his to repair his damaged back. Soon all that remained was a tattered shirt.

"You will be a bit weak for a while, after using that much energy," Mandy sympathetically advised. "Let me get you some water and something to eat."

Jon realized that he was very thirsty and hungry. He felt depleted of energy. Evidently, there was some physical backlash to the use of so much mental energy. It would be only one more thing he would have to ponder. "Wait, Mandy, I have my lunch in my pack."

In a few minutes, Jon felt more like talking. He had devoured his entire lunch in a ravenous manner! However, he still felt weak; he minimized walking.

Mandy was very much in awe of Jon now. "You realize what you did? When I use a mind blast, if I am very lucky, the creature will just die, though usually they just go away. You — you entirely disintegrated it! That's incredible. I would not have believed it if I had not seen it with my own eyes."

"But Mandy, I would have been dead if you had not told me how to defend myself! I owe you one great big thank you." Jon blushed, and his face got red. The thank you that he had just thought of was a loving kiss. Just as soon as he thought of it, he became shy and embarrassed about even having such a thought.

Mandy saw that he had become embarrassed again and instinctively picked up his thoughts. "Jon, you should go with your first reactions." She touched him gently, pulled him close and tenderly kissed him. Jon's embarrassment rose and then eroded.

*You are truly beautiful, Mandy.*

"Say, I had better close that portal," Jon suddenly remembered. Mandy at once became keenly interested.

"There it is. There is the trident. Remember, I told you that the trident is the key to passage. Well, I am just going to remove the trident."

It was carved into the side of the wall of a house at the very edge of the village. The wall was made of a fairly soft rock and the trident was not carved too deeply in the stone. Jon guessed that it would not be too difficult to remove it. The villagers, who had been terrified by the coming of the demon and ensuing battle, now slowly gathered courage to face their Savior once more. Some of the braver folk began to chisel off the stone, following Jon's directions. In an hour, no trace of the trident remained.

"Well, Mandy, I'm certain that in someone's book, a page has now gone black. Goodbye and good riddance."

As everyone walked back toward the center of the village, Jon had another sudden inspiration. "People of Brunsway, I do not think that you will be further bothered by the slavers. Their portal here is closed. However, should danger ever come and you wish to contact me, fly a red flag by my trident." He added as if in after thought, "Fly a white flag, if you merely wish to speak to me. Gwendolyn can show you the place." *Mandy? Do you read me?*

*Yes.*

*Let's get out of here before they decide to celebrate. The last time I was nearly mauled by good intentions.* They quietly slipped out of the village. Behind them, a noisy celebration had begun.

Without much thought to where they were going, the pair headed back toward Stilmar Pond. Jon said, "Mandy, thank you. Without your aid, I would have failed. You have taught me many things in a very short time. I — I feel that I have *so* much to learn."

"I understand," she replied. "You have power but not the knowledge of its use. I would be honored to teach you what I know."

Jon felt a very big relief. He was dreading leaving behind such a woman as Mandy. "You are an incredible treasure, Mandy." Jon thought that she had a slight blush, but he did not probe.

As Stilmar Pond neared, Jon realized that he would have to return home shortly, leaving Mandy. "I have another problem, Mandy. I — I will have to return to my world shortly."

"I know, Jon. Do not worry about it. I too ought to return to mine. We must meet again." That was what he most wanted to hear.

"How shall we arrange it? I do not know where your world is. Nor do I know exactly how soon I can come back," Jon added. A hint of sorrow was in his voice.

"Likewise. But I know your entrance to Stilmar Pond, and you know mine."

"What! exclaimed Jon in complete surprise.

"I love hills, so I come in by the chalky trident way. Why don't we use the same principle that you suggested for Brunsway? Red means extreme urgency; yellow, need to meet; and white, come when you can."

"Excellent, Mandy!" He grinned broadly; all of his mounting tensions of parting from this beautiful woman vanished in an instant. Jon knew that he now had to go. It was getting dusk. He hesitated and slowly backed toward his side of the pond.

"You are not going to leave me without a goodbye kiss are you?" she taunted.

Hesitantly, Jon went over to her unsure what to do next. She grabbed him and gave him a strong, passionate kiss. Boom! Jon's tentative control over his mind evaporated. He had never known such embarrassment! Yet he craved the gentle caress of her lips upon his. "I'll be thinking of you," she whispered and smiled, when she let go of him.

"And I, you," Jon whispered hoarsely, just barely able to speak, wholly unable to think properly. They parted — each fading out of Lindy and back into their own worlds.

# Chapter 5 Alison d'Ambrose

Jon sat in his easy chair staring at the picture of Stilmar Pond. He could still taste Mandy's kiss — sense her warm touch. The most beautiful woman that he had ever seen had just said that she would be thinking of him. Jon basked in this new felt emotion. *That someone **that** stunningly beautiful should would even be thinking of **me**! Wow.* His face became even redder than before. *Why am I so embarrassed if a woman should or might like me? I just don't understand it. Now if she were ugly or even just plain looking, why it'd be ok — I would not have this problem. The prettier they are, the worse it is for me. It's weird. I must be neurotic or something.*

At this point, someone began pounding on his door startling him. "Jon! Jon, you in there?" He recognized Harry's voice at once.

"Yes. Hang on. I'm coming." He opened the door.

"Hi. Come on. We're almost late. You know Mel serves greasy chicken every Thursday night. Hey, what happened to your shirt?" Harry noticed his sliced up shirt and the dried bloodstains. "You all right?"

"Uh? Yeah. Slight misunderstanding. I'm fine. Let me change my shirt, and I'll be right with you."

Shortly, they headed toward Mel's. "What are you so bubbly about?" Harry probed, noticing that Jon was acting a bit different than normal.

"I met the most beautiful woman that I have ever seen this afternoon, and she said that she would be thinking about me." Jon replied, animatedly.

"Whoa. Oh no, not you — Jon the confirmed bachelor! This is hard to believe! Better than Raquel?" Harry teased.

"She makes Raquel look like Plain Jane!"

"All right! When do I get to meet her? What's her name? How come I have never seen this one?" Harry taunted.

"I don't know. Mandy. She doesn't live around here. And I'm not so sure that I want her meeting you — you might just try to rip her off from me." Jon teased back. *No one can **own** her, but she could easily **own** men.*

"Boy, she sure has you hooked! How long have you known her?"

"About four hours, I think."

"Well, she must have been something to get you hooked in so short a time! Come on, let's find some not so greasy chicken before it's carted off to the guys," Harry replied, as they entered Mel's. The aroma of chicken and grease overwhelmed all senses as they entered the kitchen.

While running the dishwasher, Jon had time to reflect on his day. Besides meeting Mandy, he had probably rescued Brunsway from the ravages of the slavers. He had fought a totally weird monster of which he had never heard — that likely didn't even exist. He had somehow disintegrated it by sheer mental energy that he did not even know that he had. He had made some unusual discoveries about the pictures. It had been an unusual and eventful day!

However, Jon now had quadrupled the number of unanswered questions that he had. Somehow, his simple life had become enormously complex and confusing — all since he had acquired that picture book! Life was getting very, very confusing to him.

Furthermore, he had his Senior Music Recital coming up in six days and final exams after that. It helped to throw dishes into a noisy machine, to pull them through cleaned, to take them out, and to dry them. This was a comfortingly normal routine. *If only things would or could wait just a couple of weeks! Then I'd have all the time in the world.* He slammed another load into the steaming machine.

The next three days, Jon spent in studying for exams and practicing for his music recital. For variety, he did some shopping and acquired some mountain boots that looked more the part of an adventurer. He picked up some western style shirts and some new jeans. He knew that he wanted to get a present for Mandy, but he had no idea of just what. In the end, he felt too embarrassed to get her clothes or jewelry. He settled for a fancy Buck knife and a good Silva compass. These he felt comfortable about giving.

He spent several hours dreaming about weapons for himself. Obviously there was danger in these new worlds. He needed to be able to defend himself. *But I'm a musician, not a fighter. I hate fighting — probably because I'm such a weakling and have no idea of how to fight. I certainly do not like pain.* He toyed with getting some kind of sword-like weapon, but vetoed it, rationalizing that he'd probably only cut himself. A gun was the modern answer. However, he did not know how to use one and they were heavy and required ammunition. *Somehow a gun just does not fit the style of the places I've been!* In the end, the sense of style or appropriateness won. No gun. A solid oak walking stick became Jon's choice. It was something that he could use normally; and, if the need arose, he could strike with it.

Four days had passed. His concert was now only two days away. Of necessity, he had avoided thinking much about Lindy and his adventures there. The unanswered questions were just too large to grapple with just now with everything else going on. It is an ability of a musician to lose himself or herself in repetitive practice and to ask the unaskable through sound. He did, however, keep alert for possible signals — colored flags beside the tridents in the two pictures.

They appeared Monday noon. As he glanced at Stilmar Pond, he noticed a yellow piece of cloth hanging from some brush near the chalk trident. Instinctively, he examined the picture of Brunsway. There were two white ones fluttering beside the wall with the trident. Gwyn evidently wanted him too. His heart rushed, and he blushed, thinking of Mandy. Now all of the things that he had wanted to think about — to resolve — came back into his mind. He was as confused as ever. "Damn! Why can't things just wait for a few days?" He sighed and began to make preparations. Just in case he did not get back in time for supper, he phoned Harry to fill in for him. He packed his few things into his red rucksack and was off.

The first stop was to see Mandy. Quickly, he steeped through to Stilmar Pond. The pure beauty of the pond and swans washed over him once more, and he opened a box of crackers for his friends. They honked appreciatively. Then he walked around the pond to the chalk trident and bushes. There she was, lying in the sun relaxing. Two horses were grazing nearby.

"Hi Mandy!" Jon called out. Immediately, his face grew redder and redder. She was gorgeous.

She got up and seemed especially radiant. "Hi Jon. I see you got my message." She moved to him and kissed him in one determined motion. Jon got redder, but enjoyed it.

"I've been thinking of you too," he blurted, trying desperately to regain his composure a little. "I — I brought you something."

"Oh! Let's see it. What is it? I do like presents!" She bubbled with delight.

Jon brought out his offerings. Embarrassedly, Jon mumbled, "I don't know if you'll like these, but I tried to get you something useful." He faltered, "Darn, I'm just no good around beautiful women."

"Ah, stop that gibberish right now, Jon. You are perfectly fine! Come on now, stop stalling. What did you get me?"

She opened the knife first. She smiled and examined it closely. "This is a quality knife! It's perfectly balanced. A good one. Thanks!" Jon felt some composure returning. She evidently liked it. He flatly refused to probe her mind to see what she really thought about it. Yet, he could see that the compass had her both baffled and extremely curious. With an excited gleam in her eyes she queried, "Whatever is a compass?" After Jon explained how it worked and demonstrated it to her, Mandy's awe of Jon increased. She referred to it as her "magic direction finder." He did not need to read her thoughts to see that she loved this gift! She gave him such a strong thank you hug and kiss that Jon nearly fainted from the emotion. Now he really was red. Sensing this, Mandy made much small talk, until Jon had recovered his wits.

Then she explained her message. "Well, Jon, it looks like you have got me for a while. I went home and informed my goddess, Reylona, about the events here in Lindy. She seemed most interested in you, Jon. That's quite a high honor — a goddess taking a keen interest in one of us mortals, especially Reylona. Most of her worshipers are females. She requested that I stick by you at all times and give you all the aid that you need. I told her that that suited me just fine." Her eyes grinned at him.

Jon's face reddened once more.

"She said that she thought that you might be a catalyst or some such. I'm not too sure just what she meant. I think that she knows more about what's going on that she is telling me. But then she IS a goddess. Now then, Jon, it looks like you've *got* me," she charmed at him and kissed him once again. "Wherever you, so go I," Mandy said between kisses. She enjoyed watching Jon's flustered face.

Jon mumbled something that sounded like an "Ok."

Then Mandy began once more. "I know that Gwyn has a message for us — rather for you," she corrected herself. "I bought us some horses. It beats walking. These are the finest that I could find. I assume that we shall go with the best?"

"Huh? Yeah. That is perfect." Jon exclaimed, clearing his throat. Then he realized that she meant for him to ride one. "Ah, I know that this is going to sound rather silly, but I — I don't know how to ride. I have never been on a horse. In fact, this is as close to a horse as I have ever been!"

She stared at him in disbelief. "Whatever do people in your world ride? Surely they are not so backward as to walk everywhere?"

"Oh, no! We go by car, bus and train. Horses are solely ridden by a few for pleasure, except perhaps out west or racing."

"What's a car?" she asked, her face held an expression of complete bewilderment.

Jon realized that this was rapidly becoming a mess, so he replied, "It's a four wheeled, metal vehicle that propels itself."

Her face suddenly lit up in a big smile, "Oh, a form of magic transportation. That IS much better."

Since she seemed totally happy with this explanation, Jon dropped it at once. "So I guess you'll have to show me how to ride."

Mandy was a good teacher and Jon, a trusting student. Quickly, they were headed to Brunsway. As they rode, Jon noticed that Mandy was an expert rider and that she and the horse seemed to move as one. His admiration of her grew even more. She seemed to radiate individualistic freedom, as well as immense beauty.

When they reached the village of Brunsway, Jon muttered, "Looks just like a Swiss mountain village — minus the mountains, of course." Mandy gave him a frowning, questioning look.

The two were met by the smallest crowd yet. Several villagers welcomed them, and Gwyn took them at once to her home. Jon noticed that she now had an air of importance about her. The other villagers now respected her even more. Evidently, this job of being a go—between had raised her social standing and self-esteem. *She needs it — a small comfort to replace losing her boyfriend, Hank. She is pretty, though.* Jon thought.

*Prettier than **me**?* appeared in his mind. Jon's face flushed instantly, and he glanced at Mandy. She was smiling coyly.

Gwyn began in a formal tone. "Sir Giles Grescham, Lord of Rothwood Castle, has requested your presence at the castle for an audience at your convenience. Although, I might add, I think that he really means for you to come at once. You see, he expects that of us. If he summons anyone, we're to go at once. Yet I think that he thinks that you are or might be a god, and he does not want to take any chances." She giggled a bit over this.

"We'll go at once, Gwyn. You seem to like your new job as my personal communications officer for Brunsway."

She blushed and replied excitedly, "Yes. It is such a nice feeling to see all these Lords and important men asking me to help them. I feel so important, now."

"It's self-respect, Gwyn. That's all. Don't ever lose it. Each of us is important in our own way." She blushed even more. *That was a really nice touch, Jon* — Mandy sent him. Jon blushed too.

Then Gwyn remembered her other message. Her face now became very serious. "There is something else too. It's why I put out the second banner. A stranger has come to the village, and she has been asking a lot of questions about you?"

"Like what?" asked Jon curiously. Mandy became concerned at once.

"Well, she seemed most eager to find out all about you. She was especially interested in how you come and go, and where you lived. I didn't tell her much. But there are others that I'm sure would tell her anything. She is rather pretty. And she has money! She spent more than one hundred gold coins in the inn for information about you! She does not seem evil, but you never can tell. So I thought you ought to know."

"You did well — yes, extremely well." Jon replied, thinking quickly of the ramifications to this new turn of events. "Where is she now?"

"I don't know. She comes and goes. Sometimes she just seems to disappear in thin air!"

"A magic user, I'll wager," Mandy said decidedly.

"What is her name?" Jon thought to ask.

"She never said."

"Well, since she is not here now, I think that we can ignore her for the time being. Let's go see what Sir Grescham wants. You have done extremely well." As an afterthought, he said, "Here, you should be rewarded. It looks as if the others got theirs by blabbing. You shall get yours by being alert and silent." Jon gave her several of the strange golden coins that his grandpa had left him in the shoebox.

She seemed awed at first. "This — this is nearly a year's wage!"

"You deserve it." Jon replied. "Let's go, Mandy."

As they were leaving, Mandy whispered, "I did not know that you had money from this land. Every place has their own official coins. Where did you get them?"

"I did not know they were from Lindy. Grandpa left me a bag of these. Well, now I know where the coins come from. It may be useful." *At least now I know where Grandpa got these coins. I wonder what he did to earn them.*

They headed for the village edge where they had left the horses. A number of villagers stopped to say hello and wish them well. It gave Jon a nice feeling to be so well respected. It was a feeling that he was not very accustomed to having. It was close to fame. Secretly, he hoped that he'd have some fame after his Senior Recital that was coming in two days. Jon wanted respect for his musical ability. *I am a musician. But do I really want fame? Will fame tend to destroy my musicianship?* It was another unanswerable.

As the two untied their horses and got ready to go, Jon had an uneasy feeling of being watched. Mandy, too, felt unseen eyes were upon them. She sent to Jon: *We're being spied upon.*

They discreetly looked around but saw no one. Jon thought, *It's like invisible eyes are watching me.* He saw Mandy carefully examining their surroundings. *I don't like this; I can't see anyone. There must be another way to see.* He thought about this as he adjusted the stirrups, absent—mindedly. Suddenly, an idea formed. *If I cannot see with my eyes, perhaps with my mind, I can sense the spy's mind.* Jon began to probe for the presence of other's minds. He found Mandy's at once. The idea was working. Slowly, in expanding circles centered on himself, Jon probed, looking for another's mind. Suddenly, he felt another's mind over by the corner of a chalet across the street.

"Hold the horses," he requested of Mandy, and he strolled over to the corner of the chalet.

"Well, whoever you are, I can sense you, if I cannot see you. You might as well be visible," Jon challenged.

Mandy quickly joined him, straining her senses. "I sense it, too," she whispered, drawing her sword.

"Come on, Alison, we see you." Jon suddenly realized that he had begun to read the mind.

At once, he felt a shock of recognition, but it was not his own shock — it was hers. Her thoughts came to him as if sent over a public address system. *Egad! He can sense me, even if I'm invisible and doing nothing to attract his attention! He read my mind like child's play. He knows my name! Alison, you'd better be cool. This one is not going to be easy. Watch your step.* Then, both Jon and Mandy heard a strange word spoken, and at once Alison appeared before them. Her spell of invisibility was canceled.

"Watch out, Jon. She's a magic user," Mandy quickly cautioned. "Don't make any sudden movements or try to cast any spells or I'll run you through!" Mandy declared, holding her sword in a striking position.

*Damn! Another beautiful woman! I'm plagued!* Jon thought and his face crimsoned once more.

Mandy, senses alert to trouble, picked up Jon's thought. She could not control herself. She burst out laughing at him. "You are the strangest man I have ever known, Jon Brown!" She lowered her sword, for Alison did not seem threatening.

Now Alison was growing confused. First, this man discovered her against her best preparations. Then, she was accosted by the ranger — a possible tight situation. Now, the man was red in the face, and the ranger was laughing at him! "What *is* going on?" she demanded, totally confused.

Putting her sword away and between giggles, Mandy replied, "Jon, you'll never make an adventurer this way!"

With both women staring at him, Jon felt very ill at ease. His face was as bright as a beet. Alison demanded, "Will someone please tell me what's going on? Oh, never mind! My name is Alison — Alison d'Ambrose." She added that last very forcefully, as if there was a tremendous significance to it. She held out her hand, as if expecting Jon to take it, bow, and kiss it.

Off—stride as he was, Jon reacted instinctively. He shook her hand and said, "Jon Brown. Pleased to meet you." Recalling Mandy's reluctance to give her full name freely, he said only, "And this is Mandy."

This was not what Alison had expected and her confusion grew.

Mandy winked at Jon and said, "Hello. We heard that you wanted to see us. Here we are, but I think that we should move on out of the village. Prying eyes and ears, you know."

"Good idea," replied Jon, restoring some resemblance of order into his mind. "This way," he motioned to Alison. He retrieved his horse and walked it northward from Brunsway. They followed, but Mandy stayed in the rear. She was watching for any others that might be following them and the mage, Alison.

The walking cleared Jon's head. He began, "Sorry if my actions seem a bit unusual to you. I am not from this land. However, Gwyn said that you were looking for me. What do you want?"

This explanation seemed to satisfy Alison, who had been carefully studying Jon as they walked. "I think that you may have something that belongs to me — or my family, rather, but it is a long story."

"Tell away," encouraged Mandy without any hesitation. "We are going to Rothwood Castle and walking will take time. I don't think that you are an evil wizard. So let's have it. Spill it all!"

"Don't mind her; she's a bit brash. I would like to know, but I do not have anything that isn't mine, though," Jon added.

"Where should I start?" Alison queried, mostly to herself.

"The beginning is as good a place as any," teased Mandy. Jon gave her a frown.

As they walked along, Jon examined Alison. She was a very pretty young woman — about twenty-three. She was the same height as Jon — five feet eight inches. But she was thinner, probably about one hundred twenty pounds. She had blue eyes and straight, long, dark brown hair that fell nearly to her waist. While she was pretty, Mandy was stunning. Alison had a mellow alto voice. Both women, Jon noticed, kept themselves very clean and neat.

"My name is Alison d'Ambrose. My father was King Basil d'Ambrose of Verbenloc." She watched both for any signs of recognition, but found two blank faces. *Well, they don't know of daddy or of my country.* "Verbenloc is a small country, and daddy used to rule it from Castle d'Ambrose. I was his eighth child. When I was born, daddy commissioned the famous Bard Wendell Theodore Zandras to make eight identical picture books — one for each of us children. When I was three, some evil people raided our castle, leveling it to the ground by some witchery. They killed my father, my family, and most of our servants. I was crying in my room, holding onto my book, when my nanny came and took me away. Somehow, we escaped into the hills east of the castle." Tears formed and she was quiet for a time.

"I know part of your feelings," Jon said in sympathy. "I am now a loner myself. My folks were killed when I was barely able to remember them. My Grandpa looked after me. He died just a few weeks ago. I'm all alone now too. Still, everyone says that you get used to it, in time." Secretly, he wondered if this were really true.

"Thanks. Yes, you do get used to it, but it does take a lot of time. Well, where was I? Oh, yes, she and I hid in the hills and watched these black-cloaked men destroy the castle. Then after everyone left the ruined area, we went back but could find no one. So my nanny took me into town and raised me. I grew up and I found that I had a natural talent for magic spells. I have become a fairly powerful magic user and have acquired some wealth. Nanny passed away quite some time ago. I resolved on her deathbed that I would both restore the castle and that I would recover all of the lost picture books."

"At first, I held out hope that others of my family had escaped as I had. However, I have found no trace of any of them. I have been tracing the lost books for years now. I decided that the first step would be to recover the books. So that's what I have been doing. For a fair price, I have recovered one of the set. So I now have two. Six remain at large."

"What do these books look like?" inquired Mandy. A strange, curious note was in her voice.

"Well, they look like simple picture books. Some pages are representations of that village back yonder. There is one of Stilmar Pond and there is one of Rothwood Castle. Others represent other places not here in Lindy."

"Can you show us one?" Mandy interrupted. "Perhaps, we have seen one."

"Sure. But we will have to stop."

"Well, this is as good a place to stop as any," Mandy laughed. Her arm made a sweeping passage over the endless low rolling hills.

Everyone laughed. Mandy tethered the horses, which were pleased to get the opportunity to eat all of the lush grass that they had been walking over.

Alison wore a white, nondescript robe that tended to obscure much of her body. She had a small pack on her back, which she took off. Much to Jon's surprise, she then proceeded to take off her robe. Underneath, she wore another set of clothes. These were most becoming! She obviously had excellent taste and expensive clothes. She wore brown pants that matched her hair and a belt of fur, possibly ermine, which encircled her narrow waist. When she began unbuttoning her white silk blouse with lace edging, Jon hastily turned around. His face was red once more. Mandy laughed. Surprised, Alison looked up and saw Jon. Then she realized his confusion. She laughed as well.

"No, I am not undressing, Jon. Here, silly, look. See. I am merely getting to the hole."

Jon turned around bashfully. With her last word, he flushed even redder. Both girls caught it at once and burst out laughing at his confusion.

"We know where your mind is!" Mandy teased.

"I meant the portable hole. I thought everyone knew about them," Alison explained.

Clearing his throat, Jon muttered, "What is a portable hole?"

"It is a magical device that is like a huge foldable pocket or bag. I could put several people into one. The actual space is in another dimension. There is no air in there, though. You can stuff it full and it weighs nearly nothing. Further, you can fold it up as tiny as you like. It is really the only way to carry infrequently used gear!" Alison seemed pleased that she knew more than Jon did about magic. Some of her former confidence had returned. She carefully unfolded her hole on the ground. When it was fully spread out, she reached into it and pulled out a book.

Mandy replied first. "Well, what do you know? It looks just like mine does — even has that same trident on the cover."

Alison's body jerked to attention. "You've got one of the matched set? You don't know what they mean to me! Can I see it?" she implored with such force that Mandy could not resist. Both girls were so completely absorbed in their discoveries that they failed to notice Jon's reaction. The description was also the same as his book! His startled face told all but no one noticed it.

Mandy slipped her hand under her halter top and pulled out a small black spot. Carefully she unfolded her portable hole. When it was its normal size, she rummaged in it. She had to bring out numerous quivers of arrows before she found it. "Here it is. See, mine is exactly like yours — at least the cover is. We had best compare contents."

"Let's!" exclaimed an excited Alison. Jon looked over their shoulders as they flipped through the pages. They were indeed identical and to his as well. He had a sinking feeling in his stomach. Maybe his precious book was not his after all. He dreaded the thought of its loss. The girls' backs were facing him so they did not see his reactions.

Finally, Alison proclaimed, "Yes, Mandy. This is one of the lost set of eight picture books of my father. It belonged to one of my brothers or sisters. I will give you a fair price for it. How much do you want for it?"

Mandy grimaced. "Sorry, Alison. It is not for sale."

"I'll give you one hundred thousand gold coins."

"No."

"Five hundred thousand!"

"I'm sorry, Alison. It really is not mine to sell. But it sure is magical!" Alison's face fell. Mandy shrugged and said, "I guess I must tell you. It is not mine. It belongs to my goddess, Reylona."

Alison seemed genuinely startled by this. "You mean that your god owns it?" she asked in near disbelief.

"Well, you see, I am known as the Ranger of Reylona. She personally gave the book to me along with this mission." Mandy had no real choice but to tell Alison her story.

A month before Mandy met Jon, a band of Kagor's raiders descended upon the northern edge of The Gnarled Oaks Wood. They destroyed a section of the woods, carted off the lumber, and took many slaves. The guardian of this section of The Gnarled Oaks Wood, Drom Talloak, a druid, was powerless to halt such a party. So she kept close watch on them. She discovered that the strange book the magic user held was some kind of teleportation device. She observed that he had to concentrate on it to get it to function. A plan formed. She shape-changed into an eagle and soared above the raiders, watching. As she suspected, when they were leaving, the magic user was the last one to go through the portal. Finally, when he began to concentrate to return himself, she attacked with her spell. A finger of death hit him in the back. He died at once. Drom recovered the book and prayed to Reylona for guidance. Reylona herself came. Apparently, she had heard the cries of agony from her woodland creatures. After hearing Drom's tale, Reylona asked her to repair the damaged forest. The goddess took the book and came to Blackthorn Castle."

"She told me about the raid, gave me the book, and asked me to investigate. Then I met Jon," Mandy finished. "So, Alison, since you seem to have a valid claim to the book, when the need of its use is done and Reylona is satisfied that all is well, then I will ask her about returning it to you. If your claim is just, I'm sure that you'll get it back. Gods must set good examples or lose their followers."

"You are in that close a contact with a *real* goddess?" Alison asked, rather disbelievingly.

"Certainly. Reylona has personally spoken to me at least six times now. And, through Glenda Appleblossom, a cleric of Reylona, I have had numerous messages. Glenda has a temple somewhat near my castle."

"Your castle?"

"Yes. Blackthorn Castle. I own it. It's a large one. My father left it to me when he was murdered. I got revenge on the culprits within two weeks. Mom died when I was young. Dad never remarried. I grew up as his substitute son — at least until I developed." She giggled. "I've been a ranger for years now."

"Well, Mandy, I will take your word about the book. Rangers must be good of heart or they cannot become a ranger. So I trust you. But if possible, I should like to meet this goddess and state my claim personally."

"That is the best way to do it!" Mandy declared.

"It is interesting what Reylona had to say about Jon here. He must be important." Alison declared, turning her attention finally to Jon, who had very much enjoyed not being the center of the conversation for so long now. Jon sensed that her opinion of him had changed from tolerance to interest. When both women turned to him, he automatically blushed.

Quickly, Jon asked, "You said the books were magic. Can you tell us more about them?"

Her eyes sparkled. "Sure. It looks like a book of oil paintings, but it is a whole lot more than that. I have studied their history so much that I think I am an expert on them. It's a long story. Since you are going to Rothwood Castle, why don't we pack up and travel on while I tell you about them? I can ride well."

"Now you are thinking!" declared Mandy, who preferred action, not sitting. "You take Jon's horse. He can ride double behind either of us. He's never ridden much." She had a devilish grin, wondering what Jon would do now.

Before Jon could react, Alison nimbly mounted the horse and offered a hand up for Jon. Without much thought, he crawled crudely up behind her. *Oh, no! I've got to put my arms around her to hold on!* Uncertainly and clumsily, Jon put his arms around her. Mandy stifled a laugh, while Alison, catching on to Mandy's game, smiled and urged the horse forward. Jon couldn't think of anything to say.

Alison continued as if nothing unusual was happening. "The story is wrapped up with the gods. Now I don't personally believe too much in all this god stuff. I have never seen one, though my father was a high priest. But I do believe in the one supreme God. These lesser ones, I don't know."

"I can see that you and I are going to have to have a talk some time!" Mandy resolved. She shook her head in disbelief.

Alison began, "Some fifty-five years ago, Wendell Theodore Zandras was born in the free city of Wayward, but I do not know where that is."

"It's just north of where I live," Mandy interrupted.

"By age eight, everyone knew that he was to become a great artist. By the time he was ten, he could paint like a god, it is said. And by the time he was fifteen, his works of art were in great demand. He dabbled in fighting and in the art of lifting pockets for a brief time. However, by the time that Wendell was eighteen, he had become a bard."

"About forty years ago, Wendell's artistry had attracted the attention of the gods and devils. One was named Jous, the Uncaring."

"Jous is the major god among the lesser deities where I come from," Mandy inserted. "He is the god of magic, arcane knowledge, foreknowledge, and foresight."

Alison nodded. Obviously, she was learning some new facts as well.

"As I was saying, Wendell got the attention of Jous and Dispater, who we all know is the ruler of the Second Plane of Hell. Well, so real and alive were Wendell's paintings that Jous felt that they should be endowed with a great magic. Dispater agreed. Between the two, they decided that every painting could become a gateway into the world represented on canvas. Thus, if Wendell painted a picture of a seashore, then it would be possible for someone, who knew how, to step into the painting and arrive at that sea shore."

"Dispater insisted that the only way the special magic could work was to have an image of a trident somewhere in the painting. If that trident were present in the real place that was represented in the painting, then that painting would serve as a gateway. He insisted that if the trident were not in the "real" area, no transport would be possible — the magic would not work. Jous agreed. Jous visited Wendell and explained the gift to him."

"How could a god willingly work with a devil?" Jon asked rather disgustedly.

"Jous is neutral with respect to both good and evil," Mandy explained.

"That explains much," Alison agreed. Jon just looked confused.

"Wendell was awed by the gift of the gods and saw his life's work to be a helper of man. He knew that he must wander the universes painting for mankind, spreading both music and art. His special talent grew to the point where he could paint images that appeared in his mind. If he painted a trident in some obscure point in the scene, he knew that a corresponding trident would suddenly appear in exactly the same place in the "real" world he was imaging. He knew further that those who understood could then transport themselves to that place. He endeavored to paint the most beautiful places he could find or dream of."

"Soon he discovered that he could paint worlds that did not exist except in his imagination. When he would transport himself to this new place that he had just painted, he would find it exactly like his work, except that the world did not seem to exist beyond that that was painted in these cases."

"Thus, he painted beautiful places of his world, of other worlds, of places of his own imaginings, of places that others would commission him to paint, and of places that just appeared to him in his mind — regardless of how they got into his mind. He had many commissions from we magic users, for we seem to be the ones who can most easily use the paintings' special properties."

"For more than six years, I have been on the trail of the missing books from my family. As I have said, I have my own and one more that I have recovered. Six remain unaccounted for. With yours, Mandy, there are only five unaccounted for. I am glad that you have learned how to use yours, Mandy."

"Yes, I seem to step into the picture, but I hold onto the book — that's for sure." Mandy declared with emphasis.

"I do too," added Alison.

"I don't," shyly added Jon, who knew that it was now time for him to be honest. "I just come and leave that book behind."

Both girls were stunned; Alison, doubly so.

"You — you've got one?" Alison asked, meekly. She had been putting off this confrontation with Jon. At one time, she had almost been convinced that he might just be a god! Now she had to deal with him to recover her book.

"Yes, it is exactly like yours. Grandpa was given it and he, to me. Yet, just now, I do not want to give it up. When this is all over, maybe then," he cringed just thinking about losing his book.

"I promise you both, on my honor, that I will not ask either of you for the books until this situation has been resolved to everyone's liking. I swear on the honor of my family name d'Ambrose."

"We accept that, Alison." Jon replied calmly. Then he asked what he wanted most to know. "How did you find out about me?"

"Oh, that is easy. I figured that anyone who had possession probably would use it. I have been periodically going to every place in the book. I keep a constant eye on every picture for changes. I discovered that a seascape picture went blank a few years back. Fortunately, I knew an alternate route to the place. That's how I found out about the significance of the tridents. Erosion had taken a chunk of the cliff side down. Along with it went the trident. The picture went black. I am afraid that that one is gone forever from the books."

"Say no more," cried Jon, catching on, "You saw that one of Brunsway turn black and came to investigate. Then you heard about me and what I did."

"Yep."

"Don't worry, Alison. Another picture is *not* permanently gone from our books. I have been experimenting. I have discovered that if you put the trident back nearly the way it was, the picture comes back. I did it to the chalk trident at Stilmar Pond." Jon carefully explained the events of that rainy day.

She then asked him numerous questions about healing Gwyn and slaying the evil creature. Mandy added explanations, for she also had strong mental powers, which she referred to as psi power. Alison listened in awe as Mandy discussed how cell adjusting — Jon's term — was done and other effects that she could do. Evidently, Alison had heard of psi powers, for she asked if Mandy could do a full mind blast. Mandy then gave them a fifteen minute lecture of how she had used mind blasting. When she was just a fledgling ranger and not much good with a sword, if the fight went against her, then she merely mind-blasted the enemy. Some were killed outright; others entered a coma; some went unconscious for a time; others went to sleep; others merely became enraged; and a very few ignored it entirely. The stronger, more intelligent the opponent, the less the effect it had on them.

"It sure is a good thing that I did not try to take back my books by force!" Alison declared, smilingly. "Do you have as strong a psi power as Mandy, Jon?"

Jon shrugged, for he did not have any idea.

Mandy replied, "He's got at least ten times more power than I have! Perhaps more than many gods. I assume that you know about the magic disintegrate spell. Jon, here, totally turned a shadow demon into dust grains!"

"That's unreal!" Alison exclaimed in awe. "Shadow demons fairly easily nullify our magical disintegration beams."

Mandy added, "Yes, you see he does not know fully how to use his ability. Perhaps, that is what Reylona wants me to do help him learn about the power. Either that or else protect him. He doesn't know anything about fighting!"

Jon agreed. "Yes. I am just a musician — a flutist. Nothing more."

They rode onward in silence for a brief time. Each was lost in their own thoughts. Jon, confused by the presence of two beautiful women, tried to ponder his growing powers and sense of responsibility. Mandy alternated between wondering about what was really going on here and the amusing state of Jon's mind and powers. Alison thought about her quest to find the missing books, her great luck in finding two more, and how she could acquire one from a goddess. Then, memories of childhood came unbidden. She held back a tear.

# Chapter 6 Rothwood Castle

The horses ambled on north by northeastward, while each companion reflected upon their own private thoughts. Jon was quite depressed. *I really must give up my book from Grandpa. This stranger, Alison d'Ambrose, obviously has a claim to it. The fact that Grandpa and now I have it means that one of her brothers or sisters certainly has been killed. Poor girl. But it's now my only link to Grandpa. How can I even think of letting it go?*

Mandy had no such worries. On the contrary, the sooner she finished this business, the sooner she could return to her own world. *Things here certainly are confusing. I can't tell who's what! Take Jon. Magic User? Cleric? What **is** he? In the Gnarled Oaks Wood, things are as they should be understandable. Confused, Mandy Blackthorn? Yes! Maybe it's because I'm just not as smart as those two, but I'll never tell them that!*

Alison was also troubled. Things were not working out according to her plans. Back at the ruins of Castle d'Ambrose, it had been simple. Find a current possessor of the book and buy it from them for a fair price. Nice and tidy, but now things were different. *I don't really believe in gods and goddesses — a Supreme God is different, of course. Here you are, Alison, flippantly talking about getting a book back from a goddess! Well, if she is a lawful one, then I will probably have a chance to stake my claim. Otherwise, I just don't know. And then there is Jon. Under normal circumstances, I'd have just ignored him. Yet, he is somehow involved in this even more than Mandy. And his grandfather gave it to him! Alison, he really does have a valid claim to the book unless I can show that his grandfather stole it from — from,* she faltered. Painful, childhood memories returned. After a deep breath, she thought, *No, if his grandfather is at all like him, he would not have stolen it. Still, I wonder who gave it to him.*

The party rode up to the top of a slight rise among the sea of rolling hills that were covered with tall, waving grasses. Just as they crested, all around them hideous forms jumped up from concealed hiding places. They were humanoid looking with reddish brown hides, bright red faces and stood nearly seven feet tall. They were ugly. Forty of them were spread out around the hill's base. Standing impressively bold among them was a giant of a fighter. The sunlight reflected off his shiny plate mail and shield. He held a wicked looking broadsword. He commanded, "Spears!" In reply, a hail of spears flew at the startled riders. It all happened in less than two seconds!

"Ambush! Hobgoblins!" screamed Mandy, as her horse reared from the surprise of creatures lunging at them and flying spears. Alison's horse likewise panicked and reared high. Jon found himself floating in the air like a ballerina. Then the ground seemed to be coming for him. After the thud, he watched as Alison gracefully somersaulted off the rearing horse and landed on her feet. *Such dexterity!* Jon thought, suppressing the jolting pain of the landing. However, Mandy was even better. She kept her poise on the maddened horse, as if it were still just walking along! In this confusion, all the spears missed their targets.

Mandy cried, "I've got that fighter!" Without even a glance at her companions, she charged straight for the shining fighter. Jon did pick up a strong thought from her: *A ranger caught in an ambush! I'll never live this one down!*

Simultaneously, Alison issued orders. "Mandy, you take that fighter. I'll sleep these hobgoblins that are close to us. Jon, you —" She never finished her orders. She saw his body crumpled upon the ground. "Oh, well," she added. Quickly, she began gesturing and chanting in a strange language. Jon could not make out even a word of what she was saying.

His body seemed to be hurting all over, but he managed to raise his head in time to see a wall of ugly, red faces coming closer to him. They had nasty axes in their hands. Then, there was a flash of magical energy, and the entire front line of the hobgoblins collapsed gently upon the ground. Jon heard snoring sounds. This was unbelievable. He struggled up to a sitting position. Farther off, more were coming his way. Surprisingly, they halted as if following some unheard command. Perhaps, they did not want to go to sleep just yet. Jon looked at Alison. She seemed tired — as if casting that spell somehow drained her of energy. For a second, he was worried though, as he watched her, she seemed to recover quickly.

He saw Mandy hacking her way rapidly through a wall of hobgoblins, trying to get to the big fighter in the rear. Then, something near the fighter caught his attention. Another person was there, unseen before. He mumbled, "Look, by the fighter."

In her low, breathy, alto voice, Alison cried a warning. "Magic user. Look out! He's casting a fireball! Duck everyone!" And she dove for the ground, covering her hair and head. Jon hurt too much to move. Mandy ignored it.

Jon thought. *She's right. That man is muttering just like she did. Fireball. That does not sound good.* He picked up an image from Alison's mind. Suddenly, he understood a fireball. He thought: *In just one second, a streak of energy will flash from the now pointing mage. It will zap out to the center of this little hill here. It will detonate in a blazing flash of fire. All of us will burn!* Jon got an image of being totally immersed in a ball of fire. He moaned. Then, he imagined what would happen to his two girlfriends. He cringed thinking of Mandy getting hideously burned — her mostly naked, magnificent body seared by the heat — and then Alison's long pretty hair going up in flames. *I've got to do something in less than a second.*

Now he saw a faint line of magical energy streaking out from the mage's finger coming straight at him. He watched it racing toward him. It arrived. He acted.

Jon shut his eyes. With his mind, he saw the magical particles begin to detonate. He felt the energy being released. *I need the opposite energy. Blizzard.* Carefully, he created a tiny snowstorm that was exactly the same size as the tiny, emerging ball of fire. As the fireball increased in size and fury, Jon caused his blizzard to match it. He poured more and more energy into his private snowstorm. He could now sense the nullifying forces — heat and cold. It was working. Yet, the ball got larger and larger. It was now nearly ten feet in diameter. This was demanding work. He put his full concentration on reinforcing and expanding his storm. It was getting harder and harder. The fire zone was now approaching twenty feet. Jon strained every ounce of mental energy he could muster to keep pace. He started to falter. At once, he remembered his images of burned girls, and he renewed his efforts. When at last, Jon could no longer keep up, he collapsed into an exhausted unconsciousness. The fireball flamed into fruition.

It was the weirdest fireball that wizard ever cast. When it finally went off, there were the usual flames and low roar but only in the tiny edge of a sphere thirty feet in diameter. A peculiar one foot circular patch of grass began burning around the hill. The hilltop and his targets were unscathed. The mage was demoralized. No one had ever before so nullified his most awesome spell — and with no weapon or spell. Fear began to erode his confidence.

Alison could not believe her own eyes. She shook her head several times in disbelief. She got up for a better look. The hobgoblins were now retreating — actually they were routing, running away at top speed, led by the wizard himself. Finally unfettered by all of the hobgoblins, Mandy charged toward the fighter.

It was a brief battle. The fighter attempted to parry her charging blade with his shield. Unfortunately for him, her sword pierced straight through his shield and on through a joint in his mail. He died rapidly. Mandy cursed him soundly, for she could not pull her sword out of the mess. Alison heard her swearing and cursing, as she had to dismount and struggle to get her weapon free. By then, the enemy had disappeared over the hills to the west.

When Mandy calmed down and had returned to the hilltop, she found Alison sitting on the ground. Jon's head was in her lap and she was wiping his face with a wet cloth. "Is he hurt badly?" Mandy secretly cursed herself once more for falling into such an obvious trap.

"I — I don't know." Alison faltered. "He nullified most all of that fireball and then collapsed. I don't know." She was near tears.

"Don't worry. If he did what I think he did, he's just spent a lot of energy. He's just sort of pooped. But

I'll check him out anyway." She knelt down beside them, placed her hands over Jon's head, closed her eyes, and probed.

She quickly picked up all the minor pains from his fall from the horse. Then she sensed his mind, and he, hers. *Am I dead?*

*No. You just used too much energy too fast. You fainted. You really ought to get some lessons in this sort of thing.*

Mandy then picked up Jon's imagined picture of her teaching him how to use his psi ability. But in that same instant, she also got Jon's flood of shyness and embarrassment of being so close to a beautiful woman. She could sense Jon's mind flushing red. Alison saw only that Jon's face turned beet red. He stirred.

He opened his eyes and looked up into the worried face of Alison and the smiling face of Mandy — two of the prettiest women that he had ever known. He became even more embarrassed and struggled to his feet.

"I'm all right. Thanks — both of you — thanks." Jon seemed more than a bit flustered.

"Are you always like this around women?" Alison asked incredulously.

Mandy teased, "Boy, you should see his mind! He even blushes there!" Jon became even redder. In spite of this, he threw both his arms around the two and hugged them tightly. They were not burned to a crisp; he was very relieved.

Presently, the noise of the hobgoblins awaking broke the stillness. "Come on. Let's get out of here before they get fully awake," Mandy ordered. She gathered up the horses, while Alison helped Jon to his feet. They jogged hurriedly on north.

Mandy let out an apologetic sigh, "I am sorry that I was asleep on the job. Rangers are not supposed to be surprised like that."

"Don't blame yourself," Alison pleaded, "We were all rather lax in this. I should have handled that magic user."

"But he was not even visible before he started that spell," Jon interrupted. "No, none are at fault. It was just a surprise attack. It looks like someone knows about us."

"And they want us dead," Alison added. "By the way, Jon, thank you very much for whatever you did to nullify the fireball. We would have been fried. It was supposed to be a most powerful one." Her awe grew once more.

"Yes," Mandy added, "Thanks. I'll make a warrior out of you yet!"

"But what did you do?" queried Alison, "And how did you know what to do? You are not a mage."

"I only figured it out at the very last instant. I imagined you girls being fried alive, and I refused to let that happen." Jon's face reddened once more. The girls ignored it this time. He continued, "At the last instant, I realized that the opposite energy of fire is cold. So I created a miniature blizzard, but then the fireball grew so much that I had to create a larger storm. I kept expanding my blizzard matching the growing ball of fire. In the end, I could not keep pace, and it passed me. Then, I felt so tired that I just wanted to sleep."

"That's when you fainted," Mandy said with authority. "You seem to have developed some form of energy control. It's a major discipline of study, I've heard. There are those that can nullify any kind of energy directed in their vicinity. Yet, it is a demanding science. I do not know how to do it myself."

"I just wonder who wants us dead." Jon replied. "The slavers, I'll wager."

Trying to satisfy his now familiar ravenous hunger, Jon munched on some jerky Mandy produced. He vowed in the future to always be prepared with some food.

The trio mounted up once more and rode onwards to the castle. The hills became more rolling; buttercups, more frequent. At last rising above the hills, the castle could be seen, just like Jon's favorite picture in the book — only from a different angle. They arrived from the south, while the picture was from the west.

Jon grew more and more excited. "Wow. A real castle! I have always wanted to see one." Mandy shrugged her shoulders. This was a rather ordinary castle at best. Hers had far more to offer. Alison felt saddened, because her castle lay in ruins. For some strange reason, she had a strong desire to show Jon her castle as it used to be when she was just a small child.

Jon excitedly exclaimed, "Rothwood Castle is built of real gray stone!" *I'll wager those outer walls are ten feet thick at least and probably twenty high. It's even got battlements lining the top. And there's the large gatehouse with a real portcullis facing the south.* The walls were roughly octagonal, and there were several guard towers that overlooked strategic positions by the walls. Several huge stone buildings could be seen rising from within the walls as well as numerous wooden structures. To Jon, it seemed very impressive. He was inspired and enthused.

Mandy halted before the gatehouse. A sergeant at arms stepped up to block the way. "Halt. Who goes there?" came his challenge.

*Just like in the storybooks.* Jon waved hello to the solemn faced guard.

"Mandy, Alison, and Savior Jon Brown. We come at the request of Sir Giles Grescham." Mandy spoke commanding tone.

"Follow me. Been expecting you. Stables are just to the right. You can leave the horses there." The chain mail clad sergeant led the way into the torch-lit passageway into the castle.

As they rode through, Jon saw arrow slits in the walls on either side and small holes in the ceiling. *Oh, yeah — these were — are — known as murder holes. Any enemy that got through the front portcullis would be greeted by boiling oil and arrows.*

There were a lot of people and activities going on inside of Rothwood, but Jon could only catch glimpses of the castle life. They were being ushered into the audience chamber without delay. He wished that he could have a proper tour of the castle.

Sir Giles Grescham sat on his throne at the end of a large, windowless, stone room. Several fireplaces blazed, and there were dozens of torches in wall holders crackling away. Overall, it was dimly lit. Numerous tapestries graced the walls. Several weapons and armor displays occupied the corners. At least a dozen guards stood in attendance, along with two councilors and numerous servants. A long, central table was covered with food and drink: roasted pig, squab, capon, bowls of various vegetables, ale and wine — just like paintings of medieval life.

Sir Giles was a gracious host. He bade them eat their fill, before talking at length. He was a slightly overweight, husky man, probably in his fifties. When he spoke, Jon noticed that he chose his words very carefully. Evidently, Sir Giles had not yet decided if Jon was a god or not and was taking no chances.

Once the customary traditions were completed, he directed the conversation to the situation at hand. "I thank you for coming so soon, Savior Jon Brown. I must also thank you for being of such a great aid for my southern village, Brunsway. The slavers have been a great problem for us."

"That's ok," Jon replied, "But how about just Jon — forget that Savior stuff."

"As you wish, Jon," Sir Giles replied, smiling. "I trust that you had an uneventful trip here."

"Well, no. As a matter of fact, someone tried to kill us in an ambush," Jon explained. There was a general discussion about the attack. The trio found out that the hobgoblins came from Trundle and were indeed part of the slaver's army.

"Where is Trundle, anyway?" Jon asked.

At once, Sir Giles' face became worried. Long lines of age now seemed more pronounced. "We do not know. There is no place by that name anywhere in our world. I had the wise men search through every scroll in my kingdom. Not even a clue. Nowhere is there even a slight mention of that name."

"When did the slavers come?" Jon inquired.

"Well, it first began nearly two years ago. One day, strange men came walking up the hill from the west. They said that they were from Trundle. They needed strong bodies to work in their mines. Well, to make a long story short, they threatened us with destruction if we refused to send them men. I expelled them from the castle, but they returned in force. They had some gooey stuff that they lobbed onto the walls. It ate huge holes right through the stone! I had no choice but give them men."

"I have tried various tactics to discourage them from further attempts. Nothing has worked. They just appear when they want and then vanish into thin air. They must be very powerful mages or — or else they are some kind of evil gods!"

"I see. By why not defend Brunsway? " Jon asked, remembering all that Gwyn had said about their attempts to get aid. "They do not even have a soldier there to protect themselves."

"Well, I have fewer and fewer men to spare from the defense of Rothwood. And besides, nothing I have tried has stopped them. Why waste precious manpower defending a village? All is needed here."

There was no refuting his logic — at least without starting an argument. "So what do you want of me — of us?" Jon already knew the answer, but he wanted the leader to say it.

"Well, I have heard of what you have done for Brunsway. It has worked. No slaver has reappeared there. I would like you to do the same for Rothwood Castle. I will make it worth your while." He gave Jon a long, cold stare.

Even Alison could almost read Sir Giles' thoughts. "How much is this going to cost me?"

Everyone was surprised by Jon's answer. "Well, I want two agreements from you, and then I will do what I can. However, there is no guarantee that it will permanently stop the slavers. They may just find another way to get here. You can always get word to me via Gwyn in Brunsway. After I seal their passage here, you won't be able to get in touch with me directly from here."

Sir Giles did not know whether to be relieved or not. Agreements were sometimes the cause of wars! Cautiously he said, "Magic is hard to fully defeat. I can accept your qualifiers. Just what are the agreements?"

"First, you must send a small garrison force to permanently guard your village, Brunsway. Secondly, when this is over and I have the time, I want a guided tour of Rothwood Castle. It's my favorite," Jon added.

Mandy stifled a sudden urge to burst out laughing at the requests. Jon could have asked for a king's ransom and gotten it. All that he really wanted was a tour of a second grade castle! It was hilarious. Alison beamed and smiled; she was proud of Jon. She thought, *Perhaps this man is different.*

Sir Giles roared with relief. "And I thought that you'd want a quantity of gold or gems! It's agreed! Will a dozen soldiers be sufficient for the village?"

"Sure," smiled Jon, and they shook hands on the bargain.

On their way out of the castle, a young lad in his early teens hailed Jon. He wore a blue tunic with a large, white cross blazoned prominently on both the front and back. "Excuse me Sir, but are you Jon Brown?"

"Yes. Yes, I am." Jon wondered how this young fellow knew his name.

"I have a message for you from my liege, Sir Wayne Gilbold. He requests an audience with you before you leave the castle, Sir."

Jon started. *Grandpa! He said that he had aided Sir Wayne Gilbold!* "Let's go. Lead on!" Jon replied hurriedly. As they followed the young man, Jon explained to the girls, "My Grandfather came here years ago and aided Sir Wayne Gilbold. I — I must meet him." He felt the loss of his grandfather once more.

Presently, the lad led them to a small room. A white cross was upon the door. He knocked twice and took the party inside. The room was very plain, yet well lighted. It contained only a bed, table, and two chairs.

In one corner was a small altar. In another was Sir Wayne, lying upon a couch. His aged voice began, "So glad you could come. You may stay, Lonnie."

Jon introduced Mandy and Alison. Lonnie bowed and Sir Wayne nodded.

The knight was much older than his grandfather had been. His hair and beard were both snow-white, and his body was thin and worn. Age lined his face, but his eyes and mind were still alert. He looked Jon over carefully. "You do look a lot like your grandfather. Johanas has told me much about you. How is he anyway? He hasn't been here for several years?"

Jon faltered, "He — he passed away about a month ago."

"I am sorry. The world will be less with his parting. He was a kind, honest man. Did you know that he was of great assistance to me back in the Holy War?"

"Not exactly. He told me that he had helped you, but he never said what he did. Did Grandpa come here often?"

"Yes. We were good friends for many, many years. One time, he saved my life — I got careless and was caught in an ambush. Bad bit o'luck. Johanas bailed me out with a clever bit of trickery. I nearly had to beg him to accept a token reward for his aid. Good friend, old Johanas. We traveled together after that. He had the strange habit of disappearing a lot as I recall. However, I know that you are urgently needed elsewhere just now. Perhaps we can visit at another time. The reason I have asked you to see me is so that I may beseech you to aid the Lord of Rothwood Castle. All of this slaver business has frustrated him."

"We know," Jon replied.

"He is not totally pure of heart," Sir Wayne pointed out, "but then so few men are these days.

However, he is not evil. I would have tried to aid him, but alas, my body fails me. I have given him my council, though. Is there anything that you can do? I'm sure that he'd pay a kingly reward to have the slaver's threat ended."

Jon smiled and told him that they were on their way to prevent further access to Rothwood by the slavers. Sir Wayne and Lonnie smiled broadly when Jon told them that his only reward was to be a tour of the castle.

"You are as honorable as your grandfather. I am grateful to have known you both," replied Sir Wayne. "However, I am tiring just now. Please come back and visit me when the affair has been settled."

"I would be honored," Jon said. "I'd like to hear more about what my grandpa did."

They shook hands and left. Lonnie led them back to the castle gate. "I bid you god speed. Thank you for not tiring him too much."

Shortly, the trio rode out of the castle heading westward, down the hillside. Once beyond hearing range, Alison explained, "Sir Wayne is a holy paladin — the holiest of fighters." She saw that Jon did not fully understand. So she explained further. "A paladin cares little for wealth. Honor and service to his god is supreme. You saw he had his own personal altar in his room. If he ruled Rothwood, the evil would have been attacked! I'd guess Lonnie's a paladin in training — perhaps a squire of Sir Wayne."

"Aw, paladins are just too holy," interjected Mandy. "You can't even joke with them. They're always so serious!" Alison scowled.

They continued riding. Jon knew what he had to do. Alison suspected and was saddened at the prospect of the loss of another irreplaceable picture in the book. Mandy didn't care.

Presently, Alison said, "Jon, I was proud of the way you handled Sir Giles back there. He seemed like a man interested only in is own well-being. A true lawful ruler would have most certainly sent much aid to Brunsway at the first sign of trouble and certainly would not have let a little disintegrated stone sway his decisions."

"Yes, but he was not really all that bad a ruler, either, Alison. He was basically a good man. It's just that he did not know what to do to protect his realm."

"Yes," put in Mandy, "But I would have just charged and fought the slavers every time they showed up. Eventually, they would get the message that they were not wanted!"

"Boy, what a group we make!" exclaimed Alison, with a big grin. "Mandy tends to be chaotic with individualistic freedom above all; I believe in lawful obedience to the rules of society; Jon tends toward neutrality. What a trio!"

"Yes, but we are all basically good!" put in Mandy decisively.

"Well, ladies, here we are." Jon said, as they arrived at the bottom of the hill. "There is the rock outcropping, and there is the trident. From here, it looks exactly like the picture. Isn't the view just spectacular?"

"The hills and the flowers look very nice, Jon," Mandy replied, "but it still looks like a slightly run down, second-class castle."

"No accounting for taste," Jon teased.

"She's right, Jon. Rothwood is not that great a castle. I wish you could have seen mine, before it got destroyed," Alison lamented.

"Now what do we do?" asked Mandy, becoming a bit impatient. There was no action here.

"Do we really have to destroy another of the precious pictures," Alison asked, grief was slowly building once again. She knew that Rothwood needed to be defended from the evil slavers — but at such a cost?

Jon understood. "Look. This is my favorite picture in the book. It grieves me to lose it. But I can see no other way. Besides, I only intend to make this a temporary black out of the picture. Come on. Let's see what we can do to block this trident. One of you get your book out and monitor the progress." Jon ordered. Alison complied at once.

The trident was carved into a small outcropping of rock on the hillside. Jon decided that the best way to temporarily hide the trident was to bury it.

Jon suggested, "Say, we are probably being watched from the castle. I did not try to tell them about the books and the tridents. They might not understand. The villagers certainly did not."

"I agree fully," put in Mandy.

Jon declared, "Well, then, we need to disguise what we are really doing. I don't want prying eyes to see what we actually going to do here."

"Smart move," put in Mandy.

"Yes, but that is not being very truthful," protested Alison, who held truth in high regard.

"But they won't understand the truth. I am certain that if Sir Giles knew about the trident he would insist that it be permanently destroyed! I do not want that to occur. I like this view too much," Jon countered.

Secretly, Alison agreed with him, but it violated her sense of honesty to deceive Sir Giles.

"Now we need a cover show. Sir Giles thinks that I am a god or mage or some such. Let's put on a display that looks like that. That way I'd be believed. Can you girls make a big show of magic while I cover up the trident carving?"

"Sure," exclaimed Mandy, excited by the possibility of action.

"I — I can't be party to — to outright deception," protested Alison.

"All right. You won't have to," said Mandy. "I have an idea. Can you just walk back and forth like this?" She demonstrated by walking thirty feet to the north and then thirty to the south.

"Well, I can do that," Alison said gruffly.

"Good. Now help me gather some wood for a fire. We cannot create great works of magic without piles of smoke. Come on." She took Alison with her to fetch wood. Jon began to hunt for rocks to pile over the trident outcropping.

Soon they had a smoking blaze obscuring Jon. Mandy began to cast one of her druidic, nature-like spells, a fairy fire. She outlined herself and Alison in a glowing, pale, green light. Against the billowing smoke, they looked eerie. Mandy danced around the fire while Alison, grumbling, paced to and fro before the fire.

Jon quickly began piling rocks carefully over the outcrop. He built a small cairn that totally obscured the trident.

"Jon," called Alison excitedly, "It is working! The picture has gone black."

For Alison's benefit, he partially uncovered the trident. "Is it coming back?" he yelled.

"Yes! You were right!" called Alison, now much relieved.

Next, Jon threw some brush over the cairn and tried to disguise it further. Then, he joined the girls. "It is done. Now what?"

"Let's get totally out of sight of the castle," suggested Mandy. So they knocked the fire down and led the horses off on over the next hill to the west.

When they were several miles from Rothwood Castle, Jon asked, "Now what should we do? Soon, I have to go back to my place. I'm a musician. I have my Senior Music Recital to give. Any suggestions?"

"Well, I think that the only thing to do is to go check out Trundle," Mandy proposed.

"Let's just step into a picture of Trundle and see what is going on there. Only I don't know which picture that'd be." She felt suddenly very ignorant compared to the others, and this troubled her.

"It is the one with the tower — Rhones Tower — Grandpa told me," Jon replied.

"You are correct," added Alison.

They discussed other options, but none was as good as going to the land of the slavers and seeing firsthand what was going on. It had to be done sooner or later. Jon had the feeling that if he did not go now that, when he left, Mandy'd go by herself. Jon didn't like that at all.

They tethered the horses, and the girls got out their books. Jon looked over Alison's shoulder. Jon said, "Now!" Then, they all proceeded to move into the mountain hillside just outside the red tower in Trundle.

The low sun cast ruddy rays over the bleak landscape. Far into the distance, the jagged, high red mountains loomed. Nearer was Rhones Tower. A red stone wall with a battlement encircled the tall red tower. High on top stood tiny figures looking their way. They were on a low, rugged, bleak, mostly barren hill.

Only a few scrub bushes grew. The place lacked even a single tree.

All around the hillside were ranks upon ranks of hobgoblins. Some had bows; some had spears; some had axes and swords. Safely behind the wall of creatures stood a dozen fighters and a half-dozen magic users.

When the trio appeared, Jon heard a harsh cry and saw two lightning bolts arcing straight for the girls. They'd get fried. Quickly, Jon tried to alter the electrical energy, but discovered that he did not have any ideas of how to do that. Just as the bolts were about to strike the arriving girls, Jon forced the bolts downward. They struck the ground at their feet in a mighty explosion. Rocks flew everywhere.

A nasty chunk smashed into Alison's leg, and she fell down upon the ground. Next second, a hail of arrows came flying at them. Jon feverishly tried to deflect each one as it flew at them. He heard Alison chanting and knew both girls would have a hard time of it. They still carried the large, clumsy books. He saw Mandy struggling with the book. She could not shoot her arrows, nor effectively wield her sword. So in frustration, Mandy let loose with blasts of crushing mental energy. He watched as numerous hobgoblins collapsed before her. Others shrieked in terror; some began to fight their neighbors. *Damn. I've been hit!* Jon thought. Pain was flooding in from an arrow that had pierced his left arm. He stopped trying to protect the girls and put his full concentration on himself.

"It's a trap. They were waiting for us. We've got to get out of here," yelled Mandy, between blasting her opponents.

Jon saw that the magic users were beginning to chant once more. He had to act at once. They had to leave. He heard Alison cry out as an arrow hit her and her chanting ceased. *Where do we go? There isn't time to get the girls to find the right pages. And no time to concentrate. He* looked at his friends struggling valiantly, but with no hope. Then, he saw Alison's mental picture of a ruined castle. *It's got a trident. Ok. Here goes nothing!* Jon concentrated on Alison's mental picture. He decided that everyone would go together, and he stepped through, bringing the girls with him. He saw the ruined castle become real. The yelling and arrows stopped. A great stillness swept over him. They were safe. He relaxed into a deep sleep before he could even lay down.

A little while later, he heard voices on the edge of his consciousness. It sounded like Mandy. "Well, we are all safe and alive, anyway. Yes, he's all right. Just resting, I think. That certainly took a lot of energy. Now let's look at that leg of yours."

"I — I think it is broken, Mandy. I am surely thankful that bolt hit the ground instead of me."

"Jon, did it. Did you see it bend down just as it hit?"

"Yes, but how'd he do it?"

"I don't know. He also was deflecting arrows from us, at least for a while." Mandy added.

"I guessed as much. I tried to put up a protection from missiles spell over all of us, but I got hit here in the shoulder before I could get it said. It broke my concentration, and I lost the spell. There was just no time — it happened so fast!"

"It's not a serious wound either, Alison. Bad bruise or strain, I think."

"How did you fare?" Alison queried, gritting her teeth from the combined pain in her leg and shoulder.

"I got hit twice in the legs — nothing serious. We are three lucky adventurers! But I certainly would have liked to stay there a little longer and teach them a few manners!"

"We'd have been killed, Mandy!" Alison exclaimed. After a pause, she asked, "But how did Jon get us here? We did not use our books."

"I don't know that either. A funny thing, both of our books are now open to the picture of this place. Where are we anyway?"

"My castle — or rather the ruins. Welcome to Castle d'Ambrose," she said mockingly. Mandy sensed a note of extreme sorrow behind her stoic face.

"Look. He's coming around," Mandy observed.

Jon groaned and sat up. Immediately his arm throbbed. "What hit me?" he moaned.

"An arrow," Mandy replied. "Here it is. I took it out. Want to keep it?" She joked.

Jon managed a feeble laugh at that.

"Well, I see you are feeling better now, Jon. We had best get on with the healing. Since I am feeling the best, I will patch you up first." She began to gently adjust the cells in Jon's arm. It felt fantastic, and, when she was done, Jon relaxed completely.

"What an incredible feeling! Thanks Mandy. Let me fix you up."

Jon proceeded to heal up her wounds. Then they both went to work on Alison.

It was a new experience for Alison. "I have had clerics cast healing spells on me before and even drank healing potions. But this is — is — well it is *so* intimate! It is really a fantastic feeling," she proclaimed when they were finished.

"It brings us very close together. I would not want to do it on just anybody," Jon replied, sincerely.

Immediately, his face reddened, and the girls began to laugh hysterically. Both Alison and Mandy kissed him, and the three held each other in a loving, solid hug for several minutes.

"Look, Mandy. He's not red anymore!"

Just as soon as Alison pointed it out, Jon became embarrassed once more.

"Well, at least we got your barrier down once!" declared Mandy. She and Alison winked knowingly at each other. Jon didn't see that or he would have become even redder.

He was looking at the ruins. They reminded him of pictures of archeological ruins in Mexico. Undergrowth grew over crumbled blocks. Not much stood above a height of ten feet. Rubble lay strewn everywhere. Still, one could get a strong sense of size and could easily imagine the grandeur that had once been Castle d'Ambrose. Jon now remembered seeing this place in his book. "What did it use to look like, Alison?"

He saw her flinch and said at once, "Why not just show us memories of what it looked like when you were little?"

She smiled and then frowned. "I do not know how to send you pictures. I am not like you two."

"Aw, there is nothing to it. All that you have to do is recall images of what it looked like. Mandy and I will just look at them as you look at them — that is if it is all right for us to look at your thoughts. I do not like reading another's mind without their consent." They spent ten minutes marveling at what once had been.

Now Alison felt much more comfortable with the two, and she asked what she most wanted to know. "Jon, what did you do back there? How did you get us out of that mess? How did you know about this place? How did you do it?"

"Whoa a minute," Jon laughed. "Actually, you were the instigator." She looked totally baffled. Jon explained, "I knew that I had to get us out of there. You two could not turn the pages, much less concentrate enough to step through. So I knew that I had to do something. I could not figure out exactly where to go. Then, I saw your mental image of here. I figured it must be your home or at least a safe place. It had a trident in it. So I stated that I wanted us all to go through at the same time and pulled us all through and into here."

"You make it sound so simple!" Alison declared. "Yet, I suppose it is like my magic which is so easy for me to do."

After a moment's silence, she exclaimed abruptly, "Jon, do you realize that you did it *without* looking at a *real* picture in the book!"

For an instant, Jon had a startled look on his face. "How about that! I can go simply by looking at a mental picture of the picture, fascinating. Even someone else's mental picture! That is quite incredible, isn't it?"

Everyone agreed. "Well, it did have a trident in it. Now I wonder if I could do it if there is no trident?" mused Jon.

Aghast, Alison said worriedly, "Jon, leave well enough alone. Only gods, demons, and devils can jump between universal planes at will! Powerful mages can teleport between places in their own world, but there is always some risk. I don't want to see you splattered in some universe."

Touched by her sudden outburst, Jon said, "Don't worry. I won't even try. Now what do we do? Say, I had better be getting home. I still have that concert to perform. Is there anywhere that you two can stay for a while until I can get back?"

"Sure, I live here — in the underground cellars of the castle." Alison showed them a hidden tunnel that led to what used to be the underground dungeons.

"Ok. I'm heading home now." Jon proclaimed. "You two rest up and make some plans. I'll be back here as soon as I can. If you urgently need me, put some flags out by the trident. Mandy knows the code."

They agreed. However, before Jon could leave, both girls took turns giving him a goodbye kiss. Jon grew red, of course, but he relished their tenderness. Then, he remembered his room and imagined sitting in his chair looking at the book. He faded from Castle d'Ambrose.

## Chapter 7 The Rescue

Tuesday, the day before his big concert, came and went at a rapid pace. Jon had a million things to do. Now, it was late evening. Only the dull roar of the spinning dryers down below rumbled in his apartment. Jon poured himself another cup of Earl Grey tea and reflected on his day. It had been productive. He felt that he was ready for his recital.

He had paid his rent for the next six months, so there would be no problems if he were gone on an extended "vacation." He had even taken a precaution against losing his "book" to Alison. Smiling, he straightened up his large pile of Polaroid photos. He had taken a snapshot of every page in the book, including all of the "black" ones. He knew that he could use the photographs just as easily as the real pictures. This was a very big relief to him. So now he sipped his tea and pondered for the tenth time what he might get the girls for surprise presents.

They had asked him numerous questions about his world, but he found it exceedingly difficult to explain many things that he took for granted. Thus, he resolved to take some pictures of the campus and life here, and he would buy some postcards of some of the scenic wonders. *Mandy will enjoy that I'm sure.* Yet, somehow his real desire seemed unfulfilled. He wanted to share his concert recital with them. Partly, it was ego; he wanted them to know that he was really a musician. Also, Jon wanted to share with them some of his favorite music — share it for the pure aesthetic beauty of the music. Baffled and restless, Jon went for a late night walk.

Jon strolled down a nearly deserted Green Street. Only occasional noises came from the few taverns nearby. Once in a while, he met a few staggering couples and groups. Otherwise, it was a quiet, still, solitary walk. The dewy air filled his senses. How absolutely bored he was of life here. So much more going was going on in the worlds of the girls. His life seemed so dreary now that he was at home.

*No — that's not it. There is no sense of adventure, that's really it. Here, life is a routine. The big adventure was riding my bike to the lake for a swim! But with the girls, there is always something going on. No — it's that I can more easily find or create purpose, action, and adventure there.* Slowly, a realization hit him. *I'm an explorer! I like to visit new places, new people, new things! Now that is it exactly!* Jon brightened up considerably. *I'm not nuts or weird or crazy. I just like to explore, and it really is much harder to do that in my world. The unknown frontiers are fewer and harder to get to. I could go to Afghanistan! What a hassle. That's why I like Lindy and Verbenloc so well. It is almost trivial to explore, because everywhere I go, I am exploring something new!* He strolled on for a time in a state of serenity. He was at peace with life and the universe and himself. When he at last climbed up the steps to his apartment, he knew what he would give the girls as a present. He went to bed and slept soundly.

The day of his recital, Jon spent visiting stores to get his presents, to get his tuxedo for the concert and to get film and postcards. Tina and Jon practiced one last time in the afternoon. Jon worked well with her because they were just a pair of musicians. And then the biggest event of his music career was upon him. Harry had agreed to come and take several pictures of the old music hall and the concert, though he wondered why Jon wanted a few discrete photos of the crowd.

Backstage, Jon felt a little uncomfortable in his tux, but Tina — solid, dependable Tina — was downright nervous. Stage fright had come. As they went onto the stage and heard the welcome light applause, Jon calmed down a bit, but Tina became even more nervous. As they played their first duet, Jon couldn't help resist the temptation to help Tina relax. So he mentally placed quiet, serene pictures into Tina's mind. Jon could sense her nervousness dissolve. They both became absorbed in their music.

Soon, Jon began to notice the audience. Not by sight, but rather their collective minds. Some had come only because they had to — other undergrads were under orders to attend. These people were in a bored to antagonistic mood. Others had come because it was a social event where they could look their finest and receive admiration for their looks or apparel. They were not really listening to the music so much as they were covertly looking at others. Then there was another group who had come just for the music. They were engrossed in the music. For these, it did not matter what they played so much as long as they played it well. Then, Jon realized a simple fact. A true musician plays to his audience, not just for himself.

This entire point had been neglected in his education. How does one sense what the audience wants and then deliver it? The program had been decided in advance, printed up, and handed out. Yet, he could now sense their audience. Tina was playing mechanically well, so Jon decided that he would play off of Tina. He began to insert subtle ornamentations that would prick listening ears. Soon, he knew that they had immediately gotten the interest of two-thirds of their audience: the listeners and the bored had-to-comes. Soon, the others began to notice that something was going on at this concert, and it was not in the audience. And they began to listen.

Now, Jon really began to enliven the duet. Tina also realized that somehow they were really getting into the music. Jon played with renewed vigor and expressiveness. When they reached the intermission, there was a large round of applause. Jon could hear a loud buzz of conversation. He knew that they had given the people something to talk about.

After the break, it was solo time. Tina went first, playing a catchy baroque piece. Then, it was Jon's turn. He knew what he what he wanted to do, and he did it.

He walked on stage. Instead of beginning, he faced the audience and spoke softly. "Ladies and gentlemen, thank you for coming. As some of you know, my grandfather has just recently passed away. He was my only living relative, and we were close." He paused for dramatic effect. Then, he continued, "I beg your indulgence. I am going to depart from the prepared program to play a piece in his memory." A murmur arose. However, he felt support and began to play the music that he had improvised several weeks ago when he had returned from the funeral. It was then only his doodles. He began as he had at that time — slow, mournful, and low. It was an impressionistic work. Once he felt sure that he had most of his listeners enwebbed in the dirge, he began to pick up the tempo and the volume. Soon, notes came faster and faster. Now higher and higher came the notes. The audience's emotion peaked in a fury. Now Jon let it slowly melt away. Slower and lower he played, until the last notes subsided into nothingness. They were in an emotional vacuum. He ended.

For a moment, Smith Music Hall was in an absolute silence. Then, the audience responded. They sensed greatness and the applause was deafening. Eventually, Jon had to return to receive a standing ovation. He spent the next half hour shaking hands and listening to all the numerous congratulations and expressions of thanks. He knew that he had scored a success. He knew that he was a musician, and Harry had gotten it all recorded on cassette tape for him. He was pleased.

The next two days were spent in taking final exams. Then school was over and Jon had his music degree. More important, he was free — no commitments until at least the fall, if he chose to go to grad school.

So on the twenty-sixth of May, Jon prepared to return to his other worlds. After a glance through the pictures, Jon found no flags or banners flying anywhere. He was content. Apparently, Lindy had had no further problems with the slavers. Then a pang of emotion hit him. The girls also had not signaled him. He could not explain his emotions. Somehow, these two women were having a profound impact on him, but he did not know what or why or how. He had never felt this way before. He knew that he missed them — missed them very badly. And he was glad that he was about to rejoin them.

Carefully, he packed his rucksack. It was now heavy and bulging. He was ready. On a whim, he used the photograph of the picture of the ruins of Castle d'Ambrose. He stepped through. The fresh odor of the green underbrush greeted his nostrils. Grey stone ruins protruded here and there, refusing to be beaten, even in destruction. "Alison. Mandy." Jon called. No reply.

He went to the secret doorway, opened it and hollered once more. "Come on down," Alison's voice echoed up from the dark passage way. Jon hesitated, then retrieved his flashlight and headed down the old steps. Ahead, he could see light coming from a chamber to the right. He entered Alison's front room. The girls had been sitting around a huge table and they rose to meet him.

"Hi," said Jon, meekly. His old embarrassment returned in a flash. They were not shy. Both hugged him and gave him a welcoming kiss. He really wanted this, but still was too embarrassed to say so. Still, he did not get nearly so red in the face this time. They noticed this too.

"We're glad you came back," Alison said. Jon detected a note of shyness in her voice that had not been there before. "Did you get your things done? How was your concert?"

"Everything's all set. I am here as long as I want to be this time. The recital went perfectly." He beamed.

"I'm so glad," Alison replied, evidently much relieved. She smiled broadly.

Mandy smiled and winked knowingly at Jon, but he did not know what to make of this. So he said nothing, while Mandy hinted, "We are glad that you are back, in more ways than one. Alison, why don't you show him around? I'll make us a snack. Leftover rabbit stew all right?" She left without waiting for a reply. Mandy knew that Jon now was curious about them, but also she knew that he would not pry into their minds. She thought, *This will make a good game.*

A bit more shyly than when he had last seen her, Alison showed Jon her underground home. This central hall was the old food storage room. She had it nicely redone. Some salvaged tapestries hung on the walls. Much of the furniture was old and had been carefully repaired. Alison had salvaged much. She had some strange light fixtures. They looked like quartz crystals. A soft light seemed to come from each. Most were clear quartz and emitted a clean, bright light. Little bags or pouches hung from the fixtures. A total of ten currently illuminated the room. Jon saw bags over another four.

"What are these strange lights? They are really beautiful!" Jon inquired, obviously impressed.

Demurely, she answered, "I cast a permanent light spell into the quartz crystals. When I want to turn them off, I put the little bags over them."

"That's incredibly neat!" Jon exclaimed. "Are these others more of the same?"

She blushed, but Jon refused to read her mind. Softly, she said, "No. They are special ones. Go undo one," she suggested.

Jon saw at once that they were rose quartz. The light that came from the others was a pale rose color. "With only these for light, why the room would look — " Jon did not finish his sentence. He flushed red, while her eyes focused on the floor. Jon recovered and said, "That is a gesture of genius! I think that is really an exquisite touch. My compliments."

She smiled appreciatively. "It does get lonely being here all by oneself."

"I know how you feel. At times I'd give anything just to have someone else to share things with, especially beautiful things."

"Thanks." She seemed more at ease now. "You'll never guess what Mandy said when she saw them."

"And you'd better not tell him, either!" She called out as she entered the room carrying a tray of snacks.

"That is, if you value your tongue." Then, she laughed playfully. Alison did likewise.

Jon felt left out but didn't dare say anything. He knew he'd mess up everything if he spoke. So Jon said, "Let's see the rest of the place."

Another ten rooms were in use here in the underground section of the castle ruins. The dungeon had been converted into two bedrooms and numerous storage rooms. If one looked carefully, one could still see that these rooms had once been meant to hold prisoners. Alison's room was done in a white lace motif. Her bed was a large one with lacy curtains surrounding it. She had several wardrobes and cabinets. There was no doubt that this was an elegant woman's room. Mandy had been put up in the spare bedroom, which was finished in royal reds. It was very rich looking.

They merely passed by four other rooms that were used for storage. Jon saw that she had kept much of the furniture that had been broken by the raiders when the castle was destroyed. He knew why she could not just discard it. It was her last touch with her heritage, her past.

When they entered the next pair of rooms, Alison cautioned, "Don't touch anything in here, Jon. This is my wizard's laboratory. I've got lots of protection spells cast on things in here. You could get yourself fried easily."

"I won't. Thanks for the warning," Jon replied, once more acutely aware that Alison was a magic user who had powerful spells.

"I conduct my research in here. Over here, is my study."

Jon saw racks and racks of books, and one wall was filled with a huge case full of scroll tubes. "What are all of those scrolls?" He inquired.

"I have copied some of my spells on them for quick use. Others, I have acquired adventuring; some I have bought. I spend a good deal of time in here studying. Knowledge comes only to those who study." She explained didactically, as if she expected Jon to belittle it.

"I agree. I don't have nearly a tenth of the number of books that you have. But I have spent the last four years with my nose buried in them."

Although Jon did not know why, Alison seemed extremely pleased with his comments. Since she seemed a bit more cheerful now, Jon said nothing, but was curious.

The bathroom was a very cleverly done room. High above was a strange jug. From it came several sets of tubes. One came down to a wash basin made of white marble. It was spectacular. Another came down to what had to be a toilet. The third came down to the largest bath tub Jon had ever seen. It was shaped like a maple leaf. There was a fortune in jewels ornamenting the solid jade tub, which could bathe three people at one time! Jon was impressed. He noticed little corks in each of the three fixture's ends.

Alison explained, "The jug is a decanter of endless, pure water. Just pull a plug and water comes. Magically." Jon talked of nothing else as they went back to the main hall.

As they had oolong tea with the warmed stew and round, heavy biscuits, Mandy explained, "We've been busy while you were gone. Actually, more like Alison's been busy!" She amended.

"Well, you *did* help," Alison offered.

However, Mandy knew that if she let Alison tell the news, she'd only say two words. Mandy wanted Jon to have a full appreciation of things. So she continued,

"That next day, we were talking about the book and the places. We decided that it would help tremendously if we knew what and where each one was — a map, in short. Of course, there isn't any."

"Alison got the bright idea to take her book to her local magic user guild and see if anyone there could shed any light on it. She discovered that many knew of Bard Wendell Theodore Zandras and his works. They discovered that there is a magic command word that causes the title of each painting to appear above it for a short time. Now we know what each is called. I have made a complete listing. She also spent fifty thousand gold coins for this treasure!" She paused for effect. When Jon reacted sufficiently, she pointed to a large map that was spread over the long table.

"It seems that some thirty years ago, a mad, unbelievably wealthy mage appeared nearby and found the mage's guild. He gave them a small fortune just to let him stay for a few weeks. He called himself Kalanos, the Great — but really he looked old and worn out. Nevertheless, he seemed to be a powerful Mage. He left them a large collection of maps and scrolls, saying that he would not need them anymore."

"Alison, here, in a stroke of pure genius, found that this map corresponded to the picture book's places." Mandy smiled in satisfaction, but Alison beamed with well—deserved pride.

"Actually, Jon," Alison explained, "Only about half of the pictures correspond to the map. All of those of Lindy are not there, nor is my place. The clue lay in their names. The pictures of places that are on the map all had the name 'Rochelle' after them. Like 'Rhones Tower, Trundle, Rochelle.' I figured that Rochelle must be the name of the whole world. When I saw that this map had Rochelle in bold letters across the top, I figured it was what we were after. I bought it. It really was quite simple."

"Simple for you, maybe, but I say it was a stroke of genius," retorted Mandy. She knew that she would have never figured that one out. She did not have the patience. "We've been studying the map and correlating pictures with the places on the map. We are nearly through. So you can help us finish it." She sounded relieved to have help. This type of work was not what Mandy cared to do.

Jon praised them both very highly for their tremendous successes. Then, he told them about what he had been doing. When he got to the part about presents, they both became very excited and eager.

He had brought a small battery operated cassette tape recorder for each of them. Each got four tapes: one was of Handel's Water Music; another was the Bach Double Concerto; another was a collection of baroque flute fantasias; the last was of his recital. Also, he brought a spare set of batteries for each. They were impressed, to say the least. To them, the recorders alone were obviously great magical devices. But the music, well they were both enthralled. Several hours passed as they listened to each.

After listening to the tape of Jon's concert, both were convinced that Jon was a musician, and a good one. He received numerous hugs and kisses. He felt pleased and not so embarrassed. He also gave them each a set of photographs of his world — the campus and of the concert — and the postcards. Mandy enjoyed most the series on the national parks. He spent hours answering their many questions on people's clothes, cars, and the like.

When they finished the map correlation project, they held a conference on their next action. He found that Alison had already given this some thought. She gave each a magic ring that when worn made one invisible. It was Jon's turn to be surprised and awed. Mandy was already familiar with them.

"We may be able to sneak past our welcoming party," Alison explained.

"I surely would like to know more about what is going on in Trundle," Jon agreed, as he yawned. He realized that he was getting tired. The girls were too. He suddenly became very red.

Mandy teased, "Now, what?" Then, she picked up Jon's plight. She went on teasing, as Alison was left wondering. "Where shall we all sleep? Or where do we have Jon sleep?" Now Alison caught on.

She grinned broadly and said, "Well, I could put him up with you for the night." She watched as Jon grew even more redder and looked down at the floor. Stifling a giggle, she said as seriously as she could, "Of course, I could put him up with me. My bed is larger." "Oh no," Mandy exclaimed as if suddenly disappointed, "We'll fit, I'm sure. Maybe we all should use your bed. It's probably large enough. It does get cold here in the dungeon!" They both giggled at Jon's plight.

Jon mumbled something about sleeping on the couch. However, he knew he had not seen one on his tour. "I — I like you both very much — very much indeed. But — but." He faltered.

Mandy finished his sentence for him, "Ah shucks. He's just too virtuous to just go to bed with just anyone." Both women had apparently already discussed this topic and had come to just such a conclusion. They were correct. Jon just did not feel it was right to sleep with them, but he wanted to — very much. This was perfectly clear to both women. The idea that they might have wanted him had not occurred to him yet; hence, his plight.

Alison took pity on her embarrassed guest. "Calm down, Jon. We were only teasing. We had already decided that Mandy will sleep with me. My bed is large. You can have the guest room. We both promise to leave you alone."

"But only if you promise to leave us alone," teased Mandy.

"Enough, Mandy. Can't you see that he's embarrassed enough?" Alison spoke seriously. "We've had our fun. Come on. Let's get to bed. Night, Jon. Thanks for the presents." She gave him a good night hug and kiss.

He felt so warm when she hugged him. She felt herself flushing. She hurriedly headed for her room.

Mandy said rather apologetically, "You are something else, Jon. Thanks for everything. Night." She hugged and kissed him as well. Then, she followed after Alison. Over her shoulder, she called back to Jon, "Last one out of the room has to turn off the lights."

Jon knew that he had been had one last time. While he sat there a moment longer, he could still feel their touches and kisses. Then, he put the bags over the lights and headed for the red room.

Everyone slept well. Jon awoke to the smells of breakfast, compliments of Alison. Over breakfast, Mandy proclaimed, "We need to decide upon a division of labor. We girls do not want to do all the work."

Indeed, Jon had a difficult time imagining Mandy in a kitchen for hours on end. He suggested, "I'll volunteer to be permanent dishwasher."

Both girls stared at him in disbelief. "You're on!" exclaimed Alison with a rather amazed look on her face.

"Why are you both staring at me?" inquired Jon grinning.

"Around here, most men would not be caught dead doing women's work," explained Mandy.

"I don't care. If you two do all the cooking, I'm very willing to do my part. I have been washing dishes for my meals for several years now. I don't think that you two should have to do everything. Just don't burn too many pans," he ribbed.

So while Jon cleaned up the mess, the women got themselves ready. Alison put her hair up in a bun and then covered it with a pointed cap. Soon they were all ready to go. However, when they opened the picture book, they were surprised to find that it was nighttime at Rhones Tower.

"We can wait," proposed Alison. "The nighttime scenes are very short. I have timed them, and they last for less than a half hour of our time."

"Maybe it would be better to go at night. They might not be expecting it," Mandy offered.

All agreed. They put the rings of invisibility on and held hands. This was to avoid losing each other as well as coordinating action. Jon then stepped them all onto the hill near Rhones Tower. This time, the girls would not be fettered by a bulky book in their hands should trouble arise.

All was dark and quiet. They were not expected. Carefully, they made their way down the hill to the walled tower and city. Just north of the walls, numerous mineshaft openings were seen. Red torches marked their entrances. Slag piles were everywhere. The party ducked behind an especially large pile to discuss their next move. They took off their rings.

"We need information," Mandy declared. "I know how to get it. You two stay put until I get back."

"You cannot go out there alone," protested Jon.

"There is an encampment there by the gate into the walls. I'll be fine. They'll never recognize me. Here, I'll show you another thing you can do with psi powers. Actually, this one is my major effect. Watch."

Before their eyes, Mandy's body began to alter, to change its very form. In seconds, a huge, ugly hobgoblin stood before them. Jon touched her in complete disbelief.

"She's real!" he exclaimed.

"Darn right," Mandy replied. "If I change into a Pegasus, I can fly too."

"What?" cried Jon not understanding this at all. "Tell him about a Pegasus, Alison. I'll be back soon." And she marched toward the gate guards like she totally belonged here.

"She told me about her special ability," Alison began. "She can change her shape into anything that she desires — with some restrictions on size. She said that it took just too much effort or energy to change to something huge or very tiny. She can alter herself to be very pretty or to be very ugly. It really is incredible."

Stunned, Jon mumbled, "I wonder what she really looks like — if she is really as pretty as I always see?"

With a sigh, Alison replied, "Yes, I'm afraid she is. The way we see her is the way she really is. Some have all the luck." There was a note of envy in her voice. "Oh, yes. A Pegasus is a winged horse. They are highly individualistic, prizing personal freedom above all, much like Mandy. They are basically good. However, they usually avoid contact with mankind."

"They are only mentioned in legends in my world. They really exist?"

"Yes, I have seen two. They are very beautiful creatures."

They now became quiet and tried to hear what was going on. They could not. As though they were still invisible, they held onto each other's hand waiting. Jon felt a strange joy surging through him from her touch, but he said nothing, glad the darkness was hiding his awkwardness; Alison, likewise.

After about a half of an hour, an ugly, red faced hobgoblin suddenly appeared behind them, startling them both. "Got you both!" They immediately recognized Mandy's voice.

"You scared us," criticized Alison. "We might have yelled and sounded the alarm."

"You didn't. I'm just practicing my ranger abilities. Here's the news." She proceeded to tell them what she had learned. "The leader is a mad mage who calls himself Kagor Dougal, the Merciless Mage of Rhones Tower. He is preparing to start a war with Mariane — a country that lies to the east. He's been using the slaves to dig his mines for gold and ore. Apparently, he's a real slave driver. Most all of the men are now dead. There's only about twenty still alive." Mandy reported.

"We have to rescue them," declared Alison. "We had better do it right now!"

"Ok," Mandy agreed. "I thought Miss Goodie Two Shoes here would want to do that right away, so I found out where they are being held. They are in yonder mine. Apparently, it's a fizzle of a mine, full of some kind of slime. They keep the slaves penned there."

"Then, let's get going. It'll be light in another hour," announced Alison. "I'll go first, because they will not recognize me. You two guard the rear." And Mandy was off.

Putting the rings back on, they followed behind — invisible and holding hands. Alison whispered to Jon, "Rangers really hate hobgoblins. We had better keep an eye on her."

Once in the tunnel, they stopped and took off the rings. Jon took out his walking stick, and Alison readied her spells. They continued. Soon they noticed that the ground became slightly slippery. There was something covering the floor. Then, they heard a shout of alarm and the sounds of a brief struggle. They rushed forward to see Mandy finishing off the guards. Jon noticed that she had her old stunningly beautiful form back. Instantly, he knew that she would never go into battle wearing a disguise. It would be foreign to her basic nature.

Jon found the keys and released the captured slaves. It took some time to convince the twenty men that a rescue had come. Acting on impulse, Jon asked, "Is anyone here named Hank?"

"What if there is?" came a dubious response from several voices.

"Well, I come on behalf of Gwyn — Gwyn Saxbury. She asked me to rescue you." That did it. Hank rushed forward and asked all about her. While Jon brought the young man up to date, Alison got the others out and into some order. Mandy had already headed for the entrance.

When they all reached the entrance, Mandy asked, "Ok, Jon. Now what?"

That was a good question. After a moment's thought, he concluded, "I'll take a few at a time back to Brunsway. Mandy, you and Alison defend this spot. I'll hurry as fast as I can."

Alison started to protest, wondering if he would not become too tired or energy drained. Meanwhile,

Jon took five men aside. He had them hold onto each other's hands. Then he took hold and proceeded to get an image of the village and its trident on the western side. He held that image in his mind. He got the idea that he had arrived there and stepped certainly forward onto the plains, bringing the five startled men with him.

Seeing their village, they were overjoyed and began yelling and running for their homes, free men. Jon smiled and returned stepping back into the tunnel.

"Next," Jon said as he arrived. Then, he saw Alison's shocked stare. "What's wrong?" he asked suddenly very concerned. Mandy also looked quite surprised.

"There — there is not any picture of this place in the book! No trident! Nothing! You just came directly back here — not to the hill top over there," she pointed, awestruck. "Oh," said Jon meekly. "I did not even think about that," he confessed. "We'll figure that one out later. I had best hurry, because it's getting light."

A half hour later, he was ready to take the last home. Mandy, Alison, two others, and Hank went on this final trip. Hank had insisted that he go last; his pride had returned. By staying to the end and helping rescue the other men, his stature in his village would rise considerably.

When the group arrived outside Brunsway, it was now daylight. The last two men headed for the village, Hank saw Gwyn waiting nervously for him. When their eyes met, Gwyn rushed to Hank. He grabbed her, swept her off her feet, spun her around in joy, and then embraced for a minute. While Jon watched, he saw that Hank was covered with a black slime. "What is that stuff?" he finally interrupted.

"I don't know. We dug a tunnel and hit a huge pool of the stuff. It's slippery and hard to wash off. You'll see."

Gwyn now kissed Jon on his cheek, saying, "Thank you ever so much. I don't know how to ever repay you."

"Just have a good life, you two. Now get going. It's morning," Jon replied.

"We are rather slimy," protested Alison. Jon now noticed that both he and the girls were rather messy as well.

The girls began a hurried discussion about how to clean the slime off. However, Jon yawned; he felt extremely tired. He wanted to just lay down and sleep. Then he did so.

After a time, he awoke. He was back in Alison's guest room, in bed, and all cleaned up. "What happened," he said rising up on the pillow.

Mandy bounced into the room. "Alison brought us back. We got you cleaned up and into bed. Sleep well?" she teased.

"Yes," Jon replied and started to get up. Then he remembered that he had not undressed himself and did not know what he still had on. He faltered.

"Oh, go get dressed. Alison is off in her lab studying that black stuff. I have lunch nearly ready — roasted capon." Then she left.

Jon did get dressed and went looking for Alison. "What do you make of this?" she asked when he came into her lab.

She had a tiny vial of the black stuff. Jon studied it and then said, "I think it must be a form of crude oil."

"That's what I think, too. It definitely has an oil base. I'm not sure what use it has, except to make a big mess. But it does burn." Mandy called for lunch and they left the lab.

Over lunch, they discussed what to do next. Mandy won all arguments. "If they are massing for a war, we cannot hope to defeat them — just the three of us. Still, I surely would like to know the size of the army. Besides, Alison here could then go and warn all of the neighbors of the impending attack."

All agreed. Mandy then suggested that they should check out other parts of Trundle. "See," she said pointing to the map, "There are three other cities in the land. I wonder if they are also massing armies for war. We need to find out. But the problem is there are no pictures in the book of them. We cannot get there directly, unless you can get us there, Jon."

"I do not think so, Mandy," I was able to do it back in the tunnel because I was familiar with the tunnel. These other places are nothing more than a spot on a map. I don't think I'd even care to try."

Alison let out a huge sigh of relief. "Magic users can get into trouble when they try to teleport to an unknown destination," she explained rather didactically. "Sometimes, they arrive too high and fall down to the ground — if it's many feet above the target, ouch. Even worse is arriving too low. You materialize inside of the ground. Death." Jon grimaced. He had not realized this magic stuff could be so fatal.

They all looked at the map. No one wanted to trek over the Red Mountains or the Baren Range either. The Blue Ice Barrens did not sound inviting. That left only one choice. Hollybine Wood. There was one charming picture of the woods in the book. So that clinched it. They packed up more gear and headed for Hollybine Wood. Mandy seemed particularly excited about the prospect of being in woods once more.

# Chapter 8 Lady Ursla of Hollybine Wood

The trio arrived at the picturesque glen. A dozen, huge, tall oaks bordered the edge of the central, open area. Beyond the oaks the forest stretched densely in all directions. Jon recognized oaks, maples, aspens, elms, and even a hickory or two. There were scattered large patches of dense underbrush and some wild grapevines. Wild flowers were fragrant; the air was humid and warm — noticeably cooler than around Rhones Tower.

Jon could sense Mandy's excitement and joy. This was Mandy's type of environment. Although it was not exactly like her home in The Gnarled Oaks Wood, Hollybine Wood was fairly similar. Her happiness bubbled forth unrestrained. "This is a really fine wood! Just look at those oaks!" She proclaimed to her companions. "I wish Rolinda could see this place."

"Who is Rolinda?" asked a slightly bored Alison. To her, the forest was a pretty place, but nothing to get so excited about.

"She is an elfin archer friend of mine, who lives near me. She is the one who makes all of my arrows of slaying. I bring her the necessary blood of an evil red dragon, for example, and she creates magical arrows of slaying. If one hits, there is a good chance that it will kill the evil dragon — clean and effective and no mess. She loves forests as much as I do."

Since Mandy seemed in no hurry to leave this secluded glen, Alison laid down on the soft central grassy area to wait. She was patient and amused by Mandy. Jon sat down by her.

"This is really a very pretty glen," he began slightly awkwardly. "Do you like woods?"

"Oh — well, they are all right. This one is very pretty. You can hear all of the forest noises. What I like most about it is the sense of great peace. So many of the other places in the world are so hectic, but this glen radiates tranquility. Why don't you play something, Jon?"

Mandy seemed engrossed in exploring their surroundings, so he thought, "Why not?" So he got out his flute and began playing Greensleeves. Alison seemed enthralled by his music and even insisted that he play it again.

Jon liked her very much. She looked so beautiful, lying back on the grass — a jewel in the forest. But then, so did Mandy. He sighed and played to the forest. *Why do I like her so much? Mandy is prettier, but what man could handle her? Maybe it's her voice? Her face? Her figure? No, I think her mind. She's smarter than I. No, but that's got to be part of it. I guess I really don't know.*

Presently, a whisper from Alison brought him out of his reverie and playing. "Don't stop playing, but we have company. Dryads. Must live in these oaks."

Jon played on but watched the slim, shapely, and alluring females standing beside their trees. Even their pale greenish skin did not detract from their comeliness. They were even listening to his playing. He thought, *They seemed to be calling to me.* His mind echoed with their beggings and pleadings. *They want me to come to them. Each one is calling to me. I want to go to them. They appreciate me. They love me.* He played with his heart in his song. They were entrancing. Jon told himself that they were the most beautiful creatures he had ever seen. He knew that he must go to them — to join their lives forever in bliss. He played on, because he could not decide to which of the twelve lovely creatures he should go. It was a horrible, unresolvable dilemma.

Now Mandy was walking among them. *How could I have ever thought that she was so beautiful? Next to any one of these lovely dryads, she is positively ugly! How dare she talk so roughly to these beautiful, harmless creatures! I should stop her. Now, Alison is standing over me. Oh, she looks so grotesque, and her chanting is so crude. I should stop her.*

There was a flash of magic over Jon. He jerked and blinked. His mind freed.

"What happened?" he looked blankly up at Alison and then over to Mandy. They were so beautiful. He saw the dryads. They were frowning and complaining to Mandy about him. Next to the two girls, they were only just pretty. Well, pretty in their own way. What had he done, he began to wonder? Then, he heard Mandy's soft, commanding voice.

"I'm sorry, but the man is ours. Jon belongs, as you would say, to us. No, we do not want to share him with you. Yet, we appreciate your good taste. He is a fine man specimen and you are most welcome to listen to his music. It is quite good. We will not harm you."

They seemed disappointed but resigned to the situation. Jon hesitated, but Alison urged him to play once more. While he played, she whispered to him. "You had a close call. The dryads had cast their charm spells over you. If we had not intervened, they would have carried you into their trees. You would never have seen the world again. You would have spent the rest of your charmed life inside of their tree."

She saw Jon react in a disgusting manner. Hastily, she continued. "I dispelled their magic, and

Mandy intervened and put them in their places. You should feel honored by their desires, Jon. It is only the finest males that they choose." She blushed and was silent, hoping that Jon didn't see her face just then.

But he did and was confused. He knew that he did not really understand women and their deepest feelings.

Mandy called out, "Enough Jon. We should get going now." He was only too glad for some diversion.

"This way. We will follow this faint path that the dryads suggest." Mandy ushered the party off down what was obviously a worn path from the glen.

Once beyond the glen, she explained what she had learned from the dryads. "That was a sacred glen back there. The great druid herself comes there to conduct services. This path here will lead us to the retreat of the druidess. I figure that we can get some information from her. By the way, Jon, that was a close call back there. You almost became their man!" She teased him a bit about this.

Jon retorted, "How can you believe the dryads? Maybe they are sending us into a trap. They will ambush us or something!"

Mandy laughed and Alison smiled. The ranger replied, "Dryads are not evil creatures. They are merely neutral in most matters. They must live their entire lives straying no farther than thirty yards or so from their trees. They share life with the tall oaks back there. When the oaks die, they die. They just wanted a male for a time. You can guess why," she winked knowingly at him. She teased further, "They only choose the best, highest quality males, you know." Jon's face crimsoned, as Mandy knew it would.

Alison said nothing, but thought, *Mandy, sometimes you go too far!*

They continued down the path. Soon, Jon was certain that if it weren't for Mandy, he would have lost his way. It was a barely perceptible trail, at best. Mandy was an excellent guide. She marched determinedly forward as if following a boulevard.

They heard many forest animals in the distance. However, Mandy did not seem concerned. In matters involving the woods, both Jon and Alison trusted Mandy implicitly. They hiked on for several hours before Jon became aware of the lions.

They made a good deal of noise hiking down the path. However, the low, deep, growl of lions caught everyone's attention. Mandy halted, trying to locate the animals. Cleverly, they stayed out of sight. They continued more cautiously, and Jon now felt sure that they were being followed by an entire pride of lions. He became edgy and concerned. Their roars of challenge grew more frequent and louder. Jon estimated that there were at least eight on their trail. Finally, they became visible.

Eight mountain lions trotted up behind them along the path they had been following. They spread out to either side, leaving open only the direction that the party had been heading. Then, they slowly advanced toward the nervous trio.

"Come on." Mandy called. "I think that they just want to make sure that we don't lose the trail."

"You mean that they are guiding us?" Jon asked incredulously.

"That's what I think. Remember, we are in the woods of a powerful druid, attuned to nature. They can easily charm animals. In fact, often they will have animals for servants and protectors."

They continued. Soon, there was a deep roar, much louder than the mountain lions' call. Directly, the largest lion that Jon had ever seen joined the others from the rear. This female lion was substantially larger than Jon and weighed four or more times as much. Her canines were nearly as thick as his wrist. The other lions acknowledged the new arrival knowingly. Jon grew even more nervous. Still, they continued on down the path. Jon failed to see that the trail had now become well worn and broad.

Within a few minutes, they arrived at a little clearing. A tiny settlement lay before them. The small, log cabins were scattered about the bases of oak trees. Each blended perfectly with the woods, as though the cabins themselves grew from the forest floor as well as the trees. Here was a very subtle blend of mankind and nature — a harmonious union.

"This is a remarkable place, Alison," Jon exclaimed, forgetting entirely about the lions.

"Someone does have impeccable taste," she replied. "It must be the great druid's place. Who else would have the skill to create this?"

"I agree," Mandy added and then called out, "Is anyone home? Anyone here?"

All was quiet, even the lions. The lions, Jon suddenly remembered. He looked around for them and saw that they had melted into the wood's edge. All were lying on the ground waiting and watching. However, the large one had disappeared.

"Who comes unbidden through Hollybine Wood?" came an unexpected challenge from the open doorway of the largest of the cabins.

The party whirled around. Jon was speechless. Before him stood another positively stunning woman, who could not be over twenty. She had long curly black hair with a circlet of garlands around her forehead. She was very shapely, and her exquisite form was delightfully visible through the sheer gauze of a white dress that she wore. Nothing was left to one's imagination. Yet, her eyes captivated Jon. Cold, coal black eyes seemed to pierce him, laying his innermost feelings bare to her probe. Her rich voice was likewise cold, yet commanding.

Mandy recovered first and spoke for the group. (Jon was unable to speak for several minutes.) "I am Mandy, the Ranger of Reylona. These are my traveling companions: Mage Alison and Musician Jon. We seek an audience with Lady Ursla of Hollybine Wood. Are you whom we seek?"

"Nay. I am Darless, a humble servant of the Lady. What is your business here?"

"That is a matter between us and her ladyship," retorted Mandy, ignoring the icy stare and the cold, penetrating voice.

For an instant, Darless' eyes seemed vacant. Then, she resumed. "Her Ladyship will see you now. Step this way," and she motioned for them to come inside. "She will be with you in a moment."

The central room of the cabin was rustic. The floor was wooden, as was all the furniture. However, each piece was exquisitely made. None showed even the faintest mar or scratch. The floor was immaculate. The light shining through the windows gave everything a natural yellow glow. The room gave off a warm and regal mood, in stark contrast to Darless, who motioned for them to be seated.

A rear door opened and in stepped Lady Ursla, the great druid of Hollybine Woods. *Here is some woman!* thought Jon. She was about fifty years old, but still every inch of her looked regal. She could have been a queen. She still had a breathtaking beauty. Slim and tall, she wore an elegant green dress made of silk. Her long, wavy black hair had scattered patches of pure white, nobly reflecting her age. She wore numerous jewels, but none were gaudy. Each was just the correct size and shape to accent her appearance. She looked as immaculate as her home. Few women could hope to be so stunning at fifty! She paused long enough to have the proper effect. When she spoke, her voice was commanding, yet soft and smooth.

"Thank you Darless. Would you please bring my guests some refreshments? You may join us as well. Now then, I am Lady Ursla."

Mandy repeated her introductions once more. Lady Ursla kept eyeing Jon as if expecting him to be the party's leader. Soon, Mandy's talk convinced her that he really was subordinate to her. From then on, she gave Mandy her full attention.

Darless brought in some herbal tea and honey cakes, which she quickly served and then took her place beside Lady Ursla. Jon noticed that Darless now seemed just a bit more friendly. While the Lady's tone was definitely aloof and noncommittal, Darless's tone was definitely cold. That she did not like the visitors, Jon felt certain. Nevertheless, he did not probe her mind.

"I seldom receive unbidden guests, but in this case I have made an exception for several reasons. First, my dryads have told me that Jon is an excellent musician. They have asked me to try to bargain with you girls for him." An amused look spread over her face; Darless stared straight at Jon. He shuffled his feet as his face reddened. She continued. "You did not harm them, nor even affront them. You followed their advice. You did not harm anything in my Hollybine, unlike so many ignorant ones. You understood and followed my pride. You have been polite. Even though Darless tells me that it is only because you are all good at heart, I feel that you have been more than honorable to my woods and me. So I have agreed to see you. How may I serve you?"

Jon wondered how Darless knew that they were all good and how she had told Lady Ursla. There had been no time for that.

Mandy began, "We are not from this world of Rochelle, as you probably have guessed. That may be why we are so different. We are basically trying to stop some slavers from troubling our worlds and some others." She found this was rapidly becoming too difficult for her to explain. She doubted that either Alison or Jon could have done much better, but she knew that she had better remain the spokesperson. She was very familiar with druids.

"You see, my goddess, Reylona has asked me personally to halt the destruction of our woods, The Gnarled Oaks Wood. The slavers were destroying much timber and inhabitants." She purposely left out the people being captured, for she knew that all druids were truly neutral in these matters. This would have meant little to her. However, the preservation of forests was another entirely different situation. Druids live for the welfare of their woods.

"The others are here for similar reasons. We have provided some protection for our forests and friends and have now come looking for the source of the slavers. We traced them to Rhones Tower in Trundle — southeast from Hollybine Wood. We tried to visit the tower, but were attacked and forced to leave. However, we did learn that the mad Kagor Dougal, the Merciless Mage of Rhones Tower, is raising an army! He intends to wage war on his neighbors, the country Mariane. Perhaps, he will strike here as well." She paused to see what effect she was having. She saw only expressionless faces. "We came to warn you about this. Also we are planning to explore the northern part of Trundle to see if the other cities are likewise raising armies of hobgoblins. If they are, there are only two reasonable routes to Mariane: through Hollybine Woods and through the Bleak Hills. Alison, here, insisted that you be so informed." She wondered what the druid was thinking of all of this. Then the thought struck her: *Maybe she knows all about this already.*

"I thank you, Alison, for your concern. I am aware of Mage Kagor's designs. He will not come through Hollybine Woods. Of that I am completely certain. It will be both closer and easier to move an army south through the Bleak Hills. The affairs of both Trundle and Mariane are, of course, no concern of mine. If they wish to destroy each other, so be it. I appreciate your thoughtfulness. And as for your ideas of wandering about in northern Trundle, I should advise against it. The people there do not take kindly to visitors. Few have ever come back out of Trundle alive. It is much too dangerous."

"Well, we must at least try," protested Alison.

"I assumed that you would, my dear. But do not worry, you will have safe passage through my woods."

Jon felt immensely relieved with this news. He had been getting concerned that she would somehow try to stop them. He relaxed.

"But a few questions remain and I have a request to make of you. How did you get into Hollybine Wood? The forest tells me that you first appeared at the Sacred Glen of the Twelve Sacraments? How is that possible?" She eyed each one carefully.

Jon suddenly felt another presence attempting to probe his mind. At once, he blocked it out. He assumed that Mandy did likewise. He felt frustrated, for he could not tell whether it was the Lady Ursla or Darless or even someone as yet unseen that was probing. Then, he thought of Alison. She had no defense against mental probing. He grew very worried.

Alison knew that they were in a predicament. Neither Mandy nor Jon would voluntarily divulge the secret of her books. If either should be mind probed, she knew that they could and would bar access to their minds. There was no way that she could stop a mind probe. Since she definitely did not want them to find out about her books, she would have to alter the truth slightly. That she would even consider such a thing, she assigned to being in so close a contact with Mandy and Jon. However, she resolved that if necessary at a later date, she could return and explain about her books to the two women. They would understand. She spoke at once. "It is my doing."

As she spoke, Jon felt the foreign mental probe leave him. He knew that it was now examining Alison. He worried about her safety, but he also felt another emotion that he could not explain. He wanted desperately to protect her.

Alison continued, "I am a powerful mage in my own right. We simply teleported here. We came on foot because we could not bring the added weight of three horses."

Jon thought, *She's a genius. What a reply! Even if they are checking on her, nearly everything she's said is true. What an amazing woman!*

"Yes, that would explain your sudden appearance. And you are not one of those ultra-powerful wizards that could transport an army. If you were, you would not be dabbling in such affairs as these. Oh, yes. One other thing, since my dryads spoke so highly of Jon's music, I really should hear you play. I have not had really good music here in a long time. Besides, I must at least be able to tell them that I heard you. They will be so disheartened when I return to them empty-handed. I'm sure the girls here do not want to bargain for you." She smiled as if she were thirty years younger.

Jon blushed again. The girls laughed and chorused, "No."

Jon got out his flute and played several pieces for her. He found that she was most receptive to Greensleeves. Lady Ursla and Darless began waltzing around the room. Alison and Mandy joined them. Jon had an appreciative audience, and he played several more waltzes. He ended on a sudden inspiration. He finished with the Saber Dance. Both of his hosts seemed to enjoy this one the most. He was royally thanked for his playing.

A little while later, the trio was back on the trail heading southeast toward Trundle. They spoke little because Mandy cautioned that druids can easily talk with plants. They did not want to be overheard. By nightfall, they reached the edge of Hollybine Wood, and before them stretched the rolling grasslands of Trundle. Mandy suggested that they make camp in the soft grasses.

"It looks as if we will camp under the stars tonight," she began.

Alison interrupted her, "I do not want to camp out here in the open — even in a tent. It might not be safe. We'll have to post a guard. Besides, I relish my sleep. I will create my mansion." She slipped off her robe and retrieved her portable hole. After a few minutes of rummaging around in it, she produced a scroll and a small bag. "Watch this, Jon," she said, amusingly.

First, she took the bag off of a quartz crystal light. Then, she very slowly and carefully read the scroll. Jon watched over her shoulder. It was amazing. As she read the words, the writing disappeared from the page. When she was done, the scroll was blank. A flash of magical energies lit the area. A shimmering door faced Alison.

"Wow!" exclaimed Mandy, "This is one of those magical mansions. I have heard about them, but I have never seen one, much less been in one."

Jon was so awed that he said little, but his eyes were wide open. "I travel in style," was Alison's reply. "These scrolls cost me a fortune, but I do so like the comforts and security of home when I travel. Follow me." She opened the door and led them inside this extra-dimensional mansion. Once inside, the door became invisible. To the outside world, they had just vanished. She had created a mansion of about thirty-six hundred square feet. There were a grand hallway and ten side rooms.

After they toured the whole place, they headed for the kitchen and a late dinner. Here Alison cautioned them. "The food and drink are not real. That's the only catch to all of this. We must eat our own rations that we brought."

While eating various dried meats, vegetables, and fruits, they discussed Lady Ursla and Darless. Everyone complimented Mandy on her handling of the whole affair. She felt relieved that they did not think that she bungled it.

Mandy, then, explained her suspicions that the large lion was really the druidess herself. Jon found that hard to believe, but there were similarities. Alison agreed with Mandy, pointing out to Jon that druids shape change readily.

They accepted at face value her refusal to be alarmed at the armies perched on her borders. Yet, all wondered how she could be so absolutely certain that they would not come through her woods. Further, Jon just could not understand her seemingly callous attitude toward the imminent war. She had said that if they wanted to destroy themselves, it was of no concern of hers.

"Did you notice how they both became so cheerful when you played your last song — that fast, warlike piece?" queried Alison. "I think it is just a bit unusual."

"I think Darless is the really queer one," Jon replied. "Lady Ursla has a regal air about her. She is perceptive and not unkind. But Darless is cold. Not aloof. Just cold — like she has no heart."

"I think that she might even be evil in nature," added Mandy, "although I have no proof. I tried to probe her mind, just a bit. I knew that you would not do that, Jon, so I tried. I got no where. I think that she also has psi powers."

"Well, someone tried to probe my mind when Lady Ursla asked us how we came. I took your advice, and I blocked her out. I could not tell who was probing. Is there anyway one can know who is attempting to violate your mind?" Jon asked Mandy.

"Not really. All that you can sense is another mind probing yours. Even when they attack your mind, you cannot tell who is doing it. One time I was battling six evil men. Suddenly one of then tried to crush my mind, but I could not tell which one of the six was doing it. So I had to kill all of them to get him to stop."

Next morning, Jon watched quietly as Alison studied her spell book. It was a huge, leather bound book. She explained that since she had used her dispel magic spell on Jon yesterday, she had to re-prepare it for use today. He was fascinated. He watched her face as numerous expressions came and went. Her pale blue eyes seemed to reflect power. Secretly, Jon wondered if he could ever learn such spells. He wanted to ask Alison but he could not get up the nerve to ask her about it.

When they left the mansion, it vanished. "So goes that spell," lamented Alison. Jon did not ask her how much she had to pay for that scroll. He assumed it was a lot.

Mandy led them southwest across the grasslands. When they approached the town of Mader, they halted. Alison had them all put on the rings of invisibility once more. It would hide them somewhat, but it did not hide their movements through the grass. To avoid getting separated, they once more held each other's hand. They continued toward town. Jon relished the warmth of their hands.

Mader was a walled city. The adventurers had not gone far before they could see the telltale signs of war preparations. They were everywhere. Unlike the hobgoblins of Rhones Tower, here the army was composed of men.

The trio had not gone far, when there came a huge flash of magic that entirely covered them. "What's happening?" yelled Jon. He heard a cold familiar voice carefully chanting. He made out the words "I wish" and then the magical energies began to blot out all of his senses. He felt the secure grip of both girls' hands. Then the world turned dark. All of his senses failed. He felt as if he was in motion somehow. Abruptly, the girls' grasps were broken.

His arms were forced over his head. He felt cold metal around his wrists. Something cold was lying on his back. No, he was standing, leaning against — against a wall. Now his perceptions came back to him.

He was in a dimly lit dungeon, cold and damp. His arms were chained over his head and against a cold wall. He could hear water dripping. The girls were likewise chained beside him. In front of him an evil voice spoke.

"Well done, Darless. You may go to my chamber. I will join you for breakfast after I have welcomed my guests."

"Traitor," Jon screamed in his mind. He stared at Darless as she left. For a brief instant, he probed and saw a glimpse of something else standing there. He did not know what it was. Probably a delusion, he thought. Then she was gone.

Kagor Dougal was a lean black robed mage. He carried a staff which Alison immediately recognized as a magical staff of power. He had a goatee beard and a moustache, both black. His hair was unkempt and stringy and also black. A sneer of contempt was on his face as he stood before Jon. "Welcome to Rhones Tower, Jon Brown. You are my guests." He snickered for a moment, then continued. "You are chained, and I know that you cannot use a picture book to leave me now. You have caused me a good deal of trouble. However, we will talk later on — once you have grown a bit more accustomed to your room." He laughed long.

"I will now have my breakfast. After I have finished, we will talk more." His laughing could be heard echoing down the corridors as he headed up out of his dungeon. Silence grew upon them broken only by soft drips of water seeping into the dungeon.

# Chapter 9 Trapped

The silence was complete except for the faint pings of dripping water. Kagor Dougal had left the few torches burning, so there was a little light. Had he not, it would have been black. For several minutes, no one spoke. Each struggled for comprehension of what had happened. Jon broke the silence first.

"What the heck is going on? How did we get here?" He was completely confused. "I remember a flash of magical energies covering us. I sort of heard an 'I wish' and then everything happened at once."

"We were brought here by magic — very powerful magic, indeed," Mandy began to explain. "I heard it too. It was a wish spell. It is one of the most powerful magic spells that there is! Only extremely powerful mages can use that spell. I once bought a ring that had three wishes cast and stored in it by Melvin, the Mystic. It cost me more than thirty thousand gold coins! Jon, now is the time to start worrying. We are in *big* trouble."

Alison moaned and antagonistically retorted, "I knew I should not have lied. It would have made no difference! I lied for — for absolutely nothing!" She began to cry.

Stunned, Jon sympathetically asked, "Alison, what are you talking about? Please stop crying. I don't understand."

Between sniffles, she answered, "Being totally truthful is my way of life. I have violated — compromised — my own principles. Remember, when Lady Ursla wanted to know how we got to her sacred glen, I — I told her that we teleported us there. I lied. I have felt perfectly miserable ever since. I figured that I did it because of being in so close a contact with you two. But it would not have even mattered. I knew I should have told the truth to her. Darless already knew all about us! So the lie was all for nothing! I have sinned against myself for nothing." And she began to sob once more.

"Oh, Zagroot Zounds!" exclaimed Mandy.

"No, I think that's where we are," retorted Jon. "That won't help her, so keep still." She was silent. Jon listened to her sobs for a minute. He could understand her feelings. "Alison, I do understand," he began. "I'm that way about my music. But you have missed two very important points." He paused. She ceased crying. Curious, she listened.

"First of all, I'm absolutely certain that if Darless had known that we carried the books, we would not be in possession of them right now. Kagor would have all of them! Remember, he said, 'You are chained, and I know that you cannot use a picture book to leave me now.' If he had ours, he would not have said that. So as it turns out, by your tiny alteration of the truth, you may have just saved us all and all of Rochelle." He saw that she had not thought about this. He watched her as she brightened up considerably.

"What's the second thing," she queried?

"You won't like this one," Jon began, softening the blow he knew he was about to deliver. "Truth is important to me, but I can lie when I deem it necessary for my survival. I don't know about Mandy. The second point is that you are blaming contact with us for your transgression. Sorry, Alison. That cannot be the truth. Only you yourself could have chosen to distort the truth, not us for you. You cannot blame us for your own actions."

She looked stunned for a moment, then tears welled up in her eyes. Mandy groaned, expecting to have to hear more wailing and she had enough to worry about. However, Alison was brave. She faced Jon's comments with all of her intellect. She could feel her emotions wanting to cry, cry, cry for sympathy — that she was not at fault. Yet, she knew that he was right. She had felt miserable and desperately wanted a scapegoat. Just as the tears formed, she fought back and meekly replied, "You speak the truth. The fault is mine alone. I — I decided to lie." With her admission, sudden relief flooded over her. She felt as if her confessed sin had been forgiven. All of her unhappiness dissolved. She felt immense relief.

"How did you know — how did you?" she eagerly, but meekly tried to ask.

"Congratulations, Alison. I did not know if it would work. The truth will set one free, if one has the fortitude to see the truth as it really is. You are one strong woman." Jon commented. His opinion of Alison rose considerably.

"I still have one question: why did I decide to lie just then? But I think that we have more urgent problems," she added looking over at a grimacing Mandy.

Mandy said, "Well, we are in big trouble, thanks to that traitor Darless. I cannot wait to get my hands on her, I'll — I'll well I won't say what." She retorted, yanking on her chains.

"No doubt that she IS a traitor. But I wonder what happened to my rings of invisibility. You remember, we were all wearing them. I guess they have been lost," lamented Alison.

Just then, they heard soft footsteps coming down the steps into the dungeon. They became quiet.

Presently, Darless herself stepped into the chamber carrying no light at all. Apparently, she could see very well in dim to no light. Just as Mandy was about to utter a curse, Darless commanded, "Hush! Don't say anything. I know what you are thinking. But I don't have any time just now. I — I am here acting on behalf of Lady Ursla. I'm making sure that Kagor's army marches to the south and not through Hollybine Wood. It is imperative that Kagor does not find this out! So do not let him know that you already know me. If you say anything damaging about me, I shall see that you are all slain. I hold much secret power around here!"

Before they could answer, she began a low chant of strange words that Alison alone understood. Soon a filamentary, glowing door appeared. Darless stepped through and was gone.

"She is a magic user!" proclaimed Alison. "That was a spell of short distance transportation — a doorway to a nearby place. She probably means her threat!"

Jon agreed, "Yes, I suppose that we really have no choice but to honor her requests. I cannot squeal on her, for then Kagor might ravage the woods. Perhaps Lady Ursla knows or has sent Darless here. Maybe that is why she was so certain that trouble will avoid her."

"Zagroot Zounds!" cursed Mandy. She was rapidly becoming confused. She longed to take on Darless in a fair fight and put an end to this sneaking and plotting.

Soon, the trio heard the noise of several feet coming down into the dungeon. Jon took a deep breath. "Remember, no matter what happens," he whispered, "I love you both very much." There, he had said it. He felt relieved. For once, he knew that his face was not red. The visitors marched into the chamber.

Kagor had come, along with Darless and two burly guards. The bored guards took up positions by the stairs. Darless stood in the background; her face, cold and expressionless; her eyes, piercing.

Kagor began, "Well, I see that you are all comfortable." Jon's arms were aching and he grimaced reactively.

"Your traveling days are now over. You are mine — mine completely. I can even let you free right now and you'll not harm me. There is absolutely no escape, you see. No, you don't see, do you?" He laughed, basking in his power. "I will explain. You see, any time that you decide to leave me, all that I have to do is to ask my beautiful assistant, Darless, and she will simply use her wish spell to bring you back to me. You see, there is nowhere you can run to — no place you can hide. We do not even need to know where you are. She merely states my wish and, presto, here you all are once more. Neat and tidy." He laughed and snickered for some time, obviously pleased with himself and Darless. Then, he added, "And if you persist in using the book of picture portals to elude me, then I will just have to poke your eyes out. No more travel. Even blind, you can dig well enough in my mines. You will replace those miners that you stole from me! So do not get any ideas." He laughed once more.

Then, he added to Jon and Mandy, "And don't get any ideas of mind blasting me! I am prepared against the likes of thee." Lovingly, he stroked an amulet about his neck and turned to Alison. "You recognize it don't you, pretty little Mage? Yes, it is an amulet that protects my life and nullifies any mind blasts against me. Tell the others about it. You are powerless!" He gloated.

Alison explained mostly to Jon, "It's a magic amulet of life protection made only by very powerful magic users. It'll absorb all mind blasts at him." Mandy's face became crestfallen as her last plan of escape dwindled away.

"What do I want of you? It is simple. Turn over all of your magical gear, explain to me how each works, and tell me what the command words are that activate them. I know for a fact that that robe you are wearing, dear Alison, is a magical robe of the archmage. I won't touch it; it is aligned toward good. It would harm me if I tried to use it. I will simply burn it up. You all can give me your books of picture portals. I have many underlings that can make excellent use of them."

"Then, you will agree to always do my bidding — you really have no choice in the matter, you see." He snickered triumphantly once more. "And you will agree never to resist my will. When you have done these things, I will give you the status of courier and concubines. If you do not, then I will make you my slaves and put you to work in my mines, replacing those that you stole from me." Now he roared with laughter. He knew that they really had absolutely no choice. The power he had through Darless had made him invincible. He knew he was strong.

Jon, trying to change the subject, interrupted his laughter, "Why? Why the army? Why fight Mariane?"

"Poor ignorant peasant! Don't you know anything? I guess Darless is right. You are not from this world. I, Kagor Dougal, the Merciless Mage of Rhones Tower, will explain history to you."

"Mariane is a land of ship-lovers. Many years ago, they were the only sailors of the high seas. They became fabulously wealthy because they carried all of the trade for the rich Southland Ports. Then, thirty years ago, a strange wizard appeared down south of here. Called himself Kalanos, the Great. No one really lived below Trundle in the Desolation Desert. Yet, he settled in the Quatarra region, in the extreme south by the Straits of Malibar."

"This region did have a few trees and was known for its iron ores. This wizard built strange iron sea vessels. No one could see how they could float, much less move. Sail power could not move such a heavy mass. Well, he built massive magical engines in them. The magical energy source was liquid fire. Apparently, that stuff was commonly available there in Quatarra. His magic boats could go faster, farther, and carry three times the load of the mariner's wooden boats. The iron hulks were never stopped by storms."

"Within one year's time, Kalanos had wrenched the entire shipping market from the ships of Mariane. He and his followers now became fabulously wealthy and built a city there, Kalanos City. The mariners suddenly found themselves destitute. Their ships rotted in the harbor. Some became pirates; a few, smugglers."

"Fascinating," retorted Jon, "But what has all of this to do with you?"

"I'm coming to that. You see, the impoverished Mariners had no place to go. Many came here to Rhones Tower looking for a hand out. I, the Merciless Mage, in my youth, gave succor to all that came. I fed them. I gave them work. I gave them their lives! Ungrateful bastards. I was younger then. However, some thirty years ago, all the liquid fire supply was used. Kalanos became desperate. He sent emissaries everywhere looking for more of his precious liquid fire. Eventually, he stripped his land of trees and burned them in his magical engines. Soon, all of his ships were beached."

"In desperation, the Southland lords turned back to Mariane for ships. But by then, most all of their ships had rotted away. The call went forth to all mariners to return to Mariane. Work was readily available. They built new ships and became fabulously wealthy once more. All those form whom I had given new life in their dark hour then returned to Mariane and became rich beyond belief. However, not even one has ever sent me so much as a silver coin in thanks for aiding them. They ignored me. They ignored my messengers asking for remuneration. They laughed at them! I swore revenge! For ten years now, I have been plotting to even the scales. I will have my share of their wealth!"

"But what happened to Kalanos?" interrupted Jon, fascinated by the tale.

"No one knows for sure. Legends say that one night he took all of his wealth and fled Rochelle. He has never been heard of since. His city was abandoned to the desert. His vessels rust in the harbor. No one lives in Kalanos City anymore."

"Anyway, I began numerous mines — dug ore for weapons, dug gold and gems for money to hire my army. I have bred hobgoblins for foot soldiers. And soon, very soon as Darless councils, I will be ready to attack. Oh, sweet revenge."

"Then, you came along. I will not have you disrupting my plans for Mariane. You are now my slaves. You have absolutely no choice in the matter. With Darless, there can be no lasting escape from me, save to leave Rochelle forever. That will serve me nearly as well."

"But you do not have to answer me yet. I will leave you and let you think it over. Soon your arms will ache, your stomachs will cry out, your legs will tire. You will demand to be my courier and concubines. You are quite pretty, Mandy. I am not as old as you might think." Mandy spat at him. He smirked.

"Come. They have much to think about. I will return after supper. Goodbye." He joined Darless and the guards. Together, they stamped up the steps. Soon, only the slow plinking of falling water drops could be heard.

Mandy repeated herself, "We are in *big* trouble."

"But we have learned a lot," insisted Alison. "If only we can find a way to escape and use it," she added hastily, and then lamented, "But how?"

Jon said, "Well, it seems that Darless is at the center of whatever we do. Any action that we will ultimately undertake centers on that strange, powerful woman. You know the first time she left, I stared at her and she looked different. I must have been hallucinating."

"Why, what do you mean?" asked Alison.

"For an instant, she looked different, just as she turned her back and went up the steps."

"How so?" she insisted.

"Oh, well, she did not look quite human and not nearly as pretty as normal. She had these silly, little, stubby horns sticking out from her forehead. And she had some tiny, black wings protruding from her back. They were so small; you couldn't even use them to fly with. You see, I must have been hallucinating probably because I had just thought 'You devil!' when I first saw her here."

"Wow! That explains a lot!" cried Mandy. "She is no devil she could only be an alu-demon!"

"We are in BIG trouble," exclaimed Alison. "But that explains a lot."

"Hey, would somebody please tell me?" protested Jon. "None of this makes the slightest sense to me. I was just dreaming. What's an alu-demon?"

Mandy explained. "First, a succubus is a female demon with fangs, horns, and huge wings. They can appear quite beautiful, even in their natural state. They cannot be harmed by normal weapons, and they can drain the life energy of humans, usually by kissing them. They can shape change at will and are quite powerful demons. They are totally evil."

"The alu-demon is the female offspring of a succubus and a human male. These are very powerful creatures, usually evil, who have mastered the magic arts and can cast many powerful spells. They can shape change at will and usually disguise themselves as very beautiful women. In their true form, they have tiny horns and small bat-like wings. They can also drain the life energy of humans and can use it to increase their own well-being. Like their mothers, they cannot be harmed by normal weapons."

"Some are really geniuses. They can become quite powerful mages, and some even have strong psi abilities. This probably comes from the demon side of the family because I cannot see a man with any brains mating with a demon! Darless must be one of the smarter ones."

"Why do you say that?" inquired Alison.

"Well, I did try to probe her mind back in Hollybine Wood," Mandy explained. "I was effectively blocked. Psi ability and intelligence along with wisdom are intertwined. There is no such thing as a moron with psi mental abilities. That makes her a deadly foe."

"So what are we going to do?" Alison asked. There was a feeling of hopelessness in her voice. She could see no way out of the predicament, save to leave

Rochelle forever. This she knew she could never do and still be true to herself.

"First thing is to get these abominable chains off. My arms and legs hurt. Mandy, see if you can break free." Jon suggested, while struggling himself.

Mandy was the strongest of the trio, but try as she might, the chains held fast. "No good, Jon," she called back.

"There must be a way," Jon mused, straining his neck upwards to look at the lock. "Boy, these are crude locks. I forgot that this is a relative primitive culture. I'll bet there is just one slider at most. If I just had one hand free. Hum. I need a wire." He looked around hopefully, but no wires.

"Is that all you want, just to get these locks open," Alison asked hopefully? She was still pondering the larger problems.

"Well, yes," replied Jon, "I do not think so well tied up like this."

"Well, ok then — down you come." She spoke several magic words, and magic flashed. Jon's lock flew open; his arms fell down like lead weights.

"Ah, that is better. Thanks. Can you get the other locks open?"

"No. I only prepared one such spell today. Can you get us free?"

"Sure. No problem, but I need a small piece of wire."

"How about a hair pin?" suggested Alison, "Take one out of my hair." Quickly, Jon bent the end just right and began fiddling with the locks. He had both locks open, much to the relief of the girls. Mandy chuckled, "I did not know that you were a thief, Jon Brown."

"Huh? What do you mean?" He protested, "I've never stolen anything."

"Well, around here, thieves are the masters of locks and other similar things."

"Sorry to disappoint you," Jon retorted, "Where I come from, these can hardly be classified as locks. A child could pick these. I have had to unlock my door several times when I forgot my key. Ok, now what do we do?"

"Well, if we split and head for any other place in Rochelle, Darless will have us back here at once. We could return to other worlds, but then what?" Mandy replied, rather confused.

"Everything centers on Darless!" exclaimed Alison. "If only there was a way we could get to her."

"Maybe there is," replied Mandy, thoughtfully. "There is one long shot — psi coupling. She did not have an amulet like Kagor. I'm sure that she has mental abilities, but she is likely stronger than any one of us alone. If Jon and I could couple our mental force, we might have a chance. Remember what happens to Jon when he uses too much energy too fast? He falls unconscious. If we can get her to do that, we might have a chance."

"But I do not know how to do whatever you are suggesting," protested Jon. "I am untrained. I do not even know what it is that I'm doing at times."

"That is all the better. It can only make it harder for Darless. I have never actually done this coupling, but I have heard how it is done. So I will throw you my energy. Jon, you do the attacking. I will just play power plant. Alison, when we do this, you will be in charge of absolutely everything else that goes on. We will be totally engrossed in the fight."

Alison spoke determinedly, "Don't worry. I'll take care of the rest!"

Now the next problem was to get Darless down into the dungeon alone. After some discussion, Jon decided to try to probe for her mind. He felt sure that he would recognize it. It was so cold. Then, he would just send her the idea to come down alone. Mandy informed him that if they joined, the effective range of the probe could be doubled. So Alison stood guard, Mandy concentrated on Jon, Jon began to probe.

Actually, it felt to him more like roaming. He could sense his distant body down below him. He could feel the presence of the girls he loved. He began to search for that cold mind he knew belonged to Darless. Jon was methodical. He began sweeping in small circles centered on the dungeon. When he had probed in a complete circle, he expanded the radius and repeated his searching. He had gone some distance, when he began to contact minds.

Soon he picked up all sorts of minds. Mostly they were the kitchen and servant staff. His mind was filled with numerous images. These he ignored. Jon was looking for one specific mind. On and on, he probed. He passed by Kagor, himself, before he realized who it was. Then, his felt her. That cold, dark presence was in front of him. Her mental barriers went up as soon as he made contact with her. Jon sent her the idea: "Come down alone at once." Then, he dove back to the dungeon. He felt a bit tired.

"Success. She will be coming down, I'll wager. Now what?"

Mandy suggested that they pretend to be still chained up. Surprise might be on their side. She then talked to Jon about how to handle the coming mental battle. Then, footsteps were heard coming down their way. They took their places.

Soon, Jon felt that familiar cold mind probing them. Evidently satisfied that they were still chained, Darless came on into the room. "What do you want?" she asked.

She looked so pretty that Jon faltered. *Could they have been wrong about her? I hate to harm someone so pretty.* At last, feeling a nudge from Mandy, he reached toward Darless with his mind. Immediately, she threw up her defenses. Then, she countered. Jon felt a blast of mental anguish hit him. *We are going to fail. I now am sure of it. All is lost. She is powerful. I am weak. I am nothing.*

Suddenly Mandy's power boost came through. *No, those were her ideas that she hit me with.* Jon imagined a small particle before him. He threw it at her. He picked up an immediate confusion on her part. Jon imagined two particles and threw those at her. Then, he got into it. Each time, he kept doubling the number of particles. It was rather like a snowball fight, only using mental snow. He did not try for accuracy, just sheer numbers. He knew that if he threw enough fast enough, one was bound to hit.

This was going much like his fight with the shadow demon had gone some weeks before. However, Darless fought back. Repeatedly, Jon had waves of feelings of worthlessness, helplessness, and woe flood over him. He merely ignored them. He put his undivided attention onto making more energy snowballs. For variety, he turned them yellow, then pink, and then spotted green and blue.

Darless was a formidable, adaptable foe. She had not achieved the powers she had by being weak. Seeing that her normal mental attacks were failing, she stopped to analyze this new form of attack that Jon was using. Then, she countered. She made snowballs of energy and threw them back at Jon. Some of them hit his mind. When they did, he felt pain, as if a real snowball had hit him. Taking her cues from Jon, she created more and more and threw them at him.

Balls of energy were flying thick. Many nullified each other in mid-flight collisions. Many missed. Some hit Jon and Darless. Both were weakening from the strain. Now Jon changed his strategy. He put more thought into creating the energy balls larger and larger in size. When these hit, it caused more damage. Darless, of course, caught on quickly to this new variation.

Jon knew that he was tiring and that he had better devise something else. While he was thinking, he put up a shield barrier to deflect the giant balls of energy. Soon a wall had formed. He finally had to deal with the huge buildup of energy balls, for he found that their mass was becoming too much for him to hold back. He was nearly washed away from the suddenly unleashed force. Still, it gave him an idea.

He would reverse the force vectors on her. Carefully, he put up his shield once more, but this time, he put the shield around Darless, forcing his balls of energy to pile up on his shield protecting her. She paused to ponder this strange quirk. Jon was now protecting her from himself! She could not figure this one out and decided that this would make him easier to finish off. She shot more and more energy at Jon. He felt like a duck in a trap shoot. He dodged those that he could. But always, he piled his own up against the shield above Darless. He tapped all of Mandy's flows to help him make a few balls and retrieve Darless' shot ones.

Now Darless saw that he seemed to be trying to help her finish himself off. He was crazy, she thought. Still, Jon used every ounce of mental energy he could muster to hold that shield up protecting Darless from the huge, ever growing pile on energy balls. Finally, he knew that Mandy was about spent and that he could no longer hold the shield up.

In a flash, Jon dropped his shield. In one instant of time, recognition came to Darless. Suddenly, she knew what Jon had done, but there was no time to do anything about it. The huge mountain of energy balls, some her own, came crashing down upon her.

All of her barriers went down in a flash. Darkness swept over her. She knew nothing more.

Jon realized that Mandy had collapsed on the floor and he knew that he too would collapse within moments. He sent a mental command to Alison. Then, the universe went black for him as well.

For Alison, it was the weirdest battle she had ever witnessed. There was Mandy, Jon, and Darless — they were just standing there looking at one another. Soon, she saw beads of sweat appear on Jon's forehead. Then, they appeared on the other two. She knew something was going on. Quickly, she cast a spell over the entrance to the dungeon. Sticky, black spider webs now covered the entrance. No one could get to them, at least without chopping their way through the webs. That would give her time for other spells.

Instinctively, she knew that when the battle was over, Jon and Mandy would be spent. She had seen this before. She got out her picture book and waited.

She knew that she could end it all here simply by stabbing the motionless Darless with her dagger. She also knew that if she did, she could never have lived with her conscience. It would be a wrong and dishonorable thing to do. She'd rather keep her integrity and be a slave than stoop to the ways of evil.

Then, she saw Mandy fall to the ground. Almost at once, Darless fell. Then, Jon's voice echoed in her mind. "Get us all out of here at once! Bring Darless." Then, she saw him collapse on the dungeon floor. She acted without hesitation.

# Chapter 10 Darless

It was noon. It was hot. Jon had no idea of how long he had been asleep. Now that he was awake, he had no idea where he was. Then he remembered where he had been and groaned.

"Ah, you are awake. Come on lazy head. It's nearly noon." Alison ribbed him playfully.

Propping his head on one arm, he looked up at her. *She is so pretty standing there. She has her long hair down, now. Not like yesterday. Yesterday!* Suddenly, he remembered. He jumped up scattering blankets everywhere. He was breathing fast.

"Calm down, Jon." Alison cautioned, "There is no cause for alarm. Everything is under control. See." She pointed around the campsite.

Mandy was still sleeping under blankets, but Darless was already awake. Jon noticed that Alison had the alu-demon nicely tied up so that she could not cast spells or escape. Alison also had a small fire going and he smelled food.

"Want some lunch?" asked Alison. "I've boiled up a bunch of our dried rations and made some mint tea."

"You bet. Fix me some, please. I'm going to rouse Mandy."

"I did not know whether I should disturb you two or not. I do not know much about your disciplines. So I thought it best to let you both wake when you were ready."

"You were right. I feel refreshed." Then, he woke Mandy, who likewise was startled. Soon both were eating, while Alison brought them up to date.

"When I saw you all collapse, I got your message, Jon. I did as you said, and I got all of us out of there."

"But where are we?" both choroused.

"Somewhere in the Bleak Hills. I took the precaution of tying up Darless. I was scared that she would wake up first and attack me. And in fact, that's just what happened. She woke up first and is taking this all really rather nicely, I'd say. She hasn't even complained. In fact, she returned the rings of invisibility." Alison finished. She felt a pride in being able to have done her part in the struggle, even if it was minor. "I have been wondering what we do next? I don't think that we can take Darless along with us everywhere we go. Although, she does seem much more pleasant now."

After finishing lunch, Jon called for a conference with Darless. He now knew much about her. Her defenses had collapsed just at the end of his attack and he had gotten a brief view of her innermost thoughts. An idea was forming.

Surprisingly, Darless spoke first. "My congratulations, Jon Brown. You are the first person to so take me out since my father. When I went down, all of my mental defenses were lowered. I assume that you discovered much about me. Do you know my true name?"

"Yes. And for our mutual protection, I will reveal it to the girls. Her full name is Darless Hugo Dogoroth. Hugo is her father's first name; Dogoroth, her mother's last name. But will someone please explain to me why you three consider that to be so vitally important?"

To his surprise, it was Darless who replied. "You are not from this or a similar world, are you? Names have power here not by themselves — but rather the use that they can be put to. Let me explain in my own case.

I'm an alu-demon — spawn from a succubus and human mating. I would like very much to alter that, but I cannot!" She was so sincere and emphatic that Jon began to sense something deeper in her than just an explanation.

"I am these days about as powerful a mage as Alison is and stronger mentally than both of you. Plus, I have inherited many of my demon mother's special abilities as well as my looks." At this point, she dropped her shape alteration. She looked downcast. She was still quite comely, but she had two short, stubby horns protruding from her forehead and tiny bat-like wings placed on her shoulders. It became obvious that she did not like this image.

Jon said, "I still think that you are very attractive in your true form, Darless. But I know that you hate it. Please, you do not have to lower yourself any further."

That act of kindness brought a long, searching look to her face. "Thank you." She altered her form back to the shapely human with whom they were familiar. She continued her explanation. "If someone knows my name, then by proper arcane spells, they can summon me from wherever I am. I have no choice but to appear before them — much like I did with you. It does not matter what I am doing at the time or whether I want to come or not. I have to come. Further, if the summoner has taken the proper precautions, and most all do, I cannot retaliate. I am then forced to do their bidding — whatever that is — whether I like it or not. It is *most* degrading! I hate it."

Jon looked aghast. "Is there nothing that you can do?" he asked lamely. "Only guard my true name. That is the only way. For me, it is almost as precious as life itself."

"I agree with you!" he exclaimed. "I — I am sorry now that I have discovered it. But I swear that I will not divulge it nor use it."

"I trust you and I believe you, Jon Brown. That is why I am talking to you now. The same goes for Mandy and Alison. You may not believe me, but I really do admire you three."

Her unexpected compliment startled him. It was so very unlike the way she had acted before toward him and the girls. He realized that the combat victory must be very significant in ways that he did not yet understand.

"But what are we going to do with her?" queried Mandy. "What's to keep her from wishing us back to Kagor's dungeon?"

"Let me tell you my story; perhaps it will help."

"Wait. We are not being very civilized," broke in Alison. "Will you promise not to do anything that we might regret if we untie you?" Darless agreed. Jon thanked Alison and apologized to Darless for overlooking this. Mandy protested. She did not trust a demon.

"Recently, by name calling, I have been forced to serve the goddess Morrigan, the goddess of war. She is thoroughly evil and delights in watching bloody wars. If I fulfill her request this last time, she has promised to release me."

"What is it that you have to do? Oh, I'll bet it has to do with Kagor Dougal's proposed war with Mariane!" exclaimed Alison.

"Yes. But it is a long story. Kagor himself nearly touched upon the truth when he was telling you the history of this land. However, he failed to mention two very key points. First, thirty years ago Mariane was suddenly forced to rebuild their sailing ships so they could regain all of the profitable shipping for the Southland Ports. What Kagor failed to tell you was that the mariners were very short of oak trees. In their haste to build new vessels, they raided Hollybine Wood. They cut indiscriminately. Every oak tree on the western edge of the forest was cut. Many poor dryads died. Many forest creatures were made homeless. It was a terrible wound to Hollybine Wood and Lady Ursla was utterly powerless to prevent it."

"The second point he failed to tell you was his own destruction of Hollybine Wood. Ten years ago when he swore revenge on Mariane, he began great mine works. He opened many, many new shafts, looking for gold and iron ore. There are very few trees in Trundle. He raided the eastern edge of Hollybine Wood for trees to make supporting beams. His destruction was very like Mariane's. Again, Lady Ursla was powerless to prevent it."

"She swore revenge on both lands. About two years ago, Lady Ursla conducted a great ceremony that cost her a small fortune. She summoned the aid of Morrigan herself. Well, Morrigan responded to her request for aid. She gave Lady Ursla two gifts: two copies of the picture book of portals and me. My allegiance is to Lady Ursla, by command of Morrigan. Under her orders, I took the books to Kagor and offered them as gifts, if he would let me assist him in his revenge. After I showed him how to use them, he trusted me completely. I have now got him completely under my control. He will do nothing, unless I ok it. Periodically, I teleport to Hollybine Wood to keep Lady Ursla updated on the progress. Soon, he will strike."

"Lady Ursla will get her revenge. Both of those who have so horribly wronged her will be destroyed by their own hands."

Mandy interjected, "Wow! That is some druid! But it is typical, Jon. That is how a druid would react. That is some plan. She is quite a lady! I certainly would not want to cross her."

"Yes. But over these last two years, I have found myself growing very close to Lady Ursla. I — I love her like a mother." Emotion swelled and caught in her throat. She had to pause.

Curious, Jon asked, "What was your mother like? I'm afraid that I am very ignorant about so many things."

She looked sorrowfully at him and said, "She was evil. She killed my father; I killed her. Let me explain. Mother was Myleen Dogoroth and ruled a castle in the Abyss. Father was Hugo; he never revealed his last name. That way, he explained to me, he could never be summoned against his will. He kept it hidden even from me. He was a great mage, nearly twice as powerful as Alison or I am. He had strong mental abilities as well. As I got to know him, I discovered that he was really truly neutral. He believed in the balance of all things: good with evil and law with chaos. Apparently, he and his wife — he never ever spoke of her were childless. He wanted a daughter; it was really an obsession with him. So he left his wife and went to some desolate place. There he cast powerful spells and eventually summoned Myleen to him."

"He struck a bargain with her. I never knew what it was. They became lovers, and she eventually gave birth to me. They lived in her castle for five years. I think that he was performing some magical services for her. When I was five, he pronounced the contract complete. He took me away with him. He had a castle, and we lived in solitude for many years. Those were the happiest years of my life. Every day he would teach me magic spells and how to use my mental abilities to their fullest. When I grew older, we would attack each other mentally. He wanted to prepare me for the hard life that he knew I must eventually lead. I have often thanked him for that. Over the years, only my father has ever been able to best me mentally, until you, Jon."

"Well, when I was eighteen, my mother, in an act of deceit and treachery, raided his castle and killed him in his sleep. Mentally, he warned me of what was happening, and I came to his aid. Although I blasted her into bits, I was too late. She had already killed him. Without his great magical protections, my fate as a demon was sealed. At least, Morrigan has promised me my freedom when this war is done."

There was a long period of silence before she spoke further. "You might as well know. I do not really have the free use of the magical wish spell, but I can freely teleport twice a day. When I need to fulfill another's wish, I simply call upon Morrigan. She wants this war badly. She lusts for war and bloody battles."

"Well," Jon began, "Thank you for honoring us with your innermost secrets. I shall honor them as your father would. You really haven't done anything evil to us that is of any real consequence. What I propose is a truce. We do not want to find ourselves back in that dungeon. I certainly do not really want to harm you. We do not wish any ill to Lady Ursla. Still, we have or feel an obligation to at least let the people of Mariane know about the impending war. At least they can be prepared. What say you that, if we stay out of Trundle and Hollybine Wood and not attack Kagor in any way, then you let us alone here in the rest of Rochelle?"

"I know that you must tell Mariane about the war. There is really nothing any of us can do to prevent it. When a goddess has her mind set on having a war, she will have her war. But if you will not directly intervene with Kagor and mess me up with him, I will see to it that he does not bother you or your worlds any longer."

"Yes. So how will you explain all of this to Kagor?" wondered Mandy. "He's sure to ask questions. He'll demand that we be returned."

She smiled. "I have a way with him. He really is under a permanent charm spell from me. He cannot go against me. He does not know that he is charmed, of course. I will say that you have returned to your own worlds — that you are afraid of him."

"Well, if you need anything, just let us know," volunteered Mandy. She had somehow taken a liking to this alu-demon, in spite of her best warnings to herself.

"Thank you. And thank you, Jon, for the great mental game. You are a true master. Now, I must really be getting back." She spoke a few strange words. Magical energy flashed, and "poof" she was gone.

The trio sat in silence for several minutes.

Jon broke the silence. "That was quite a story. Darless is some — well, I want to say woman, but I can't."

"I know," put in Mandy. "She's caught in the middle of the eternal struggle between demons and gods. She is a pawn in the great struggle between good and evil."

"Somehow I think that she is not really on either side anymore!" Alison declared with rising passion. "And I think that she really wants to be human."

Sighing at the futility of her position, Jon asked, "Now what do we do? Should we head for Mariane at once — to let them know about the war coming their way?"

"That's what I think we should do," put in Alison, hoping that they would agree.

"If we don't, Alison will go there by herself!" laughed Mandy.

Jon looked at the two in turn and then smiled. *She is right, of course. For Alison, it is her solemn duty to immediately warn Mariane of the impending war. I wonder what Mandy would really like to do?* He did not have long to wonder.

Mandy then added, "I would like to go back and teach that Kagor a few things, but I did give my word to Darless. So let's head for Mariane."

From their recollections of Alison's map, they knew that they should head eastward. The question was how far. If they had a long way to go, Jon suggested that they go back to Alison's castle, research Mariane, then enter via a painting of a place within that country. Alison was all for making straight for Mariane at once. Mandy became the deciding factor.

"I'll find out where we are. Besides, Jon, you really did not get to see me change into something worthwhile. A hobgoblin doesn't count." She winked knowingly at him. He flushed, and Alison smiled. "This is one of my two favorite shapes, besides my own, of course," she quickly added.

Jon watched fascinated. He wanted to know how Mandy did her shape-changing feat. He concentrated his attention on her carefully, but the effect was just too much for him. He ended just as awed as Alison. Mandy had turned her body into a horse.

First, a silver-white glow surrounded her body. Next, her familiar shape whitened rather like an apparition, which then seemed to flow into the larger silhouette of a horse. Finally, the white solidified into true horse form. No. It wasn't a horse. It was a Pegasus!

Pure white, she looked like a beautiful Arabian horse, but from her back enormous wings extended and flexed. Her head was held proudly erect. She whinnied and pranced about the two awe-struck companions. Then, she galloped and lunged gracefully into the air.

Great white wings majestically fanned as the Pegasus slowly circled her way high into the sky. Jon commented, "Mandy sure knows how to create effects!"

With a twinge of jealousy, Alison replied, "Yes. And not only in the sky!" Jon looked at her out of the corner of his eye and wondered.

Mandy kept circling ever upwards, until she saw what she wanted. From the ground, she was only a tiny dot of white in a vast sea of blue. Then, she slowly circled her way downward, landing on the ground as if she were a swan upon a gentle pond. Then, she was Mandy once more.

After a brief rest, she exclaimed, "Jon, you really should try it! Well, we are in luck. Alison picked a good place to bring us. We are in the extreme eastern section of the Bleak Hills. Mariane lies north of us. It's only about thirty miles or so to the grasslands. I thought I could see that town — Zaire — in the extreme distance. I say, let's walk for a while."

They did so. The Bleak Hills were aptly named. There were no trees and very little water. Located just north of the expansive Desolation Desert, the hills were fairly arid. It was hot, but not unbearably so. The ground supported only stubble grass and was primarily a gravel base. These were the foothills of the Baren Range, moderately tall, but quite rugged, mountains.

"You know," Jon began, "It seems everywhere I go in these worlds, I encounter gods and goddesses. I just do not understand it. Darless is being forced to work for this Morrigan goddess."

"Well, I work willingly for Reylona," replied Mandy, cockily. "Whom do you worship, Alison?"

She sighed, "Well, I'm rather like Jon. I — I do not have any patron. I do believe in the Supreme Father, though. You see, my nanny raised me from just a baby. She had just seen my entire family barbarically slain. All of her world had been destroyed. The gods did not intervene. No aid ever came. She became totally disillusioned with gods. So as I grew up, she never mentioned them. A child never knows enough to ask about such matters. Hence, I am ignorant. I do not even know what gods and goddesses there are in Verbenloc! Or even what god my priest father worshiped. In a way, I envy you, Mandy. It must be a fantastic experience to be so close to and favored by a real goddess. I would not even have the slightest idea of how to even go about looking for a god — much less what to say to one."

"Well, you don't just say that you believe in a god and then he comes to your aid."

"How did you get to be so favored by Reylona?" asked Jon fascinated.

"I came by her naturally. When I was a young girl, I roamed The Gnarled Oaks Wood around father's castle. I guess I have always loved the woods and creatures that live there. I befriended the denizens of the woods. In fact, when I first went adventuring as a ranger, my companion was a brownie. He and I shared many adventures."

"What happened to him?" asked a delighted Alison.

"Oh, when I range too far from his home, he stays behind. We still get together whenever I am at home in Blackthorn Castle. Well, the goddess of the forest is Reylona. So I naturally pray to her and worship her. As my adventures grew, so did my fame and prowess as ranger. Then, I met Glenda Appleblossom, who is, among other things, a priestess of Reylona. We shared some adventures, and I actually freed a temple of Reylona that had been desecrated and taken over by some evil bandits. I did it singlehandedly and Glenda said it was done with style. Anyway, after Glenda re-consecrated the temple, Reylona visited us."

"I was awed to say the least. A real goddess actually spoke to me! She even thanked me — a mortal. Right there, I swore that I would be her special ranger. Ever since, I have been known as the Ranger of Reylona. I had more adventures. During one of them, I rescued numerous forest animals from destruction. Reylona then appeared to me and gave me a special spell animal friendship. Was I ever honored! My exploits grew and now I am rather famous in my land. There are few who can match my archery abilities. Only my friend, Rolinda, and a strange man known only as Odysseus can challenge me."

She laughed, as she remembered that day. "My fame as an archer spread. One day, a wizard and this fighter, Odysseus, came by the castle. Ody said that he heard that I was a good shot and demanded a contest. He ordered his wizard friend to hold the apple targets on his head, while we shot them off. The wizard balked at first, but then he cast a protection from arrows on himself and played target holder. Rolinda, Odysseus, and I shot many flights. Close up, it was nearly always a draw between us — well, perhaps Odysseus did slightly better a time or two. When I moved the distance out to nearly four hundred feet, I won. But at an impossible six hundred feet, Rolinda won."

"So where was I. Oh, yes. So I have had many adventures, but always I worship and pray to Reylona. I have total certainty that she listens to me."

"It is an enviable relationship," admitted Jon. "I think that she listens is the crucial point. In my world, such does not occur. Gods and goddesses are only myths from our distant past. Yours are alive! Tell me more. Are there other gods?"

"Oh, yes. Many. Some are good; some are evil; some are balanced between. Above all, reigns Jous, the Uncaring. You see, there are greater gods, and lesser gods. Then, there are what I'll call demigods. While greater and lesser gods are ranked primarily by their powers, demigods are mortals who are extremely powerful individuals that somehow develop powers not unlike those of the gods. Also, there are demons and devils. These are rather like evil gods, especially the devils. While the greater and lesser gods have certain territories that they operate within, the devils only rule in Hell; the demons, the Abyss. It is said that the Supreme God rules above all of these."

"I'm beginning to see, Mandy. In my world, only the Supreme God is worshiped. Oh, I see. The Angel Gabriel could be viewed as a greater god. However, they do not seem to visit us. Certainly, the devils have not put in an appearance. We have had numerous mortals who worked such miracles that they became known as Saints. That would make some of the Saints demigods. I wonder why the greater and lesser gods have seemingly abandoned my world. Perhaps, it is because we are such an advanced culture! But I don't know. Perhaps, it is because we do not believe in them."

"You have a point there, Jon. Maybe it does have to do with the worshipers themselves. You see, a god or goddess must have followers. In their realms, they derive power and force from the number of believers they have. If one god can only boast of having a hundred followers and another has ten thousand, he will be viewed only as a lesser god. Followers are vital. That's why the priests are always trying to get new converts. It increases the power and force of the god."

"I can see how that could work," agreed Jon. "The greater the number of believers, the more real or solid the god becomes — the more power he will have. What is a god without any worshipers?"

"Exactly. Now you are catching on," replied Mandy. "But doesn't your world have any gods?" she asked, incredulous.

"Oh, the one God, the Supreme Being, the Lord, is a common belief and faith among many of our lands. That is about all. We are so mechanized, so automatized, so civilized, so advanced that we need no gods. Or so we think. But I'd very much like a patron god or goddess."

"Maybe you two will find yours," offered Mandy. "I'd recommend Reylona, except that usually only females worship her — a goddess of fertility as well, you know — and that you do not seem overly fond of forests."

"True," replied Jon.

"I suppose I really should find out about the gods of my world too," agreed Alison. "After all, my dad was a high priest of some god called Ukko, it was I think."

"You should. It must be devastating to have no one to turn to," mused Mandy.

Jon realized that they all three had one thing in common each had no other family. Each was more or less alone in his or her world. It was a sobering thought.

Lost in their own thoughts, they continued walking through the barren Bleak Hills. Jon was moved. *These hills are as barren as my life! I've only got my two college buddies, now that Grandpa is gone. But they are only just friends no one to be close too. Mandy has adopted the goddess Reylona and gets by. Alison keeps on looking for any surviving brothers and sisters. It keeps her going. Yet, I really have no one now — no one at all.* The current desolation of his life, now that Grandpa was gone, swelled over him. Tears formed and rolled. Desperately, he wanted to cry out, "I need you both! I love you both!" He could not force the words out. Instead, he hugged them both tightly. He did not become embarrassed.

To his surprise, the girls held onto him as well. Together, they continued walking. Somehow, the hills were not so bleak anymore.

Several hours later, they halted for supper. "I want some real food, for a change — not this dried, shriveled, preserved stuff," declared Mandy. "I'm going hunting. Jon, you collect firewood. Alison, you get to do the cooking. Now, then, I'm taking orders. What'll you have? Deer? Bear? Rabbit?"

They all sounded foreign to Jon. So Alison said, "I'd like some quail. But these hills are so bleak. There can't be many animals around here!"

"Are you joking?" laughed Mandy. She bent low and studied their supper site. Then, she pronounced, "Seven days ago, three antelope passed through here. Five days ago, a brown bear roamed past. Two days ago, there was a battle here — a mountain lion and a badger, who lost. Yesterday, an eagle landed here and ate a rabbit. See, there are the remains," she pointed to some small bones and got her fancy longbow and arrows ready.

As she left, she turned and called back, "And don't make a lot of noise or I'll have to wander farther." Mandy silently left, drifting off over the hills.

Acutely aware of the noise that he was making in spite of his best efforts, Jon went in search of firewood. Since trees were scarce, he had to settle for dried brush.

By the time that he had collected a large pile and Alison had the rest of their supper ready to cook, Mandy reappeared as silently as she had left. Tossing two quail and a rabbit to Jon, she declared, "You get to clean them, since Alison's got the vegetables and pears ready to cook."

"What a pair you two make," Mandy went on, "An enemy could have snuck up on you and attacked you before you even knew that they were there. I guess that you really do need me." She and Alison began talking about her hunting trip, leaving Jon to clean the animals.

After a minute and with a red face, Jon awkwardly broke in on their conversation, "I'm sorry to interrupt you, but I do not have the slightest idea of how to fix these."

"I figured that you didn't," replied Mandy, "but I wanted to be sure. Here, I'll show you. What do people in your world eat, anyway?" Jon tried to explain the idea of a grocery store, canned foods and jars. He failed miserably until he remembered butcher departments. This, they both could understand.

When the quail and rabbit were ready to cook, Jon offered to light the fire with a match. Alison interrupted him, "That'll take forever, Jon. Here, I'll show you and Mandy how to start a fire." She spoke a few magic words and waved her hands about. Then from her hands, a beam of magic shot forth. Flames flashed onto the brush pile. Instantly, the dried brush flamed uniformly. Nodding to herself, Alison proclaimed, "Now, that's how to get it going in a hurry." Jon was speechless. Mandy smiled.

So while the girls watched the dinner cook, Jon took out his flute and played for them. His music seemed to raise everyone's spirits. Dinner seemed more of a feast out there in the Bleak Hills. As usual, Jon cleaned up the dishes.

Since there were still several hours before dark, Mandy wanted to move on closer to the distant city, Zaire. All agreed, and they began their march once more.

About an hour later, Mandy spied a dust cloud some distance ahead of them. For a time, she said nothing about it, but watched it carefully. When she was certain, she spoke, "Something is coming toward us. See that dust cloud? Horses, I'd guess, probably a dozen. Could be a patrol from Mariane — we're close to their border. Or could be bandits, ruffians, and the like. We certainly won't see fellow travelers!"

"Should we hide?" queried Jon, concerned for their safety. "Where?" replied Alison, sweeping her hand across the barren hills.

"Right. We'll stand and do battle!" declared Mandy. "Alison, you get your spells ready. Jon, well, you do whatever you can. I'll use my bow from a distance. Then, when they close, I'll use my sword. Let's get to the top of the next hill; it's more defensible."

They hurried to the top and then waited the on comers. "We should be sure whether they are friend or foe before we fight them," insisted Alison. Jon concurred; likewise, Mandy, although grudgingly.

Soon, the riders approached their hill, spied them, and encircled them. There were fourteen men. Jon noted that they all wore chain mail and carried lances. Several had colorful banners of purple and green flying from their tips. Shields were tied to the saddles, and each had a horseman's mace dangling at his side.

To Jon, they looked like they meant business. Presently, the leader broke from the circle and rode up to them. Mandy notched an arrow.

"Hail, travelers in Mariane. We spied your campfire and came to investigate. I am Squire John, servant to His Holiness, Prince Reginald Noxwood, Archdeacon of Zaire." He paused in his obviously rehearsed speech, eyeing each carefully for any sign of recognition. Seeing the blank stares of the beautiful women, he continued coyly, "What are you beautiful women doing out here in the wilds — and all by yourselves with no one to protect you? It is a good thing that I happened by." He tried to look impressive, sitting tall in the saddle.

Jon reacted vehemently to Squire John's attitude. Always before, when he had seen a particularly beautiful woman strolling about the university campus, he had had a similar reaction. He had even whistled and catcalled once. He could sense that Squire John had that same cocky, strutting, "look at me" attitude, designed to impress the ladies that he had had at times. However, now Jon was revolted by it. He realized suddenly that the girls always had to put up with this reaction with men, everywhere they went. *It is forced subservience! In two sentences, he has pointed out that they are beautiful women, that they should be helpless, that they should be at home satisfying the sexual desires of some man, that they need protection, and that they are obviously out of place here in a man's world. But he is wrong on every account!* Furious, Jon suppressed an urge to drive his fist into that grinning mouth.

He could not and did not look at the girls' reactions, but hoarsely spoke, "Do not further insult my dearest friends. It is you who do not know your own peril. Anyone of us could single-handedly take out your whole patrol. Now, what is it that you want? Be quick. We want to continue our journey."

Jon picked up an immediate mental reaction from both girls, but he kept his attention on the rider. Rather taken aback, Squire John hastily proclaimed, "By His Holiness's orders, all strangers to Mariane are hereby ordered to answer a few questions."

He fumbled in his pocket and pulled out a folded piece of parchment. He read solemnly, "Do you know of or have you heard anything about a bard known as Wendell Theodore Zandras? Answer truthfully, by order of His Holiness, Prince Reginald Noxwood."

Jon jerked noticeably and Alison's face displayed a sudden surprise. Only Mandy did not outwardly react. No one said a word.

"Come on. You must answer. I can tell that you know something — just from your faces. Out with it, or else."

Jon hastily replied, "We know that he is an especially gifted, talented artist. He paints pictures." He did not want to say any more. This, he felt, would be merely common knowledge to anyone who knew about the bard.

"I thought as much." He stiffened in his saddle and declared loudly, "In the name of His Holiness, Prince Reginald Noxwood, Archdeacon of Zaire, I hereby place you all in protective custody. By his orders, anyone who knows anything about him at all, especially strangers, must be brought before him at once, without delay, for direct questioning."

Jon saw that the other riders had all dropped their lances into a charge position, ready for action. He inquired argumentatively, "Does that mean you are trying to arrest us?"

"It means that I have to take you at once to see His Holiness, in Zaire. You can come peacefully or you can come struggling or you can come wounded. It matters little to me, just that I get you to His Holiness as soon as possible."

Before Jon could retort, Alison replied, "Squire John, we are indeed strangers to your lands, but we come in peace. Actually, we have a vitally important message to deliver to the rulers in Zaire. If you would lend us spare horses, we can both accomplish our tasks much more quickly."

"You must forgive my harsh manners. I am not normally so brash. But these are dark days. Come, My Lady, I would be honored if you would ride behind me." Alison agreed. Jon fumed just thinking about his Alison riding behind Squire John. Two other riders picked up Mandy and Jon. Then, they were off, galloping toward the city. The girls made the best of it, while Jon had to hold on tightly in fear of falling off. At least, they would be in civilization by dark.

# Chapter 11 Zaire

The patrol ended their galloping ride just as the sun set. Ahead lay the city of Zaire. As Jon stared in wonder, all of his concerns and worries were forgotten. *This is right out of the Middle Ages!* His nose picked up the unmistakable odor of salt water; his ears, a cacophony of sounds.

Zaire was built in a land of low, sprawling, green hills. A high, brown stone wall, complete with saw-toothed battlements and periodic, overhanging bartizans, zigzagged a semicircle around the sides of the city exposed to land. The ocean and docks provided protection for the eastern side of the great city. Here was a city of a hundred thousand people at least, Jon estimated.

The patrol rode slowly through the teeming streets of the outer city — poor town. Here those in abject poverty lived in shanties outside the protection of the walls. Riding on, they passed through the massive gates into the city proper. Cobblestone streets were narrow and stone and wooden buildings crowded everywhere — masses of humanity seeking shelter and security behind the walls. Shops of every type imaginable beckoned: tinkers, tailors, candle makers, cobblers, herbs and more. Jon knew that he could spend days just exploring the city. He became alive with excitement. Everywhere, people thronged, wearing exotic clothing, as far as Jon was concerned. Leather pantaloons, held up by numerous belts of various dyed materials, accompanied loose fitting blue shirts. Most wore purple and green striped bandannas either around their necks or as headbands. His awe grew. Of course, he entirely failed to notice that others were gawking at his strange, exotic clothing.

The patrol halted by a stable and dismounted and several boys rushed out to take care of the horses. Squire John commanded formally, "From here, we must walk. Guards, fall in." The trio found themselves in the center of the marching patrol. Down and around the narrow, twisting streets, they formally marched, until they rounded a sharp bend.

Alison gasped. Instantly, Jon knew why. Before them was an immense formal garden. Towering impressively at one end stood a magnificent cathedral. Everywhere they looked were beds upon beds of irises. Some were white, some yellow, some purple, some blue, some orange, and some multicolored. White marble statues stood impressively at the centers of small fountains. However, it was not the incredible beauty that caused Alison's and Jon's reaction, but rather that this was exactly like a picture in their books! By one statue, Jon spied the small, unobtrusive trident at the base of one figurine.

Squire John, seeing their reactions, explained, "Behold the Gardens of Vainamoinen and the Church of Ukko."

The church was commanding. Built in a style reminiscent of Gothic architecture, the massive church had high pointed arches, steep roofs, stood well over a hundred feet high, had numerous elegant stained glass windows, and a highly ornamented front facade that nestled between two, great, white marble columns that led to massive doors. It was shaped like a giant cross and trimmed in gold. Huge flying buttresses held the walls in place. Over all, the form seemed to focus one's attention upwards to God. Fleur crosses of gold topped all pinnacles.

Hundreds of town folk were filing out into the gardens. "Evening services have finished," explained Squire John. "This way," and he led them inside and through some side rooms. They halted in what was obviously a waiting room. "Wait here. I'll inform His Holiness of your arrival. You may refresh yourselves." He bowed and left. At once, the other members of the patrol took up positions by the four doors, leaving the trio alone in the center of the room.

"Better make ourselves presentable," offered Alison, and the two women began to dust themselves off, comb their hair, and clean up. However, the room and contents fascinated Jon. He wandered about examining the seven huge paintings that adorned the north walls and the thirty—foot tapestry that hung on the south wall. *There is a fortune in art in this one room alone! Some of these rival Michelangelo himself.*

Squire John returned within minutes. "His Holiness will see you now. This way." He led them through the southern door and down many dim corridors. Everywhere he looked, Jon saw elegant wooden walls — some made of mahogany, some of ebony. There were numerous niches filled with small marble statues. *This is an artistic paradise!*

Then they were led into the receiving room of His Holiness. The high vaulted room was about twenty feet square with a stained glass skylight. The room was regally done in lush scarlets and aquamarines. Nearly everything seemed trimmed with gold. The furniture — a desk, small table, and several chairs — was highly polished mahogany. A white marble throne with thick bright red trappings lay before them. His Holiness stood in front of his throne awaiting them.

Squire John spoke, "His Holiness, Prince Reginald Noxwood, Archdeacon of Zaire." He bowed low and departed.

The Archdeacon was an impressive, elder man, about sixty years old. His black hair and short beard were graying, and he stood about six feet tall but was at least fifty pounds overweight. He wore a flowing red robe with gilded edges and seams and his hands held a tall, silver scepter with a golden fleur cross on top. Jon was impressed. *Here is a man who can command! But he does not radiate authority so much as great wisdom.*

His Holiness spoke slowly and quietly, yet commandingly, "Welcome to Zaire, strangers. Please forgive the rudeness of Squire John. He gets a bit zealous when carrying out my requests. Please be seated." And he sat down on his throne holding the scepter before him.

As Jon helped the girls into the ornate chairs, he noticed that each of them had a slight glow about their heads. Then, he noticed he was glowing too. *What's going on? We're glowing, but each slightly differently. But he's not glowing.*

Mandy's thoughts appeared in his mind. *Careful, Jon, this man is a powerful cleric or priest. Watch what you say. He can probably tell if you lie.*

Jon sent, *But we're glowing! What's he doing? What is this glow?*

*I don't know — maybe he's seeing if we're good or evil.*

As soon as she was seated, Alison spoke, interrupting Jon's thoughts. "Permit me to introduce our party. I am Alison d'Ambrose, a mage. This is Mandy, the Ranger of Reylona. This is Jon Brown, a musician." Each nodded in turn and felt the weight of his discerning, penetrating, black eyes examining them.

Mandy smiled and said, "Pleased to meet you."

In turn, Jon replied, "Hello." But he could not restrain his curiosity, and he added, "Why are we all glowing? Did you do that? What does it mean?"

The Archdeacon's bushy and massive, graying eyebrows raised perceptibly. "So you see the effects of my spell? Well, that is interesting. Only I should be able to see it. Have no fear. I was just inquiring about your personal alignment between good and evil and law and chaos. It is prudent to know whether one is dealing with evil creatures or not. I see that all of you are good. I am relieved. But how is it that you, Jon Brown, can read the results of my own private spell of inquiry?"

Jon faltered, "I — I don't know. I just saw that we were glowing and now we are not."

"Most intriguing, but never mind, for now. I apologize for any affronts that may have occurred in bringing you to see me. Squire John has informed me that you insisted that you were on your way here to see me. So before I ask you my questions, it would be more honorable for me to let you deliver your message."

Alison explained. "Your Holiness, we bring evil tidings. In short, your country, Mariane, is about to be invaded by a hoard of evil hobgoblins and humans."

His imposing, commanding eyebrows rose ever higher. "Do go on. From where will they come?"

"You see, it's a long and involved tale," she sighed, wondering how best to proceed and not tell any lies and not divulge more than she cared to at this time. For her, it was a hard decision.

"I, well, none of us really, are from your world — Rochelle. We are, well, let's just say that we are visitors from other worlds. Why we are here is another matter. Let's just say that we are trying to stop evil."

"I see that you are telling the truth. Please continue."

"Well, during part of our quest, we visited Trundle. There we learned and saw that Kagor Dougal, the Merciless Mage of Rhones Tower, has created a mighty army of hobgoblins and humans. We discovered that he intends to invade Mariane — and very soon now — from what we have learned."

"How do you know of his plans? Certainly, he would not make his plans public."

"Well, it's part of that long story, your Holiness. You see, we were captured. Gloating over his victory, he told us about his plans. We escaped and decided that we had best come at once to Mariane to let you know about the impending war."

"But why should Kagor do this? Many years ago during the dark ages of Mariane, he gave solace to many of our destitute people. He gave them work to do, food, shelter, and protection."

"He said that when you became wealthy once more, no one bothered to repay their debts to him."

"Ah, I see. I have long told my people that recompense would be well advised. Evidently, few heeded my words. I wonder if it is too late."

Mandy replied, "Yes. I'm sure that he'd ignore it now. It's like a festering wound to him. He'd probably think that you were scared of him and were trying to buy him off."

Jon added, "And from all that we've seen, I do not think that any mortal could prevent this war." He did not elaborate.

Reginald cocked his eye and pondered long on Jon's words. Jon squirmed; he hoped that he'd not have to tell about the god's involvement. That would raise further trouble, and, besides, he had promised Darless.

He was relieved when the Archdeacon asked, "Is all of Trundle mobilized for war?"

Alison replied, "Well, we are not exactly certain of northern Trundle. We only visited there for a short while. After we learned of Kagor's plans, I thought it best if we spied on the rest of Trundle to see the extent of the threat. In the short time that we were there, we saw no hobgoblins, only armed encampments of men. We do not know the significance of this. We were captured there before we could find out much. But we do know that Kagor plans to invade Mariane through the Bleak Hills. They will definitely not come through Hollybine Wood."

"Well, strangers, my sincere thanks I extend to you for your timely news. It has spared many lives, I am certain. I will take action tomorrow. It seems that we owe you our profound appreciation. I will see that you are appropriately rewarded."

Alison quickly interrupted, "No, we need no reward, your Holiness. It is our duty to inform you."

"As you wish," Reginald replied.

Hastily Jon added, "But I would like a tour of this immense cathedral. It is incredibly beautiful."

This brought a smile and a chuckle to the old man's face. "Such a reward for saving a nation! May Ukko be praised. Certainly, my son, certainly." Then he sobered, "Now I must ask you some questions of grave importance to me. Speak truthfully, for I will know if you try to deceive me. You know of the Bard Wendell Theodore Zandras?"

Quickly, Jon told him the same things that he had told Squire Jon — that he was a famous painter.

"We are very familiar with his fantastic work. Why do you want to know this?"

"Let me explain — then I shall ask more directly. You see, nine months ago, I commissioned Bard Wendell to paint a huge fresco on the ceiling of our holiest chapel. It was to be a giant work of praise to God and his mightiest servant, Ukko. It is now about two-thirds completed. Almost three months ago, Bard Wendell disappeared from Zaire under unusual circumstances."

He continued his explanation, "The ceiling is nearly one hundred feet high. In order to paint the fresco, Bard Wendell erected huge scaffolding and erected numerous lanterns to illuminate his work. He established a pattern of working until midnight, at which time, he would carefully clean his brushes and blow out the lanterns. Well, one night, when Adept Paul was making his rounds about eleven o'clock, he noticed that the lanterns were blazing, but Bard Wendell was nowhere to be seen."

"We became concerned the next day. The lanterns were still burning and all of his brushes were uncleaned. Something was not right. Bard Wendell could not have left of his own choosing. He has never left a work unfinished. We have searched everywhere, but without the slightest bit of success. He seems to have just vanished into the night without a trace. I assume, therefore, that he has been abducted. This, of course, is a gravely serious matter. Think of all of the ramifications should I fail to find Bard Wendell! Thus, my standing orders: anyone who knows Bard Wendell must be brought before me at once."

"So therefore, I ask you, do you know anything about the mysterious disappearance of Bard Wendell?"

"No," chorused the trio, relieved. A bit of hope faded from his aged face. "I see that you are telling the truth. Thank you for being honest."

Jon's curiosity was aroused, "Perhaps we can help. I would like to see his great work. I would like to examine the scene of the crime, so to speak. Maybe I can get a clue or something."

"Any help would be greatly appreciated, Jon Brown. However, let it wait until tomorrow. I shall see to it that you are given a royal tour and a chance to see the unfinished fresco. Please accept my hospitality for the night. Do you require three separate rooms?"

"Yes," replied Alison.

"But connecting, if possible," added Mandy, with a smile.

He rang a small bell. Then, footsteps could be heard coming.

"I have one more question," Jon asked, "That is, if it wouldn't be considered impolite."

"What is it?" asked a curious Reginald.

"How could you tell if we were telling a lie?"

He laughed. "Tell one now, Jon Brown."

"Ok. My name is Fred."

Immediately, the scepter in the Archdeacon's hand glowed perceptibly.

"Wow!" exclaimed Jon.

"I am a cleric, a priest, you know," chuckled the old man. And then, an adept entered to take them to their quarters. "Sleep well, my honored guests. I truly would like to hear your full tale, but only when you consider it proper to do so. I would like to know more about you three, especially you, Jon Brown, but only when you choose. Until tomorrow, then. Good night."

Soon, they found themselves in three of the most opulent rooms imaginable. Mandy's room was predominately done in scarlets; Alison's, in emerald; Jon's, in vivid yellows. Each room contained a huge bed with silk sheets and quilts. Each had a table, four chairs, chest of drawers, and a full sized wardrobe with mirror. All of the mahogany furniture was of the finest quality — each was priceless, Jon surmised. Additionally, three works of art adorned each room.

After inspecting their rooms, the trio found themselves in Alison's green room, discussing the day's events. Eventually, Mandy remembered Jon's upset with Squire John when they were placed in "protective custody." She was curious and inquired, "Jon, how come you were so upset with Squire John when we first met his patrol? You seemed fuming at the time."

"Yes. Come to think of it," put in Alison, "all that he did was introduce himself. Why did you get so fired up? Did we miss something?"

Jon remembered the coy, cocky speech insinuating that the beautiful women were helpless, out of place sex objects that needed his protection. His face reddened but also his frustrated anger returned. Embarrassed, Jon tried to explain, "It was his attitude and his meaning. He acted like a strutting peacock, trying to impress you! Yet, after pointing out that you are beautiful, he implied that you were helpless and out of place in the wilderness, needing a strong man's protection, insinuating that your position in a man's world should be at home in his bed! I don't see how you could just stand there and not be totally offended!"

"I don't know why I reacted that way," Jon faltered, his face, a deep crimson. "I — I can understand his view. I — I used to do that too — well, I only did it covertly. I didn't have the guts to do it openly. I'd just catcall and whistle at some of the prettier girls as they walked by me. Just now I find that attitude and those kinds of actions utterly disgusting. I'm ashamed of my conduct and appalled when I see others doing it. It is downright degrading to you. How can you stand that sort of thing? It must happen everywhere you go!"

Alison answered quickly, she knew, for Jon's sake, that she had to beat Mandy's reply. "Good observation, Jon. It is rare that a man is able to glimpse our side. It is all right to be embarrassed by your prior actions — that you are embarrassed is the healthy sign. As the Archdeacon would probably say, 'You have realized your sins.' People are only ashamed by actions they feel were wrong. Now that you have told us about them — bared your soul, so to speak — don't you feel more at ease, Jon?"

He was humbled. Most of his telltale redness had gone. "I do feel better now that you know," he replied quietly.

"As for us, yes, it is always there. The more beautiful a woman is, the more of that sort of thing occurs. At first, it would bother me. My magic user guild peers were always treating me that way at first, until I proved myself more than just a pretty toy."

Mandy could contain her reply no longer and interjected, "Yes, but we also use it. Sometimes by using our beauty and charm, we can work miracles that we could not do by sword alone. Besides, it's fun dressing up and looking elegant, making men's heads sway and eyes roll. It gives us a feeling of power and control over men."

"You talk like beauty is a weapon!" protested Alison. "It's just feeding your own ego! Isn't that just as bad?"

"Oh, come on, dear Alison. Haven't you ever dressed up really elegantly and had all of the men looking at you? Didn't you feel really excited at being the center of all their attention?"

Alison flushed. "Well, yes. I won't lie about it. At the time, I enjoyed the attention and all, but afterwards, I felt cheap! Like I had put myself on some kind of public display! I want respect for what I am, not just my beautiful body."

"But that is all that some women have," interjected Mandy. "Did you ever think of that? However, I will be honest, too. I enjoy it. I use it to my advantage. I am strong. I am a powerful fighter. I am a good ranger. I am a lover of and protector of forests and those that dwell in them. I am beautiful. I am many things. I use every aspect that I have. I am not ashamed by any of it. All is me, Mandy. I do not deny my sexuality! I use it."

While listening to their different viewpoints, in a flash of insight, Jon understood all sides. Realization came. He began to laugh, in sharp contrast to the serious attitude the girls had. They stared blankly at him. He tried to speak, "I see — I understand," was all that he could get out. Then they grasped his meaning, and his contagious laughter caught them as well.

In a while, their talk turned to other events of the evening. Finally, they retired for the night, sleeping in utter opulence.

After breakfast in their rooms, their guide for the royal tour arrived and introduced himself as Patriarch Thomas Bethel. "But you can call me Father Thomas or even Tom, if you prefer," he suggested. Then, he took them on a guided tour of the Church of Ukko.

First, he showed them the formal entrance gardens with thousands of irises in full bloom. "These gardens are dedicated to the god Vainamoinen, a great hero and minstrel or bard. He is our heavenly patron of the arts and assistant of Ukko."

Jon interrupted him, "I'm sorry, Father Thomas, Tom, but I'm not from this world and I do not know about your gods. Who is Ukko?"

Tom was delighted at the opportunity to explain his religion. "Ukko is the Lord's supreme assistant to the world of Rochelle. Ukko is seen as an old man, but his power and might is supreme. He is the master and controller of both the sky and the air. Thus, we mariners pray to him to protect and guide our fleet of ships at sea. We are a sea faring country. We are the sole shippers for all of Rochelle. Thus, Mariane is in a position of might and power. But we always pray to Ukko for guidance and support."

"Does Ukko ever visit his church here? It is the most magnificent cathedral that I have ever seen," exclaimed Jon.

"No, Ukko seldom directly intervenes in our worldly affairs. I suppose that if extreme evil were to come, Ukko would come to our aid. Usually, though, he sends his representatives, the air maidens. Their coming is held in great awe and respect. We have made a painting of them. I'll point it out to you, when we get to the holy altar room."

"Do these air maidens visit here often?" asked Jon curiously.

"Not really. The last time was more than forty years ago during the dark ages. His Holiness was just a young man then." Father Thomas briefly outlined their history. Up to their dark ages, Mariane had been the sole shippers for all of Rochelle. Then, a strange wizard known as Kalanos, the Great, came. He built a large fleet of huge iron vessels that were powered by liquid fire. In ten short years, he had taken all of the shipping trade away from Mariane. The country was destitute. During these dark times, Reginald Noxwood had prayed for divine guidance from Ukko. Three air maidens answered his plea."

"That was a divine day that will never be forgotten. Flying down from the sky, they landed just over there in the gardens, asking for His Holiness." Tears of joy swelled in Father Thomas's eyes. "We all took heart, knowing salvation and deliverance were sure to come. It did. Kalanos used up all of his liquid fire, and his fleets were left to rust in the docks of Kalanos City. His lush city became a ghost town. Now the great desert has swallowed all remains. We have regained our former position." Jon realized that Father Thomas could talk all day about his religion.

Next, Tom led them through various rooms of the impressive cathedral. Everywhere were treasures of art. Jon was impressed and moved by such a rich display of beauty. He had to personally stop to examine each piece, ignoring the growing impatience of the girls. There were great frescos, ceramics of all types, marble statues of gods and goddesses, Jon presumed. He felt as if he were touring a Greek museum. Finally, they entered the great square, high altar room.

Here, all other art was lesser in comparison. The splendor was breathtaking. When Jon saw the huge painting of the air maidens, he cried aloud, "Angels!" They appeared as women in battle armor, but with huge white wings. Jon was moved.

"And up there is where Bard Wendell's greatest masterpiece lies as yet unfinished." All eyes rose to the ceiling, a hundred feet overhead. Between mounds of scaffolding and ropes could be seen the two-thirds completed fresco. The immense painting stirred seldom felt emotions within Jon. To him, it was like witnessing

Michelangelo's work while still in progress. He knew that he had to meet this Bard. It was truly awe-inspiring.

Further, the acoustics of the huge room were superb. Jon was deeply moved and inspired. "Would it be all right if I played my flute in here?" he asked. "I am so moved that I must play here."

"It would not be sacrilegious, my son. Often, our choir raises its voice to God and Ukko here. Play, if it moves you."

Jon did. Taking advantage of the fantastic lower resonances of the chamber, he played a transposition of the Fantasia on a Theme by Thomas Tallis. When he finished, absolute stillness filled the holy room.

Then, the voice of His Holiness, Prince Reginald Noxwood, the Archdeacon, broke the silence. He had arrived in time to hear Jon play. "That was superb. Are you sure that you are not a high priest of Ukko? I'd be honored if you would play that for high service someday. It is particularly moving. Perhaps, you are Vainamoinen here in disguise!"

"No, I am no god, just a musician, but I think that I would like very much to play here. The room has the best acoustics I have ever heard. It seems so holy here. It is truly inspiring."

"That's what Bard Wendell thought as well and why he agreed to do the fresco for us. He said that this, our high altar room, was aesthetic, holy, and altogether fitting for such a work of art. Now he has been abducted."

Everyone's spirits sank. Jon inquired, "Father Thomas told me about the air maidens and Ukko. Have you called upon Ukko for aid and guidance in finding Bard Wendell?"

"Oh no, not yet! You see, I would not even consider calling upon the gods for aid until I had exhausted every means that I have. It would be presumptuous and annoying to Ukko to have every follower asking for aid for every little upset that life provides. Man must attempt to solve man's problems, before he seeks divine intervention. Still, I will beseech Ukko for aid if I cannot resolve this matter soon."

"Is that where he was last seen working?" asked Jon, pointing high above to the scaffolding.

"Yes, there by the Madonna of Mankind. You may go up and take a look, if you like."

Jon immediately began climbing up the left ladder. The girls refused to be left behind and scampered up after him. To be on the safe side, Alison slipped on a magic ring. She was not a climber by nature.

The unfinished work was even more impressive close up. After admiring it, Mandy asked, "Now what, Jon? What do we look for?"

"See if you can see any signs of a struggle," he proposed.

"Let's stay out of her way while she looks," suggested Alison. "That way, we won't confuse any tracks that may be up here."

Mandy searched the area carefully. The central painting area was formed from a platform of planks. Off to the west side was a large table of planks. On this, Bard Wendell had his supplies. Vials, bottles, and vessels of all shapes and sizes were piled neatly in ordered rows. Each contained pigments and oils and the like, all arranged by color and shade. Numerous brushes lay ordered upon the table as well. "Come here," Mandy called out. "There are no tracks, just a lot of dust. Here was where he was last working. I'd say that Bard Wendell was a very ordered person — everything is in its proper place — except over there." She pointed to the only messy area around.

There were two pallets half full of paint smears. Five used brushes had dried and were now firmly stuck to the pallets. While Jon studied this area, the girls roamed about the scaffolding looking for anything unusual. They found nothing.

Jon decided to pretend that he was Wendell and that he was painting away. There was a bar stool nearby and he sat down on it with the pallet in hand. Now he could see clearly where Wendell had been working — the colors matched. Then he spied a small canvass sketch lying just under the table. *Hum. Looks as if he dropped something.* Jon retrieved the canvas. It was done in the same colors that had now dried on the pallet. It was merely a sketch of an intriguing forest. "Alison, Mandy, come here. What do you make of this?"

They all looked over the oil sketching. "It's just an unfinished sketch," Alison pointed out, "rather like the exploration of a sudden idea. It was not meant to be a finished oil. Artist doodles?"

"Look, it is done with the same colors that are on this pallet. He must have been working on this the night that he disappeared."

"I believe you are right!" exclaimed Alison. "See. It has his trademark. There is a tiny trident in that corner."

"Let's show this to Prince Reginald. Perhaps he can tell us what forest this is. Maybe it's a clue," offered Mandy. They hurried down at once.

They were disappointed. "No, I have never seen such a forest. Look, the leaves. They are sort of queer looking — unusual shapes. But I will take this to my general staff. Perhaps some of the sages can identify the place. My thanks. Why don't you continue your tour? Say, by the way, I have ordered a general mobilization of our army. Within a month, we will be ready to meet Kagor Dougal on the field of battle."

After showing them the rest of the cathedral, Father Thomas led them to the docks. The eastern edge of the cathedral was only a few blocks from the wharves. Here was the central focus of activities for the country. Currently, twenty huge ships were in dock for cargo transfer or repairs or just on leave. Everywhere, workers swarmed like ants. Numerous lines of men were unloading several ships and storing the goods in three enormous warehouses. In the distance, Jon could see the dry docks, where repairs were going on as well as new construction. The spines of two new vessels rose silhouetted against the ocean and sky. It was a fascinating tour for Jon, but both women found it rather dull.

They returned and had lunch as the day passed slowly. After the evening meal, His Holiness returned, sketch in hand. When they were alone, he explained, "We cannot identify the forest. There is no place like this that any of my people can recall. The only hope is that perhaps a druid might be able to identify it. So thus, I think that it might just have been an imaginary area that he painted — you know, just an idea not yet complete. Certainly, there was to be no place for anything like that in the fresco here. Perhaps he drew it up for some future job."

"Perhaps," agreed Jon. Then acting on impulse, he asked, "May we keep it for a while? I'd like to study it tonight, if I may."

"Certainly. There is yet one other curious factor in this case, but, as yet, I do not know its significance. Let me explain. Ever since Bard Wendell's mysterious abduction, I have had armed patrols abroad searching for clues. In particular, we have been watching the Bleak Hills, for that is the most logical escape route for the abductors to take. Several times, patrols have encountered mysterious bands of mercenaries, who insisted that they were only traveling to the temples of their evil goddess, Morrigan. From several, we confiscated small oil paintings that they were going to offer to the goddess. Here, I brought one for you to see," and he showed them the painting.

"It looks like Wendell's work," Alison exclaimed. Jon noticed the familiar tiny trident in the bottom left corner. "However, why would he paint such a grim, bloody battle scene? That's not like Bard Wendell," she protested.

"Correct on both accounts. It is definitely his work. But why? We do not know. Even more peculiar is the fact that this is the fourth one of these that we have confiscated. All were identical!"

"Now that is really incredible!" Alison declared. "Why? What can the significance be?"

"We do not know. My sages have been researching this, but the best idea we have is that he is trying to send a message. To whom is the real question? Our immediate reaction is that he wants to be rescued, but the painting's content coupled with the fact that it was going to Morrigan discredits that idea. We are baffled. So, my new friends, I will leave this painting with you as well. Perhaps, you may have another idea."

They thanked him for his information, and the Archdeacon left. He had to conduct evening worship. Baffled as well, they retired to their rooms.

About nine o'clock, Alison found Jon in his room still pondering the sketch and the painting. She could sense that he was troubled. "What do you make of them?"

"I'm not sure. Somehow I feel that both are important very important. Chronologically, the sketch came first, then the battle painting, I'm sure. Now note: Wendell did not have any other sketches up there. It was done that very night — probably on the spur of the moment. You know, Alison, I think that he was looking at this before he was abducted. I found this on the floor, as if he dropped it. You don't —"

"I do!" she exclaimed, finishing his thought for him. "He went there — to wherever that picture represents."

"It fits. It was late. He got this idea of a neat forest. He made a quick sketch. Then, curiosity aroused, he stepped into that forest for a quick peek to see what it was really like! Only he never came back."

"I wonder why not," she mused.

"Then, we will have to go and see ourselves," proclaimed Mandy, who had just entered quietly and heard their conclusions. "Besides, I'm already bored of this city life. One day is enough for this forest lover! Shall we go right now?"

"No rush. He's been gone for months. One night will make no difference. Let's get some sleep and go first thing in the morning," Jon proposed. They agreed.

"But what about the painting?" inquired Alison.

"I'm fairly sure that it is a message, probably to Morrigan. But what and why — I have no idea. I will take it along with us, just in case." Then they retired for the night.

The next morning, right after eating, they congregated in Jon's room, dressed and ready for adventure once more. Both had their hair braided up and out of the way. Alison had on her little cap and magic robe. Mandy had her sword available and carried her bow with two quivers of arrows on her back.

Mandy pronounced, "This time, I will be ready for anything. No one is going to take this ranger by surprise this time!"

"Shouldn't we tell His Holiness what we are going to do?" asked Alison.

"Well, I don't think that he'll understand about the pictures and portals. Why don't we just leave him a note," Jon offered? Alison quickly did so. Then, they held hands, and Jon stepped them through to the queer forest in search of Bard Wendell Theodore Zandras.

Sometime later, His Holiness found the empty rooms. In Jon's, he found a note addressed to him. "Your Holiness, we have uncovered a possible clue concerning Bard Wendell's disappearance. We have gone to check it out. We will return. Alison."

The only other thing in the room was the strange sketch lying neatly on Jon's bed. He picked it up and wondered.

# Chapter 12 Caleb Durward and Dispater

They stepped out into the strange, eerie forest. From the right, a sickly light shown through the trees. It was deathly silent, except for a steady plink of falling water drops somewhere to their right rear. "Spread out and keep still," whispered Mandy in a commanding tone. They did so.

Mandy carefully studied the ground. "There was a struggle here. Tracks lead off to the right," she relayed.

"This isn't a real forest!" exclaimed Alison, excitedly. "It's made of paper."

"What?" cried Jon in disbelief.

"Quiet!" ordered Mandy. They hushed and examined the trees closely.

"They are made of paper," agreed Jon. "This IS queer! This isn't a real forest. That explains a lot."

"Let's go check out the strange light," suggested Alison, acting on a hunch.

"I'll go first," Mandy insisted. "The tracks go that way as well. But be quiet."

Carefully, the trio walked through the paper forest toward the light. "It's just as I thought," exclaimed Alison. "Someone has cast a continual light spell on a lamp on a wall."

"Wait a minute. What's a wall doing here?" asked Jon, momentarily confused. "We must be inside a building and not outside at all."

"Come on. The tracks in the sand go this way," broke in Mandy. They followed her. Soon another wall appeared. They were indeed in an underground room. The tracks led to an arched doorway and on into the corridor beyond. They stalked silently down the corridor. Around a sharp bend, the corridor led them into a well-lighted chamber — a dungeon — below a castle, they assumed.

The room was nearly fifty feet square. Opposite them, a great stone stairway rose up into the gloom. Numerous lanterns hung on the walls. The right corner was full of discarded torture equipment — all very old and rusted beyond use. To their left, an old man was sitting on an iron grill-worked chair — paintbrush in hand. Ten feet of heavy chains connected his legs to the wall. A dozen easels were spread in a semicircle about him. The odor of fresh oil paint hung in the air. Behind him were a fancy iron bed and an iron table with three more iron chairs. Jon immediately recognized the style. They were exactly like the "Gay Nineties."

Jon spoke first. "Bard Wendell Theodore Zandras, I presume. We have come to rescue you."

He gasped and cried. "Flee! Run! It is a trap! Flee for your lives! Flee before the mad wizard comes. He's due any moment! Go!"

"Not without you," declared Alison.

Bard Wendell was now about fifty-five years old. His long black hair and beard were streaked liberally with gray. Both were unkempt. He showed signs of long captivity. He was about six feet tall and well-muscled. However, he appeared long out of practice as a fighter. Both of his legs were attached to the wall of gray stone blocks by long chains.

"See if you can get him free. I'll stand guard," ordered Mandy. She took up a position off to the right, where she could shoot arrows at anyone who came down the stairs. Jon and Alison rushed over to the bard.

"Forget it. You can't free me unless you have a metal saw and about an hour. See. He poured molten lead into the lock mechanism. It cannot ever be opened! Now will you flee before it is too late?" He pleaded.

"Not a chance," declared Alison. They tried to pull on the chains, but that was futile. They tried to break the chains, but that was even more useless.

"Hurry up!" called Mandy. "It sounds like an army is coming!"

"You better get your spells ready, Alison. I'll get Wendell free somehow."

Alison moved between Jon and Mandy, covering the stairs as well. Jon heard her cast some kind of protection spell on herself. He knew that this time she was totally prepared. He concentrated on Wendell's chains.

Soon a large number of guards, rushing down three abreast, came into sight, cursing and yelling for them to surrender. Mandy replied by firing arrows as fast as she could. The entire front line stumbled and fell over and down the last few steps. Each had an arrow squarely in his heart. At this range, Mandy could not miss.

Soon the sheer number of guards charging forced new tactics. While they were delayed stumbling down over their fallen comrades, Mandy put her bow over her shoulder and drew out her bastard sword. Screaming "Reylona," she charged into them, hacking and slashing.

Alison patiently waited. Just when Mandy charged, the anticipated magic user himself now appeared on the steps, watching the events.

"Caleb Durward!" screamed Wendell, "All is lost! He'll blast you to pieces." Jon looked over his shoulder at the wizard on the steps. He was tall and lean, but not more than forty. He appeared clean and neat in his ruby and amber striped robe and cloak. He had several rings on his fingers, and his right hand held a staff.

As soon as Caleb saw the party, he singled out Alison. He decided that she was his only real opponent. *Let the boy fiddle with the chains. They are unbreakable. My fighters will soon take out that dashing woman, such a pity. But their magic user — she could pose problems.* So he launched his attacks toward her.

From the corner of his eyes, Jon saw a volley of bluish missiles fly at Alison. They hit her magic defenses and bounced off. She sent a volley back at him. He spoke a word, and they seemed to be sucked straight into his staff. He mumbled some words and made some gestures. Suddenly a tremendous lightning bolt arced to Alison. Wendell cringed. However, it, like the missiles, bounced harmlessly off of her shield. "Ah ha! You've got a globe of protection up!" Caleb yelled, "Now I've got you!"

Alison spoke and gestured. She pointed her finger at him, and a streak of fire shot from her finger at him. Jon instinctively braced himself for the ball of fire's detonation. It did not come. Caleb sucked that one into his staff as well.

Meanwhile, Mandy chopped and slashed her foes. She was forced to slowly retreat from the steps because of the growing pile of dead or wounded men. Now, the fighters swarmed at her, forcing her to fight four at one time. Over a dozen guards lay dead or wounded, but still they continued to press her back. At this point, a huge fighter slowly came down the steps. He was obviously their leader. Soon the captain of the guards would be on her.

Jon worked furiously on the chains. However, he could not think of any way to get Wendell out of them. Then he saw Caleb shoot yet another spell at Alison. This time, she had to dodge out of the way, as a beam of disintegration shot past her, drilling a hole in the side of the dungeon wall. Alison sent one back at him, forcing Caleb to jump hastily out of the way. This time, he was too slow, and the beam disintegrated his hat. He cursed her.

Next, Caleb created a sickly, yellow cloud of poison gas before him. He then commanded it to move slowly toward Alison and the rest of her party. Wendell screamed, "It's a poisonous gas cloud. We're all about to die!"

Undaunted, Alison was hastily casting another spell. Just as the cloud enveloped them, her spell went off. Her dispel magic spell canceled his and the cloud disappeared, but not before Alison coughed twice.

Jon feverously worked on the chains. He pulled and tugged and twisted, but all to no avail.

Now, the captain had reached Mandy. He ordered his men to fall back, while he took her on personally. Jon could hear the clank and bash of steel upon steel and steel upon shield. He was a burly man, and much stronger than Mandy. Jon knew that she could not hold out much longer. Beside, he was fresh and Mandy had been fighting strenuously for several minutes now. His mind raced.

While Alison was distracted, coughing from the spell that nearly got them all, Caleb quickly shot another at her. Fortunately, Jon and Wendell were far enough from Alison so they were not hit. Nevertheless, the blast of extreme cold could still be felt. A cone of intense coldness covered Alison. When the frost cleared away, Jon could see that she was badly wounded, but still alive. He knew that she could not take another blast like that again. He was on the verge of panic.

Then more trouble came. He heard a clank of steel and the clattering sound of a dropped sword. "Zagroot Zounds!" echoed. Jon saw that the captain's powerful blow had disarmed Mandy. Her bastard sword lay three feet in front of her — just out of her reach. The captain had his huge sword raised high above him just waiting for her to try to reach for it. He would cut her to pieces.

Simultaneously, Caleb, seeing victory almost at hand, prepared to launch another blast of cold. Alison was struggling to get her spell spoken. Jon knew that she would not beat him, and she would be frozen — this time permanently.

Mandy yelled, "Do something fast!"

Jon did. "Mandy, grab Alison!" He grabbed both Wendell and Alison. In the following instant, while the girls awaited certain destruction to fall, it did not come. Three things occurred. The muscled fighter, who was about to slice Mandy into pieces, suddenly just dropped his sword to the ground. Mandy grabbed her sword with one hand and Alison with the other. Caleb paused mid-casting; his arms dropped to his sides. He took Alison's magical web spell full in the face. He was trussed up like a fly in a web. In the next moment, Jon stepped them all out of Caleb Durward's dungeon.

In the next instant of time, they were all standing back in Jon's yellow bedroom in the Church of Ukko, Zaire! Everyone was shocked, except Jon, who collapsed onto the bed.

Mandy, who, at the last instant, had retrieved her sword, exclaimed, "Wow! That's cutting it a bit close." Then, she saw Wendell. There was the Bard, still in chains, which were driven into the stone block. Jon had brought a huge chunk of the stone wall!

"How? How did you do that?" cried Wendell in utter disbelief! "I have never painted this room. Did you teleport us here? And the block? How?"

Meekly, Jon explained, "I do not know what teleporting is. I could not figure a way to get the chains off of you. There wasn't any more time. I just stepped us all and some stone as well. I brought a good chunk. I was not certain how deep the spikes went — had to be sure I had it all."

"You've done this sort of thing before?" asked an incredulous Bard Wendell.

"Well, no. Not exactly. I didn't have time to recall to memory one of your paintings. So I just used the first place that came to mind."

"You can do it from memories?" asked Wendell in even greater disbelief.

"But why did Caleb just stand there and let me hit him?" wondered Alison.

"Yes, and why did that fighter just drop his weapon?" asked Mandy.

"My doing," Jon said shyly. "I'm sorry if I messed up your fight, Mandy. I know how highly you value an honorable fight. But I thought that he was about to slash you and that you were going to get frozen again, Alison," he added.

"But what did you do?" queried and impatient Mandy. "That was a good trick."

"Well, at first, I thought of creating a big hand and grasping his sword arm. Then I'd hold it from moving down on you. But I realized that that was the hard way to do it. I just borrowed his mind for an instant. Through his mind, I had his body just let it go. It was really a simple thing to do — just let go, I mean.

Once I saw that I could do it, I borrowed Caleb's mind. I commanded his body to go rigid. You then did the rest, Alison."

"You are really incredible," exclaimed Alison, and she kissed him. This time he did not blush.

Mandy added, "You are sure full of surprises. Thanks." She heartily kissed him as well. Now his face reddened.

"My thanks too," broke in the bard. "I didn't think you had a chance of rescuing me."

"How did you get captured?" asked Alison, while they tried once more to get the chains off.

"I had this sudden inspiration to sketch that forest. Then, you know, I was curious. I had to see it first-hand. It was a trap. Caleb was there waiting for me. I was weaponless. He put me in chains and —"

He did not get to finish his sentence. Just then, there was a flash of magical energy about them. Jon distinctly heard the words "I wish." The room swirled and dissolved. Grey energy clouds swept past them. Then they found themselves right back in Caleb's dungeon, approximately where they had been.

The dead bodies and the mess had been cleaned up. There were only three people present, besides themselves: Caleb, his captain of the guard, and a huge, seven foot tall man. Both Caleb and his guard were standing inside of a crude, black pentagram drawn on the floor. He heard Mandy shriek in terror. He felt Alison shaking violently beside him. Wailing incoherently, Wendell collapsed into a ball on the floor. A chilling cold swept over him. Jon felt his limbs go numb and then he couldn't move. He sensed the chill of death.

However, he could still see, and he did so. Ignoring the frigid sensations that his body was sending him, Jon examined his surroundings. At first, this took energy and concentration, but he soon became accustomed to doing it. Caleb was gloating. However, his towering captain held his arms tightly around his head in a vain attempt to see nothing.

Now Jon faced the tall man. He was towering. Two horns protruded from his bald head, right above his eyes. He had a goatee and was dressed in rich, blood—red robes with black trim. A soft furry boot was on his right foot. His left leg ended in a cloven hoof, like that of a goat! A small tail protruded from under his robes. He was handsome — extremely so. He carried a staff in his right hand and a rod in his left.

He spoke. The voice was cold and chilling, yet compelling. "So you are the ones who have dared to defy me. Welcome, Jon Brown. I see that the chill of death does not bother you like it does your companions. My servant, Caleb here, tells me that you stole his bard from him, chains, wall and all. Now that interests me. How did you manage that? What new spell have you invented? Speak!"

Jon found that he could not resist that command, so he spoke. "You have the advantage, Sir. I believe that we have not been properly introduced."

"Such impertinence!" He roared with laughter. Finally, he said, "I am the Arch-devil, Dispater, ruler of Dis, the second plane of Hell."

"I see," said Jon meekly, "I kind of figured you were someone like that. Well, to answer your first allegation, I did not know that we were defying you. You see, Bard Wendell was abducted from his painting work. We — I merely rescued him. I apologize, Caleb, for taking part of your wall, but I could see no other way left to me. If you hadn't poured molten lead into the lock, I would not have taken the stone. However, I have decided that the next time I will take your entire dungeon!"

Caleb visibly cringed. He did not doubt that this weird stranger probably could!

Dispater roared with laughter once more. "You are delightfully refreshing, Jon Brown!"

*Jon!* Mandy sent him. *Be careful! You are talking to the Arch-devil himself! He is unbelievably powerful. Watch your step.*

Another voice appeared in his mind. *Right, Jon. I am. You'd better do as she says.* Dispater smiled at Jon. Jon shook his head; it felt like he had a crowd of people inside. Dispater grinned and let out an evil, soul crushing, cold laugh. Alison cringed again.

Jon grew bolder. "Well, I always wanted to meet a god or goddess. But a devil, well I guess you'll do. You must have wished us back here for Caleb. He doesn't seem to have that much power. I take it that he has summoned you. Do you get summoned often? Does it bother you?" Remembering Darless' hatred of such, Jon was curious. Dispater was much more powerful.

"Impudence or ignorance?" declared Dispater, wonderingly. "The latter," he concluded. "You are worthy of discourse, Jon Brown. No, I am not called upon too frequently. My price is too high for most to pay. My retaliation, too fierce. Actually, I rather enjoy it. It gets a bit dull in Hell, you know. No variety. Then you come along to brighten up my night."

Caleb interrupted, growing impatient with the events."Don't listen to him, Dispater. Kill them now. Give me Wendell back. Remember our deal!" He was beginning to worry that he might lose control over his summoned devil.

Jon replied, slightly annoyed, "Caleb, I don't know what your deal is, but I don't think that you and your magic pentagram there exert much control over Dispater here. In fact, I suspect that he's just using you. So if I were you, I'd shut up."

"Jon Brown, you are very perceptive, yes indeed. You are most worthy. What else can you tell me?" asked an amused Arch-devil.

"You sent Bard Wendell a mental picture of that paper forest of Caleb's. You knew that Wendell would be curious and come to see the strange forest first hand. Caleb captured him. Part of the deal was to have Wendell paint a battle scene many times. You had Caleb arrange to have those battle paintings delivered to temples of the goddess Morrigan. I assume that you wish her to get one of the paintings. Obviously, Caleb wanted Wendell to paint him a lot of pictures — none of them the same. Thus, Caleb is hunting for something, something in particular — something that is so important that he'd risk summoning an Arch-devil. He has not yet found it."

"Tell me, Caleb, what price did you have to pay for Dispater's aid?" Jon asked.

Caleb sneered, "You're just guessing. Hah!"

"Very good, Jon," Dispater remarked. "My price is known to all. I ask only for a person's soul. A simple matter."

"It's a small price to pay," interjected Caleb, rather haughtily. "Besides, what do I care for my soul? I'll be dead!" He laughed, pleased with himself and his bargain.

It was Jon's turn to laugh. Between chuckles, he said, "Dispater, you cannot trick me. I know the truth. It is common knowledge where I come from. A simple price — hah! A soul! Man is a complex creature. He has a body, a mind, and a soul. That which is aware and is truly alive — that which *is* the person is the soul. So your bargain is that you have the person *himself*! That is no bargain. Caleb, you have sold your entire future as a spiritual being to Dispater. I hope it was worth it."

Caleb turned sickly gray.

"You are very sharp, Jon Brown, as well as correct," announced Dispater. A big smile spread across his face. "You should know the rest of the story. Then, we will see. Speak, Caleb! I command you to tell Jon your bargain!" So commanding was his intention that poor Caleb had no choice but talk.

Struggling with the major revelation of the true price he was paying, he said, "In the last days of Kalanos, the Great, I was a beginning apprentice. I was the door warden. When the liquid fire was gone, I watched the city crumble into ruins. Kalanos fled. So did everyone else. Because I was in charge of the door, I would not leave. So I stayed. I dreamed of finding more liquid fire and bringing fame and wealth back to Kalanos City. For years, I have kept two great ocean ships free of rust — all ready to sail. All I need is more liquid fire."

"Two years ago, I discovered a secret hiding place of Kalanos, the Great. In the chamber was a book of pictures. I discovered that it is a book of magic portals. I tried them all, but found no liquid fire. So I researched for six months to discover who the artist was. Finally, I learned that Bard Wendell painted them. My plan is simple. I want him to paint worlds for me to check out. Sooner or later, I will find more liquid fire. Then, I, Caleb Durward, shall sail the seas and become rich and famous and bring glory back to Kalanos City!"

"About a year ago, I summoned Dispater and we struck our bargain. It was as you have said. I created the trap and we got Wendell. So far, I have had no luck.

However, sooner or later, I will find that for which I seek — Dispater has promised me!"

"In return, I was supposed to force Wendell to paint this war scene over and over. I was to see to it that they were sent to various temples of Morrigan. Why? I do not know, nor do I care. For this, I have sold my soul. It does not seem so worthwhile, just now." He looked downcast.

"Better wisdom late than not at all," offered Jon. "Ok, Dispater, that's his story. But why all of these paintings for Morrigan? What is it that you really desire in all of this? Another soul?"

"Are you offering yours?" asked Dispater whimsically. "No. Too bad. Let us just say that I have a small debt to settle with Morrigan. But I am patient. Two hundred years ago, she had the audacity to steal back a soul right out from my very palace! It was a sneaky raid! Now, I merely wish to give her one of those paintings. Nothing more. Just a mere painting."

"I don't get it," protested Jon. "You don't have to," replied Dispater, "Unless you are willing to pay for it."

"Thanks, but I'll pass," Jon joked. "So now what, Dispater? We have a standoff."

"This is most interesting," mused the Arch-devil.

"But you promised me," wailed Caleb, mournfully.

"Ah, but Morrigan has not received a picture yet, has she?" Jon probed. "No, I'm sure she hasn't and I know why, too." Dispater looked curiously at Jon, but said nothing. An idea was forming in Jon's mind. "I need one last question answered. Where are we?" he asked, "Besides in a dungeon." There was a slight moment of silence. "Ah, thank you, Caleb. Most appreciated."

"So you read minds, too, Jon Brown. You are clever," Dispater acknowledged.

To Alison and Mandy, Jon said, "We are in Kalanos City by the ocean." However, he did not tell them that he also had gleaned one other vital piece of information. It was crucial only to himself. Besides, they would not have understood. He had seen what Caleb's two ships looked like. They were exactly like the steam driven cruisers of World War I. Jon now knew much.

"Ok, Dispater, how about a deal."

"I was expecting this. I really do not want to slay you three. You are much too valuable. I shall relish the attempts to acquire your souls, or yourselves if you please! What do you offer? Your women? They are certainly beautiful. Either one would grace my palace halls!"

Mandy and Alison cringed, but they were still basically held immobile by the chill of death that Dispater exuded.

"Here's the deal. You give me time to get Caleb, here, his precious liquid fire. You let us and Bard Wendell go free now. Further, you will refrain from hassling the Bard any further in these matters. When I get Caleb his liquid fire, he will give me his book of portals, as a thank-you for speeding up matters."

"And the price you shall pay?" he asked full of curiosity.

"I will see to it that Morrigan personally gets a copy of that painting that you so badly want her to get." Jon replied.

Dispater roared with laughter. It was a totally unexpected response. For an instant, Jon had the thought that he might not go for it. That would leave only a fight — one that he could not hope to win. Then, he discarded that idea. He was certain. He knew that his certainty would prevail.

The Arch-devil smiled, "I am patient. I hereby suspend all actions in this matter for a period of one month. I shall be watching. After that, we will meet once more. It is agreed. This has been extremely amusing, but now I must really be going. A month, Jon Brown, but I would prefer your soul or those of your women. Ah well, I have plenty of time!" He roared with laughter. There was a flash of magic and Dispater was gone.

The paralyzing, chill of death that had frozen Alison and Mandy was gone. Caleb's captain, let out a wail and fled from the dungeon.

"Caleb, you will hear from me very soon. Goodbye for now," said Jon. Caleb was visibly shaking. Evidently, he now felt that he had made a very bad bargain.

Jon got the image of the yellow bedroom in the church and stepped his party there. He collapsed onto the bed and fell asleep. He was totally exhausted beyond any exhaustion he had ever known.

# Chapter 13 Lady Ursla's Challenge

Jon awoke. He had slept soundly and peacefully. It was afternoon, and the sunlight shone through the stained glass window onto Alison's face. He stared at her, marveling at her angelic beauty.

"He's awake, now, Mandy," she said much relieved.

Now Jon noticed the ranger. She looked even more beautiful. Moved, he spoke, "I must be in heaven. I've got two angels watching over me."

Alison blushed, and Mandy replied, "Well, I see you are back. I'll go order you some food and let the others know you're awake. We all have a lot to discuss, handsome." Predictably, Jon's face reddened with the last remark as she knew it would.

Jon noted that both women had cleaned up and had evidently gone shopping in the city. Both wore magnificent new dresses. To Jon, both looked like goddesses.

Mandy added, as she left, "Alison, here, has hardly ever left your side."

Jon marveled, and, as he looked at her, both grew embarrassed.

"I feared for you, Jon," she began. "I stayed by your side in case you needed anything. I didn't want you to wake up and see some unfamiliar priest or adept looking over you."

"Thank you. You look stunning. You both do." "Mandy picked it out," Alison explained, referring to her long, flowing, lacy, yellow gown.

"You two are fantastic. Say, how long was I out of it asleep, I mean?"

"Three days. I was very worried. Mandy said that you probably had to use a tremendous amount of energy doing all that you did. I feared that you might have some permanent damage," she said, her voice full of concern.

"I feel fine — no I feel starved! Mandy's one step ahead of me. I guess I'd better get up," Jon decided. Then he realized that he was still in bed and became embarrassed once more.

"Let me get you your clothes. They have been washed and cleaned. However, the Archdeacon has sent some other clothes, if you'd rather have them."

"I'd be more comfortable in mine. Thanks." Alison got him his clothes and then waited by the door, her back turned toward him. Jon felt her awkwardness and his. Then, he felt her emotions. He slipped into his pants and hastily buttoned his shirt. "Alison, come here." She did, shyly. Jon opened his arms, beckoningly. She did not hesitate. They hugged, gently kissed, and held each other tightly for some time. Neither spoke. Jon caressed her long brown hair. She smelled so sweet. He hugged her tighter.

Then, Alison's sense of propriety returned. "You had better finish getting dressed. Mandy will be back with the food and everyone's just filled with questions and worries. Soon, they will all come at once."

Jon had just finished tying his shoes, when Mandy returned with a tray of steaming lunch. Jon hugged her and then ate ravenously. "I'm starved," he proclaimed between mouthfuls.

Mandy, he noticed, had a long blue gown whose front plunged nearly to her naval, leaving little to the imagination. Mandy made impressions! She was lovely.

While he was eating, Mandy explained, "I let the others know that you were awake. The Archdeacon and Bard Wendell are in the high altar room. Wendell has resumed his painting. He says that it will be done in just a few weeks. We are to meet them there for a council. There are only twenty-seven days left." She sounded concerned.

A half hour later, the three joined Prince Reginald and Wendell in the holy room. Wendell was high atop the scaffolding, painting furiously, determined to finish the fresco before the month's time expired.

As they entered, an inspired Wendell explained his work. "Here is Ukko himself," he pointed. Jon gazed upwards at the enormous fresco. "It's supposed to be Ukko's realm. See I have created ten air maidens — mine are so much more alive than those others down there on the wall. The Mother Madonna represents the mother of humanity; the babe is symbolic of we mortals."

The Archdeacon interrupted him, "You see, worshipers can get a symbolic view of the imagined realm of Ukko. It will make him more real to them. Their faith shall be reinforced."

Jon realized that these two could talk for hours about art and religion. He proposed, "I see. It is superb. But can we talk a while? There are some things that we need to discuss. Our time is rather limited."

Hastily, Bard Wendell climbed down. Jon could see that he had recovered from his ordeal. He had a haircut and his beard trimmed. Now he looked dashing in spite of his age. Jon realized that he could still charm women easily. Soon the five were sitting on the pews.

Wendell began, "Jon, I want to personally thank you for rescuing me. Alison has explained how you figured out where I was. Alison and I have explained my 'gift' to Reginald, and he has seen her book of portals. He understands now how we can come and go by use of the trident portal pictures. On the other hand, none of us understands you completely. It seems that you can step through even someone else's mental picture of one of these pictures. How? And even more striking, you can step through any picture that doesn't even have a trident in it — even mental pictures. We do not understand. How is this possible? Such was not part of my 'gift' from the gods."

Jon was humble, "You are right on this, but I do not know how I do it. It just works." He explained how he first had discovered the book's functions — how he had simply gotten the idea of having already arrived. He described his adventures at Stilmar Pond with the swans. "It seems that I never knew the 'rules' and I just experimented to see what would work. Even now, I still surprise myself with finding new possibilities. I do not know how I do it. I just do it. I just step through as I would one of your paintings. It works. I have complete certainty. But, Wendell, there is one thing I'd like to know about. What is the significance of the trident?"

"Alas, I do not know. It is part of the 'gift.' If I do not put it in the painting, then that painting cannot be used as a portal. Yet, if one is there, it can be. Why? I do not know," he replied honestly.

Archdeacon Reginald counseled, "I understand, Jon. You have your own 'gifts.' They are mighty. Had you known the rules, you would not have been tempted to explore your own abilities. You would tend to accept the limitations of others. You would be less than you are. You have great wisdom. Only you, my son, can know and determine the bounds of your own power."

"Could you really have brought the whole wall or dungeon like you threatened Caleb?" asked Bard Wendell, full of curiosity.

"If I was fresh, I might give it a try. No, just teasing! Unfortunately, I had already exerted myself getting us all back the first time. Then, there was that awful energy drain just to keep Dispater's chill of death subdued! That was terrible!" Jon declared.

"I couldn't move," Mandy interjected — the horror of it returning. "I have never felt so utterly helpless."

"Me too," broke in Alison. "I just shook uncontrollably! I could not have even tried to cast the simplest spell."

"A devil, especially the Arch-devil himself, has powers far beyond we mortals," explained His Holiness, Prince Reginald. "He is, of course, totally evil."

"I must apologize for my cowardice," offered Bard Wendell. "I just collapsed from the chill of death."

"No apologies are needed," Jon replied. "It was Dispater's will, that's all."

With Jon's mentioning of the energy drain, Mandy finally understood and declared, "Now I understand how you could still operate while we could not. You were able to nullify that chill. I know of other mental masters who have a similar ability to control all harmful energies in their vicinity. It does take lots of mental power to do so. I do not have that ability."

"Yes, but you were superb handling all of those fighters," Jon said. "Where I could not have fought even one, you took them all on. And you, Alison, handled Caleb extremely well! If you hadn't been caught off guard by coughing from those toxic fumes from his gas cloud, you might have beaten the wizard. You both did extremely well."

"But, you saved us all," added Alison, reassuringly. "I want to thank you for endeavoring to get Caleb's copy of my family's book back for me. That was a nice touch, but I would never have thought of doing that."

"You are certainly a rare man, Jon Brown," put in His Holiness, Prince Reginald. "There are only a very few people that would even consider challenging a devil, much less the Arch-devil himself! You were bold — yes, extremely so. Bard Wendell has described your discussions with Dispater. I am astounded by your attitude toward him."

"I don't understand," Jon returned.

The priest explained, "Most would have been cowered by Dispater's might and evil. They'd have been satisfied just to be able to straightforwardly answer the Arch-devil's questions. Yet you seemed to be challenging Dispater. You are either a great fool or extremely courageous."

Jon knew that he had to explain his attitudes at that time. "I saw his power immediately. The women and Wendell were frozen into a state of immobility. Even Caleb's mighty fighter was cowered. Caleb seemed to have confidence in his futile magic circle. I could feel that chill of death. I knew this man had power, evil power. I intuitively sensed that it was mostly a challenge meant for me, since I was the only one able to respond to Dispater directly. Either a challenge or a test — I couldn't tell which. I figured that if I was submissive, all was lost. So really, you see, I had nothing to lose by being arrogant and cocky. If I had let my self-assurance drop for even a moment, Dispater would have won. Hence, I acted as if I were in control. In a way, I was."

"I see," replied His Holiness. "You were quite right. I have not had any dealings with devils, but all of my training indicates the correctness of your basic premise. Only the hardiest can hope to interest a devil. And you are quite correct about Dispater's price being a soul, the person himself. I am surprised that Caleb did not know that. But then so very many of the people these days do not understand themselves. They come here to pray for their souls. They have become so ignorant of their own lives, but that's why the church is here."

Jon could detect a long sermon in the offing and hastily interrupted. "Yes. But it did take much energy to keep that chill at bay. For a time I wondered if I would be able to pull it off. I am sure that Dispater in some devilish way was testing me."

"Evidently, he found you worthy," added Bard Wendell. "That was some bargain you made."

"He had no choice, but bargain," interjected His Holiness. "Dispater obviously meant for Jon to bargain, but I am a bit concerned over the price. It is almost always a soul, but deliver a painting to Morrigan, the goddess of war? I simply do not understand."

"Neither do I," Jon added hastily.

"Well, it must be very significant," Alison replied thoughtfully. "We have a month in return for mere delivery. What can be so vital about that painting?"

"I surely do not know," Wendell explained. "I painted it two dozen times. It is simply a battle in progress scene — a bloody one at that. Perhaps, Dispater thinks Morrigan will like it, who knows?"

"But what exactly do we have to do?" Mandy wanted to know.

"That is the real question, and you are right in asking it," agreed His Holiness. "I do not think that any of us entirely realize what Jon has in mind in this matter. Jon, could you explain in more detail what must be done. I will endeavor to provide as much aid as I can. Much is at stake here, including your souls." That was a sober thought, and one they had been overlooking. The next meeting might not go so well for them.

With a rather perplexed look, Jon scratched his head and began to try to explain his half formed ideas. "First of all, you must realize that I do not have all of the answers just yet. I have enough to feel certain that we can do it all, or I would not have so bargained. Let me explain. Caleb is the easiest. He has a fleet of iron ships. When I looked into his mind, I saw that they were just like some ships from my world, but obsolete by some fifty years. From what I have pieced together, liquid fire can only be petroleum. Since there are no refineries in this world, Kalanos must have used a crude form to burn in his steamships." He saw blank stares of non-comprehension on everyone's face. He spent several minutes trying to describe the steel ships, oil, and the process of refining. He succeeded best when he called it a magical process. This they could accept.

"Now we have already found another possible supplier of liquid fire for Caleb — Kagor Dougal, the Merciless Mage of Trundle! Remember that black, messy oil in the tunnels?" The girls now completely realized what Jon was thinking. He continued, "Kagor wanted a piece of the action, so to speak your Holiness, but he did not get it from Mariane. He is going to war basically to get revenge and wealth and fame. Well, if he should now become a partner with Caleb, he could achieve all of his goals with far less risk."

"Yes, but we would be plunged into yet another dark age by the loss of all of our shipping rights," protested the Archdeacon.

"Not really. There was only a small supply of the liquid fire there in Trundle. All of the iron ships have rusted into worthless junk, except for the two ships Caleb has salvaged. I'm sure that two ships would make very little difference to your trade."

"No, you are right. Two ships would not be a problem. Further, if the liquid fire supply is limited, so much the better," His Holiness agreed.

"Remember, also, that it was Kalanos who designed and built the ships in the first place, not Caleb. He has only two ships. I doubt that he could ever build more. He and Kagor could make a respectable fortune with just two — enough to keep them both happy," Jon said decisively.

Jon went on, "That will handle Caleb and also Kagor. It also ends the war on Mariane, which raises more problems specifically: the cause of that war in the first place, Lady Ursla of Hollybine Wood. If her war of revenge against both Trundle and Mariane goes unfulfilled, more trouble brews. She has the goddess Morrigan behind her. From what everyone has been telling me, if Morrigan wants a war, then a war she'll have. And then there's Lady Ursla's desires."

Jon concluded, "So we must find some way to satisfy Lady Ursla's desire for revenge of wrongs inflicted by both yourselves and Trundle and appease Morrigan. This is the part that I have not yet figured out. I do not know what would satisfy Lady Ursla, other than war. Any suggestions?"

Silence. "But even if you find a way to appease the druid of Hollybine Wood, how do you propose to get that painting delivered personally into the hands of Morrigan?" queried Alison. "She is a goddess, and who knows where she is located? And what will she do when she finds out that you've stopped her private war?"

"Ah, that is the last little problem," Jon assured her.

Bard Wendell, nodding in agreement, said, "You've got three tasks. The first is straightforward — Caleb and Kagor — more or less, anyway. However, the other two pose mighty problems. You have less than a month to solve them. Grim."

"But not impossible," Jon added. "Or I would not have bargained. I think that it will be easy to get in touch with Morrigan, when the time is right. I'm not too concerned about that. Appeasing her is another matter. The only real difficulty is with Lady Ursla."

"Well, since I and my people have been partially responsible for her desperate measures, I feel I must assist you in this task," the Archdeacon volunteered. "Although I am getting too old for this sort of thing, I feel that I should go to Lady Ursla and plead our case, personally."

"We must accompany you," assured Alison. "With Jon just stepping us there, it should not be too taxing."

"Thank you. That is a great relief to an old man. I hope that I am up to being able to handle her, considering our past deeds." There was a strong note of doubt in his words. He continued, "Let me call an emergency council of the ruling senate to discuss ways and means of reparation. Shall we plan to go to see Lady Ursla tomorrow?" Everyone agreed. So the Archdeacon left to arrange the details.

"No matter which way this all turns out," Wendell said, "I want to have this supreme fresco completed. So if you will excuse me, I will get back to my love." He nimbly climbed back up to the dome a hundred feet overhead.

Now that they were alone once more, Mandy said, "There is still one thing troubling me."

"What's that?" Jon replied.

"Dispater kept referring to us as 'your women' as if we were property that could be possessed! That was an affront! Men! Devils!"

"I disliked that attitude as well," Jon consoled. "I do not consider you two as my property. Or like the dryads considered me their man. I love you both. You are individuals. Perhaps, it has something to do with his owning souls. Or perhaps, Dispater does not know everything. I am counting on the latter. I hope that he is not omniscient. But come, you elegant ladies, let's go for a walk in the gardens." They giggled and agreed. Tomorrow would take care of itself, Jon hoped.

The next morning, his Holiness joined them, dressed for a journey. He carried his scepter and a small pack. The girls were likewise dressed for adventure. Mandy cautioned them all to be alert around the lions and not harm them. Jon then recalled a mental picture of the grounds around Lady Ursla's dwellings. All joined hands, and Jon stepped them into Hollybine Wood.

They arrived in the tiny settlement with the quaint log cabins about the bases of the massive oak trees. Various woodland creatures were milling around the clearing, and Lady Ursla was out doing her morning activities among them. Their unexpected appearance right in the middle of the clearing startled the animals and Lady Ursla. For a brief instant, Jon thought he saw not the Lady but that huge mountain lion that had stalked them the last time they had come to Hollybine Wood. Lady Ursla recognized them at once, and that vision dissolved. She did not look too pleased to see them.

"Pardon us, my Lady," Jon began. "We have an urgent need to meet with you. I have brought His Holiness, Prince Reginald Noxwood, the Archdeacon of Mariane, with me. Could we have a bit of your time?" He hoped that she would not be too affronted by their unexpected appearance and also by his bringing her sworn enemy into her home. He was beginning to have major reservations about these two. He stood for law and goodness; she, for the natural balance of all things. They were far apart in their worldly views.

Lady Ursla was a grande dame. If she was displeased, she did not show it. She knew at once that she had a royal visitor. She even seemed amused. "Welcome to Hollybine Wood," she began. "You, Jon, should find a way of asking or announcing your coming before you just pop in. But no mind. I see you have brought His Holiness. Surely, he would not venture from his church unless the matter was of the utmost importance. Very well then, follow me."

She led them into her cabin. While Reginald marveled at the quaintness of her home, Jon noticed that the fire was burning and that some water was hot. *Perhaps, she expected us after all.*

The perfect hostess, Lady Ursla soon had them all sitting around her table drinking tea and eating snacks. Jon secretly marveled that a woman her age could still look so beautiful. She was striking in appearance. He wondered if she had ever been married and resolved to inquire sometime. Soon the real reason for their visit could no longer be delayed. Jon knew that now the trouble would begin, but he had to follow through.

Jon began, "I assume that it is safe here to discuss private matters." She nodded and her eyes were suddenly full of curiosity. "We know all about your revenge — about Darless, Morrigan, Trundle, and your desire for retribution." For only a brief instant, there was a flicker of anger on her countenance. He went on, "There were no betrayals of your pact. It is just that there is more to all of this than your simple matter of a just revenge. You are definitely entitled to some retribution from both Mariane and Trundle. Their irresponsible actions are appalling. I have only once met the dryads, and I found them to be lovely creatures. My heart also cries out at the thought of their deaths. No one here will deny you that some form of retribution is due you." She seemed to relax a bit. Perhaps, she was enjoying seeing her victim, His Holiness, squirm. Jon could not be certain.

"You see, Kagor abused his gift books with the picture portals. He wreaked havoc in other worlds beyond Rochelle destroying forests and people there. That is why Mandy is here trying to halt the destruction of her forest." He hoped that this view would be more to Lady Ursla's liking. "I will be totally honest with you." He then told their complete tale, although leaving much about Darless out. He indicated that they had given Darless no choice in the matter. He wanted to be absolutely certain that Darless was not compromised in any way. He had given his word. He finished with their recent meeting with Dispater. She listened to all with a keen ear and a sparkle in her eye. She enjoyed this immensely.

At last, His Holiness spoke, "So what we have come here today is to ask what would make an amends for our terrible destruction of your forest and creatures, years ago. Realize that we are not looking to save ourselves from war. We are strong and would easily repel an army of hobgoblins. However, I truly wish to make an amends for our evil act. It should have been done many years ago. In this, I am to blame. I did not pursue the matter."

"So you feel guilty and wish to buy me off to make your conscience feel better?" Lady Ursla retorted. "Hobgoblins are weak you say. Well, how about hobgoblins that are assisted by the goddess of war. Do not doubt that Morrigan herself will be on the battlefields aiding them. It won't be that easy a victory. Many will die for the deaths of the dryads."

Jon wondered what would happen next. *This is not going to be easy! She still has vengeance in her heart.* He began to think. It was just as well that he did, for the next ten minutes the two — Reginald and Lady Ursla — argued back and forth. Fortunately, both remembered a sense of propriety and kept their voices lowered. Nevertheless, they definitely were arguing.

Then, Jon had an idea. "May I interrupt?" He didn't wait for their reply, but continued, "Lady Ursla, think for a moment. Suppose you have your war. Many are slain. Punishment is dealt, but has that action benefitted your woods in any way? Not at all! Further, think of the reprisals. Many will die. Of course, they'll blame you, overlooking their own country's past evil toward you. Some may seek retribution from you. More evil. No, Lady Ursla, you cannot fight evil with evil. Only more evil results." He paused for a moment to let her absorb his meaning.

Then, he continued, "What I propose is a true and lasting retribution — one that has meaning and value for the future of Hollybine Wood. If Mariane gave something of immense value to the woods, and therefore to you, would not that be an even better solution?"

He could see her thinking as well as Reginald. "I see your meaning," Lady Ursla replied, "What exactly are you proposing that Mariane could give to the woods? They can hardly give the dryads' their lives back?"

"Well, that is the problem, my Lady." Jon paused. "You see, I do not have the eternal and all-encompassing love for the forest that both you and Mandy here have. True, I love the woods, but not like you two do. Hence, you see I am ignorant about such matters as what would benefit a wood. I am hoping that either you or Mandy could come up with an idea."

For the first time, Lady Ursla smiled and laughed. "Jon Brown, you have great wisdom. You truly respect me. That is what counts. I do not ask that you love the forest as I do — only that I have your respect. You have shown me that you do. You could have ignored me entirely. Most certainly my woods would have been defiled further once the people of Mariane and Trundle hear that I was behind a devastating war. You chose to find another way for us all. Yes, you are correct. There should be some other form of retribution. Although I cannot claim that I will be able to stop the war at this point. Things have gone too far. Morrigan may keep it going for her own edification. Who can say? Thus, I cannot make any promise, except to try to prevent the war, should I find the retribution satisfactory."

"I accept your offer," hastily agreed Reginald, before she could have a change of heart.

She laughed again. "You agree and yet you do not know what the payment will be. You are getting hasty, old priest!" Now everyone laughed, even the Prince himself.

The problem remained as to what the retribution should be. Numerous ideas from a massive reforestation project to land grants were suggested. No one could agree on anything.

Then, an idea formed in Mandy' mind. She proclaimed, "Lady Ursla, you need a formal druid's college in your woods. From time to time, I must get some tutorage from druids, and it is hard to get if there is not a formal place of learning."

"That is a really good idea, Mandy." Lady Ursla seemed very pleased with the concept. "Yes, a druid's college would benefit everyone concerned and provide some measure of insurance that the wanton destructions do not occur again."

She paused, looked them over, and spoke once more. "All right. I will consider an amends made if two conditions are fulfilled. First, Mariane must build a huge druid's college according to my specifications for Hollybine. I would estimate that you may need to spend a half—million gold coins. Furthermore, you must provide all operating expenses for twenty—five years. Do you agree to these terms, your Holiness?"

"I most certainly approve," Reginald hastily concurred. "Although I suspect that only a fifth of that sum will be needed for a fine building. Such a place would help to guarantee the sanctity of Hollybine in the future. However, there is no way that the project could be completed in a month's time."

"That is of no concern. You get it started. I know that for you, your word is sacred. You will not go back on your vow once given," replied Lady Ursla with complete certainty. "Now the other condition. The meddlers must also provide some token of an amends for interfering. You three will bring a Theos tree to Hollybine."

Blank stares faced her. No one had the slightest idea of what she was talking about. Eagerly, she explained. "In my youth, my husband and I traveled far and wide studying many forests and lands. One time, he teleported us to Melkor Woods, which is cradled against the northwestern edge of the Forlorn Mountains just north of the wild country of East Reach. Those mountains are the most rugged that I have ever seen completely impassable on foot. The lands north of this range are uninhabited by people, but there are many fell creatures there. It is a dangerous place. Nonetheless, we visited the woods there. The Theos tree grows deep inside that woods. It is an old and magical race of tree. If a woodland creature licks its bark, the tree both heals their wounds and cures their illness. Such a tree would be magnificent for Hollybine. Meddlers, bring me a Theos tree to show your good faith."

"At once," declared Mandy. "We will be honored to do it. It would help all of the animals. Forgive my ignorance, but what does such a tree look like?"

"Ah, I will show you. One moment." She retrieved an old sketchbook yellowed with age. "Here it is. We drew sketches of the things we saw on our adventures. Oh, those were the days," she lamented. Obviously, she had stirred memories long forgotten. She showed them her sketches of the Theos tree.

After some further discussions about the location of the college and other details, the party prepared to depart.

As everyone filed outside the cabin, Jon spoke to Lady Ursla, "May I have a word with you — in private?"

"Certainly," replied the druid, full of curiosity.

Jon began awkwardly, "It would help us greatly if I could see your mental memories of the place where the tree is located. You see, if so, I can get us there at once. You will get your tree quickly. Time is vital to us."

"You mean you want to read my mind?" she asked incredulously. He nodded. "You are unbelievable, Jon Brown. Anybody else would just have gone right ahead and pried. Why bother asking?"

"I like to ask permission first," he shyly replied. "I consider that it would be an offense for me just to pry into another's mind without their consent."

"Your integrity is most honorable, Jon. By all means, you may do so. What do I have to do?" She wondered.

Rather embarrassedly, Jon explained, "All you have to do is recall your memories of that adventure. Remember the tree. Just call those images back. I'll be seeing whatever you see in your mind."

Two minutes later, Jon joined the others. He had a good image of the tree, its location, and some of the wild creatures there. In addition, he had one other unexpected and rather startling piece of information, which he kept to himself, pondering its significance. Waving goodbye, Jon stepped them back to the Church of Ukko in Zaire.

## Chapter 14 The Theos Tree

By the next morning, the council had adopted the concept of a druid's college. Draftsmen were hard at work laying out the basic plans suggested by Lady Ursla. The Archdeacon personally organized the project. Engineers had to be called upon, materials arranged for, and the work force acquired. Still, it would be nearly two weeks before the crews finished traveling the long distance between Zaire and the proposed site on the eastern edge of Hollybine Wood. Construction began at once. Ten druids were waiting there, representing the Lady's interests. All went according to plan. (It is worth noting that the Hollybine Wood Druid College opened its doors four months later.)

The companions spent two days helping His Holiness establish the construction project. During this time, they also visited the local gardeners to learn how to safely transplant trees. Though Mandy had never done it, she had the basic idea. However, Jon and Alison had no idea of the correct procedure, except dig it up. Since it was neither early spring nor late fall, they would have to take some care or the tree would not survive.

They also studied the extensive maps the mariners had. Melkor Woods, they discovered, was roughly at the same latitude as Hollybine Wood. Both were far north from the world's equator. Hollybine Wood had the moderating influence of two vast plains on either side of it. Only the northern most edge felt the cold from the Blue Ice Barrens. In Melkor Woods, the climate would be different. The small forest was cradled right up against the northeastern edge of the tall, rugged, and impassable Forlorn Mountains. The range robbed the vale of both moisture and warm winds. Thus, Melkor Woods should be both cold and arid.

Another problem burned in Jon's mind. Over thirty some years had passed since Lady Ursla had visited the woods. Secretly, Jon wondered how much the forest had changed. *What if the image I have from her no longer represents the way the forest really is? What if it's changed? A lot could have been altered in thirty years. Will I be able to get us there if the image I use is not accurate? Would we still arrive? Or would we just not leave?* As the days passed, Jon's doubts grew.

Finally, the day to leave came. Jon found that the girls were all ready to go. This morning, Alison explained that she had prepared a dig spell. With it, the process would be easier to do. Mandy was bringing a shovel along, just in case. She was excited about visiting another forest.

Jon confessed, "I hate to spoil everything, but I have some doubts." Serious expressions replaced those of excitement. He continued, "What if Lady Ursla's memories and the woods today are very different? That is likely, for much could have and probably has changed in thirty years! Will I be able to step us there? Or will it just fail? Or will we end up in some weird void? Suppose we step into an open area that is no longer open, but full of trees. Will we materialize inside of trees?"

"Oh no!" exclaimed Mandy. "I never thought of that. It probably has changed some. Perhaps we should go overland. That would be safer."

"Yes, but we do not have enough time," protested Alison. "Jon, I knew this problem would arise sooner or later. There are some parallels with my magic spell of teleportation. Every time one teleports, even to one's home, there is some chance of error. One can arrive too high — falling results. One can arrive too low, materializing in the ground — death. The less familiar the destination is, the greater the chance for error. Some gamble and aim purposely too high; they are then prepared to use falling spells to glide down."

"But what does this have to do with my skills?" Jon wondered.

"Everything. Jon, I have been studying you closely, ever since we first met. I am, after all, a magic user. Spells are a way of life for me. I now have a learned opinion for you, if you want to hear it." She faltered uncertainly. Not everyone wanted criticism in their profession, especially by outsiders.

"Look, I admit that I do not know the rules of all this. If you've got some ideas, out with them, love. I'm all ears." Jon was now very curious. Could she have seen something that he'd overlooked?

She took a deep breath and began, "I think that you've got two disciplines not one, and that you've got them confused — sort of all merged into one. Traveling between worlds is one skill, but traveling to other places in the same world is another. I'll try to explain."

"Using the magical books is a fixed mode of travel. They are simply magical devices to move to the place represented in the picture. That is their function. Now, you have shown me that you can go far beyond this. You can travel to another world by using your own or anybody else's mental image of the desired place. Also, you can go to any other place within a given world from a place also within that same world. These are two different things. The latter is similar to my teleport spell. The other, I cannot do and have no name for it, except perhaps 'move to another world.' A fundamental principle of magic use is that one specific cause will create one specific effect."

"I see what you are saying. I've really got two different talents: one for world hopping and another for place hopping. Now that explains a lot," Jon exclaimed, excitedly. Many little doubts and confusions in his mind seemed to clear up and vanish. He started laughing. "You are exactly correct! I do have two different skills. I had them merged into one, because they all evolved from the book of portals. Thanks for clearing up my thinking." And he gave her a kiss of appreciation. She blushed, and felt relieved.

"Now that that is settled, Jon," Alison continued, "I think that I can safely say that so far you have been very lucky. Each time you jumped within the same world, like my teleportation, you had a high degree of certainty of the destination. No error occurred. This proposed jump to Melkor Woods is very different. You expect things to be different. The chance for error is large."

Mandy was having a little difficulty following the significance of all this. She asked, "So what does this mean — that he should not try?"

"No. I'm suggesting that if we just went normally, the chance of error would be great. I think that we'd be in trouble. That's all," Alison explained.

"Hum, you have given me an idea, Alison," Jon announced. "Since the wood has surely changed, let's error on the high side, say by five hundred feet."

"Then, we'll all crash land!" protested Mandy.

"That's where you come in, Mandy." Jon continued. "Before we go, you shape change into the

Pegasus form. We get on your back. I take us there, say five hundred feet above ground. You fly us all down safely."

Mandy kissed him. His face reddened. "Brilliant, Jon Brown. Let's get going."

In a few minutes, Mandy was now a huge, beautiful winged horse. Alison easily vaulted onto her back, while Jon clumsily struggled up behind her. Then, he carefully stepped them high above Melkor Woods.

Chilly air stung their faces as Mandy slowly circled the strange forest below. She gracefully spiraled down toward a clearing. No one was prepared for Melkor Woods.

They were about two hundred feet from the ground, when Alison spied another winged creature sailing straight for them. "Look over there. Something's coming our way."

Mandy swerved to look. Jon nearly fell off, but he managed to both hold on and see as well. The creature looked like those that he had seen in his brief look at Lady Ursla's memories. He wondered what it was.

"Oh no!" shrieked Alison. "That's a dragon! A white dragon."

Jon instantly heard Mandy's response. "Zagroot zounds!" Mandy dove for the ground, but soon she saw that they would never make it. The white dragon would intercept them mid-flight. She then furiously winged upwards, trying to gain altitude for maneuverability.

"I won't be able to cast any spells, Jon. I'm bouncing around too much to concentrate. All of my magic wands are in my portable hole. I didn't think we'd need them," cried a dismayed Alison.

Now the strong white dragon swooped in close. It was huge, dwarfing the Pegasus and passengers. Jon was instantly reminded of the renaissance painting of

Sir George and the Dragon at the Art Institute in Chicago that he and Harry had once visited. "Is it dangerous?" he asked out of ignorance.

"Hold onto me," screamed Alison. "I'll hold onto Mandy. Yes, very! It can breathe a cone of intense cold on us. If it catches us up here, we'll probably freeze to death. Don't worry. It'll be a quick death."

Jon was not reassured. Furthermore, he again had to hang onto Alison. However, this time he did so willingly and without embarrassment.

Alison continued, "If it does not freeze us, it can claw us to pieces. We cannot even dodge its claws. Also, if it decided to bite us, we could be eaten alive or crushed in its jaws."

"I see," Jon relied. "Are they carnivorous creatures?"

"They like to eat horses, deer, and antelope and the like, I've been told," she replied. "Look out. Here it comes!"

Normally, the Pegasus could easily out-fly and outmaneuver the bulky white dragon. However, Mandy was heavily laden, carrying Jon and Alison. Even though her speed was greatly reduced, her maneuverability still exceeded the dragon's. Still, if she were not extremely careful, her passengers would be dismounted. This critical information she relayed mentally to Jon.

The gaping mouth was now about fifty feet before them. Jon saw a white cloud exhaled, moving straight at them. It grew in size as it neared them. Jon closed his eyes and concentrated. He could sense the intense cold. He proceeded to nullify its effect. He expanded the area as far as he could. Then, the full cloud of dragon's breath hit them and passed on off into the sky beyond them.

Mandy sent, "Ouch, it froze my tail! Next time, don't forget my tail, Jon. Thanks for the assist."

Alison opened her eyes and exclaimed, "Why — why aren't we frozen?" "I nullified the cold around us, but I'm afraid that I missed Mandy's tail. I hope it doesn't hurt too much, Mandy." She whinnied.

"Wow! So that's what it's like — to have harmful energies dissipated around you. That's incredible. Is it very taxing?" asked Alison.

"A little. I can hold out for several more blasts. Watch for another attack. I want to think," he said.

In a minute, Alison exclaimed, "I think it's coming in again from above us this time."

Mandy sent him, "It means to attack with its claws or bite. Hold on. We are in trouble again."

Jon had been thinking rapidly — speculating on various approaches. Acting on a mental hunch, he commanded, "Mandy, head for that tiny clearing there at the edge of those hills. I think that we will find a cave or something like that there."

Mandy thought it a bit unusual that there would be a convenient cave, but did as he commanded. *Let me know if I need to dive. I can't see the dragon from this angle.*

Alison watched helplessly as the giant creature swooped down upon them. "It means to claw us this time," she called out calmly.

Jon was distracted. *Fabulous pair of women! They remain calm under stress. They are something else.* Alison's warning allowed him time to act. He expanded his mind, reaching for the approaching dragon's. He made contact. For an instant, he was overwhelmed by its basic animal urges and thirst for the flying food. Then, he commanded. The dragon fought his mental attacker for a brief instant. Now, Jon was in control. He commanded it to circle them and to guard its food.

"It's stopped its dive. Now, it's circling us," reported Alison.

"Great! That's what I told it to do," Jon said.

"We're saved," Alison exclaimed.

"Not yet," Jon cautioned. "There should be several more coming any moment now. I doubt that I can dominate more than one or two at the same time. Keep your eyes open."

They were within a few hundred feet of the ground, when Alison spotted the other dragons. "Two more coming in from the right, one from the left, one from above us."

"Keep on heading down, Mandy. Keep alert, Alison. Let me know if any get too close.

Come on cave, where are you?" Jon urged.

"There — there to your right, Mandy. There's the cave. Head for it. Come on just another minute. Hold off, dragons," Jon pleaded.

Mandy landed and began to change her shape back.

"We're going to get frozen again," warned Alison. "Two are sweeping down on attack runs."

Jon commanded his dragon. Mandy completed her shape change and collapsed unconscious onto the ground, utterly exhausted from the ordeal. She had spent every ounce of energy she had and then some. Jon and Alison picked her up and hurried for the safety of the cave.

"Won't we get frozen?" wondered Alison.

"I don't think that they will get the chance to freeze us. I told the one I'm controlling to defend its food from the others. I hope that it fights well for at least another minute; then we'll be safe." Jon urged.

The tunnel narrowed and had grown quite dark. Jon was stumbling, groping for his footing. Alison spoke a word of command and light sprang forth from Jon's forehead. It startled him.

"Now we have light. I couldn't think of a better place to put it just yet," Alison explained. "Gosh, she's heavy. How much farther?"

"Just a little more. I suspect that they cannot follow us in here. They're too big. Pray that we're beyond the range of their frost. Let's rest here. Please stand guard. I must —" Jon collapsed into a deep sleep. He was likewise spent.

"Oh well. Now, it's my turn," said Alison with a smile.

Quickly, she opened her portable hole and retrieved several blankets and made her companions comfortable. She moved her light around and explored her surroundings, wondering what else lived in here. Then, she prepared to watch.

Soon, she heard a loud commotion outside the cave entrance. She suspected that the dragons were trying different approaches to get at their food. Soon, scratching, clawing noises grew closer and closer. One was actually coming down the tunnel. She knew that it had to be a young one, in order to even fit in the tunnel. She prepared her spell carefully. Then, she stepped forward to face the dragon. Before the creature could fire its cone of frost, Alison's spell triggered. The small white dragon was consumed in a ball of fire. It retreated but died at the tunnel's entrance. Then, all became quiet.

Alison relaxed, but she did not let her guard down. She waited patiently. She reflected, *Jon could have teleported us back home at the first sight of the dragon. However, that would have been just giving up.*

*I can teleport us home from here, if things get too sticky so I think that I can handle things for a while. We do need to get that tree. I wonder if Lady Ursla knew about these dragons. Perhaps they're recent arrivals. Wait — what's that?*

She thought that she saw two eyes peering out of the darkness further on down the tunnel. She moved her light to see. It was a large, hairy, ugly spider. It hovered over the sleeping forms. Without warning, it leaped for Alison — its nasty mouth open, ready to bite and inject its poison. She reacted fast. A volley of magical, tiny arrows blasted into the spider's body. It died mid-jump, landing between Alison and the sleeping companions.

"Uck! I hate spiders! Now I'll have to move this thing out of the way," she commented to herself. She got her quarterstaff out from her portable hole and pushed the creepy thing back down the tunnel. Satisfied, she pronounced, "Where there is one spider, there's bound to be more. I think I'd better get my wands out." She rummaged in the extra dimensional hole and got out two wands. "I think I'll just shoot a fire ball down the tunnel and see if there are any more sneaking up." She said, "Fire, fire, for me burn bright." The wand responded with a ball of fire, rushing down the tunnel from where the spider had come. Though only about half as powerful as her spell, it was sufficiently hot to fry six other spiders that were lurking in the dark shaft. "I thought so."

So she got out several lanterns and fumbled with her tinderbox. Soon she had three lanterns illuminating both tunnel approaches to the sleeping party. Now she could see one hundred feet in both directions. "Now, I shan't be surprised," she declared.

However, it was boring, just sitting, watching the tunnels and her sleeping companions. She began to wander around the tunnels, exploring. In one corner, she spied something shiny. Closer inspection revealed the remains of a long dead knight. The shield bore a distinctive coat of arms, but she could not identify it. She determined that the shield and the suit of full plate armor were magically enchanted and quite valuable. The stub of his broken lance lay beside the body. His skeletal hand still held onto a magical sword. She rolled the body over with her staff. His leather pack crumbled into dust, spreading its contents over the floor.

It was the usual sort of gear, lantern, rope, tinderbox, and so on. Nothing was valuable. Most was totally decayed or rotten. One thing did catch her attention, though: the disintegrating remains of a woman's handkerchief. It was a particularly fancy one. "I've seen that kind before, I wonder where," she mused. Then she found his rotting coin purse and determined that he carried about five hundred gold coins.

She sat down pondering the significance of her discovery. At last, she remembered where she had seen that style handkerchief. "It's just like Lady Ursla's!" she exclaimed. She began wondering.

In about four hours, Jon awoke. There was dependable Alison watching over him. "Hello, love. It seems that you are destined to mother me. Thanks. Any trouble?" He stood and stretched and looked about. "I guess so!" he proclaimed.

There were about twenty dead spider bodies littering the tunnel, along with two dead snakes, a bear, and the small dragon at the tunnel's entrance. Alison smiled. "I was not too bored this time. Are you all right?"

"Yes, just a bit tired, but I'll get my strength back. I'm hungry."

"I'm sorry, but I have not had time to fix food. Also, I figured that the odor of food might bring even more creatures. I have had enough of them."

Jon fixed himself a snack from the dried and preserved rations they had brought. When he finished, Alison said, "Follow me. I want to show you something that I found." She showed him the remains of the knight and the handkerchief.

Jon examined the dead knight, curiously. "Where have you seen a handkerchief just like that before?" She probed.

Jon thought for a moment and then blurted, "Lady Ursla. She has some just like this one. He's been dead for years. All that is left is bones."

"And his gear," she added. "It is valuable. That suit of armor, the shield, and the weapon are magical and therefore quite valuable. Also, he carried about five hundred gold coins. He was not your average knight. Unfortunately, I cannot decipher the shield, since I've not studied heraldry at all. Maybe Mandy can identify it, when she wakes up."

"She will be asleep for a while yet," Jon explained. "She really overextend herself back there, but she will be all right. I'll watch for a while if you want a break."

Jon took her quarterstaff and sat down beside Mandy, leaning against the wall. Alison wrapped herself in a blanket and laid down, resting her head on his lap. Jon snuggled her close. Time passed without further interruptions.

About suppertime, Mandy awoke. Alison fixed them all a meal. After eating, everyone was refreshed and ready for moderate action. Mandy was amazed at all of the dead creatures that had tried to dine on her while she slept. She repeatedly complimented Alison on a job well done.

Later, when she was shown the dead knight, she could not identify the shield either. Next, they conferred on what to do about the body. Mandy suggested that they should take the gear back with them. Alison decided that they should take his remains as well. "He obviously died bravely. He deserves a decent burial at least." Her view won, but it was Jon who had to put the bones into a sack and carry them in his pack.

"Now for the tree," Jon said. "Perhaps, we could use those rings of invisibility, Alison. Maybe the dragons will not see us."

"Possibly, but remember that they are animals," cautioned Mandy. "They have other senses besides sight. The rings only hide sight, not smell. We must be quiet and careful."

Holding hands, the invisible trio walked out of the tunnel past the dead dragon that Alison had killed. Then, they entered the forest. The dragons were nowhere to be seen. They remained alert. Jon was very thankful that Mandy was a ranger. She led them slowly and carefully through the forest without incident.

It was not hard for them to find the Theos trees. Their golden bark and huge height marked them as something very special. Their problem was finding one that was small enough for them to manage to carry. After an hour of searching, Mandy selected one.

Alison, using her magical dig spell, soon had the tree dug out. After a good deal of effort, they managed to tie a huge sheet around the ball of roots and dirt. It was heavy and all that the three could do to lift it out of the hole.

"I'm now sure that I do not want to be a gardener," declared a puffing Alison.

Next came the problem of transportation back to Hollybine Wood. Mandy still had not recovered fully, nor had Jon. Alison spoke authoritatively, "I can teleport a maximum weight of five hundred fifty pounds beyond myself. Let's calculate weights." She decided that the total weight did not exceed her limitations.

Alison had Jon hold onto Mandy, while she held onto Jon and the Theos tree. The mage spoke a few words of command. Magical energy flashed and they were next standing before Lady Ursla's cabin.

"Well done, Alison," Jon said proudly.

Lady Ursla was most impressed with the tree. After thanking them, the four proceeded to replant the Theos tree. Jon watched curiously as her lions dug the new hole. Actually, they were just playing, scratching and digging. Jon was grateful that he did not have to dig it himself. By dark, they had the tree replanted. Lady Ursla then sent the trio into her log cabin to clean up and relax, while she prayed, chanted, and blessed her new tree.

Since it was now dark, Lady Ursla insisted that they spend the night with her. They gladly accepted. They were all very tired.

Over breakfast the next morning, Alison brought up the subject of the dead knight that they had found. Lady Ursla was most interested and insisted in seeing the shield. When Mandy produced it from her portable hole, tears swelled into the druid's eyes. She sat down stunned.

In a few minutes, she recovered. "Thank you for bringing him home to me. He was Sir Charles Silverleaf, my only knight." She paused. Everyone sensed that he was more than just her knight. After a few minutes, she said, "I should explain. I was married to Thornapple, a magic user. We were young and I was madly in love. All went well for years, except that I failed to bear him any children. At last, his driving need for children broke us apart. He left one day. I have never seen him since."

"Many years later, Sir Charles came into my life. We — we became lovers. However, his code would not permit us to marry until he had proof that either Thornapple was dead or else we were divorced. Eventually, I had him declared legally dead and we were free to marry. He wanted to get me a special wedding present. Over the years, he had heard me speak of the Theos tree. He decided that he would bring one to me so that we could marry in honor. He was so foolish. Honor is not all that important to me, but it was his life. He had to do it. He left and never returned. I grieved long."

"I'm so sorry," Alison comforted. "Each of us knows what it is like to be so alone." After a pause, she added, "When I found him, I wanted to bring him back so that he could get an honorable burial. Now, I'm glad that I did so."

The somber group carefully laid the fallen warrior to rest in honor. His grave was near the Theos tree that he had died trying to bring to his Lady.

When they had finished and had cleaned up, one of Lady Ursla's aspirant druids came to see her. She had brought a bear cub that had a nasty wound in its paw. Unattended, it would have died. Lady Ursla took everyone out to the Theos tree. "Watch," she commanded. Lovingly, she helped the bear cub to the tree. He sniffed it. Out of some kind of instinct, it licked the tree truck as though it were covered with honey.

While the group watched, the wound began to heal. In ten minutes, there was no trace of the cut. Tears of joy rolled from Lady Ursla's eyes. Everyone was moved.

When the trio was ready to return to the Church of Ukko in Zaire, Lady Ursla gave them each a gift. She presented them each with a huge, green emerald, nearly the size of a fist. "Please accept these as a token of my deepest gratitude. You have done me services beyond words. Each gem is quite similar to the others. Thus, you three will always be united by gems no matter where you are." All were touched by her generosity. Many thank you's followed. Only much later did Jon discover that just one of the matched gems was worth the equivalent of fifty thousand gold coins.

At last, Jon recalled an image of the beautiful gardens and fountains in front of the Church of Ukko. He stepped them there. Their eyes were misty.

# Chapter 15 Such a Deal

After a complete day's rest, during which Alison spent many hours preparing her spells, the trio was once again ready for adventure. "Now it is time to handle Kagor Dougal and Caleb Durward," Jon explained. The first step would have to be a discussion with Kagor, the Merciless Mage. This was a problem. Jon felt certain that after their last visit, the evil wizard probably hated them and would attack them on sight — so much for discussion. Yet, there had to be a way. Jon gave this a good deal of thought. As usual he had a plan.

He outlined his ideas to the girls. "The first and most important step will be to contact Darless. She is the key. Kagor trusts her and is under her charm spell. If she could arrange a semi-friendly meeting with the Mage, we could present our case. If Darless agreed to it, she could help sway Kagor. If all goes well, we should take them and some samples of the liquid fire to Caleb's abandoned town, Kalanos City. If the crude oil works, and I'm almost certain that it will, they should be able to reach some kind of an agreement."

"How do you propose to get in touch with Darless without Kagor knowing about it?" wondered Alison.

"There is only one way that I know will work. I must contact her mind. Telepathy might work, except that the distance is great. I have never done anything quite like this before and she is evil," Jon said.

"Ah, but I do not think that she has much evil in her anymore. Somehow, living with Lady Ursla has affected her. She has changed," offered Alison, who was quick to point out the good in people.

"Yes, I suppose you're right. She did not seem so evil once I got to know her. Perhaps, it is just her appearance to strangers that suggests a heart of evil. Anyway, I will try to contact her. You two see that I am not interrupted."

While the girls watched the room, Jon laid down on his bed, closed his eyes, and expanded his awareness, searching, groping for Darless. Actually, he was feeling for her mind. Each person's mind is different; each is unique. He reached for the alu-demon slowly and carefully. It was very slow going at first because he really did not know just how to do this. He kept refining his technique, and, at last, he knew that he found the mind that he wanted. He sent, *Darless? It's me, Jon Brown. I need to talk to you. Do you always bother your women while they are taking a bath?* She thought back. Jon hastily withdrew, offering an apology. He knew that his face was quite red. He hoped that the girls didn't notice it. However, nothing escaped the alert eyes of Alison and Mandy.

"Whoa! I wonder what *that* thought was," ribbed Mandy. Her eyebrows flicked teasingly.

"Hush. He's trying to concentrate on his spell or thought," reproved Alison.

Jon chose to be only vaguely aware of their comments. Soon, Jon sensed that Darless was ready to listen. He strengthened the contact and began, *Darless, I have met with Dispater and have a plan that will stop this war before it gets started. Lady Ursla has already agreed to it.*

*I know. She told me all about it. And thank you for not breaking our agreement. You are honorable, Jon Brown. Except for Lady Ursla and my father, you are the only person to respect me and honor me. I am more grateful than you'll ever know. But let's be quick because Kagor is calling for me.*

*Ok. Can we meet later today — say at the same place that I teleported you to the last time, there in the Bleak Hills?*

*Yes. I'll be there as soon as I can get free. Bye Jon.* She sent him a mental kiss. He blushed once more. Jon let the contact fade away. Her kiss had a fascinating power, unlike any kiss that he had ever had. Slowly he opened his eyes.

Mandy jumped on him at once, "You must have had a hot contact there, Jon. You are really red! What did she do? What did you do?" She teased, enjoying his squirming.

"I caught her at the wrong time — you know when she was well, never mind. She kissed me. That's all," he mumbled shyly.

"Must have been some kiss!" retorted Mandy playfully.

"Leave him alone," protested Alison. "Why embarrass him further?" *A telepathic kiss! I wonder what it is? What's it feel like? Must be powerful. He sure got embarrassed by it. I'd sure like to know, but I don't dare ask him about it!*

"It puts him in his place. Besides, he should learn to overcome his hang—ups," she replied. "Sorry, Jon. Well, not really! Anyway, what did she say? Will she go along with the plan?"

Jon welcomed the change of topic. He knew that he had problems around women, and Mandy wasn't making it any easier. She always seemed to remind him of his difficulties. "She agreed to meet with us today at the place we camped in the Bleak Hills. We didn't have time to discuss any details because Kagor was calling her. She said that she'll come when she is free. So we'd best get going ourselves."

They agreed and Alison teleported them to the old camping spot in the Bleak Hills. The signs of their stay were still visible on the ground. The trio made camp and waited. During their wait, Mandy went roaming in the hills. Alison asked Jon to tell her what it was like to use telepathy to communicate over such a distance. She was fascinated.

About noon, Darless appeared accompanied by a small flash of magical energy. She looked elegant and very cheerful. Her coal black eyes were penetrating. The first thing she did was give Jon a real kiss. He grew quite red.

"What — what's that for?" he mumbled.

"That is for both hello and double thanks," she replied, obviously glad to see him once again.

Alison was a bit envious. She always knew that Mandy would be a good woman for Jon. However, she had not considered the possibility of Darless. She knew that the alu-demon had much to offer him and she sighed.

Then Darless hugged Alison and then Mandy, who had come back from her nearby explorations. Alison felt that it was her genuine feelings that Darless was displaying. Despite her conflicting emotions, she was also glad to see Darless. Jon then related all of their adventures to date. He was careful to explain exactly what he had said to Lady Ursla regarding Darless. She beamed appreciatively. Next, Jon outlined his ideas and suggested plan about Kagor and Caleb. Darless agreed that it might work and was eager to help.

"Give me until tomorrow morning to prepare Kagor for your visit. The approach that I will use is that the gods wish him to listen to your offer. Whatever he wants, play along with him. If things go bad, you can teleport away or I can get you out," suggested the alu-demon.

They discussed some further details. Then Darless left to begin the necessary groundwork of the plan. The trio waited and watched the hours drift by. Jon helped pass the time by playing his flute. Still, all grew quite bored.

At last, the next day's noon came. They held hands and Jon stepped them to the hill just before Rhones Tower, where they had been ambushed once before. This time, as before, they had no weapons drawn. Mandy did not like the idea at all.

Their arrival was expected. One hundred hobgoblins armed with spears surrounded the hill top. Several human fighters commanded them. Over a dozen magic users pointed wands and staves at them. Kagor stood triumphant, yet safely out of harm's way beside his tower. Darless was by his side.

Quickly, they were ushered into the central meeting hall within the red tower. Tapestries that depicted great battle victories elegantly decorated the room's walls. The furniture was spotless. Evidently, Kagor wanted to impress them.

They were seated at one end of the long table. Kagor sat in an elaborate throne at the opposite end. Darless stood at his right. At once, servants brought silver platters of roasted venison, rabbit, and quail along with bowls mounded with nearly fresh fruits. Others carried in baskets of brown bread and mugs of ale. Although no one was interested in eating, just now, Jon sipped the ale and found it surprisingly good.

Kagor began, "Welcome to Rhones Tower. I have desired to meet you again. You have been of considerable trouble to me. Still I have spared your lives more than once. Now I suspect that the gods have been using you. Ah, well. Such is life. Still, I am curious just what the gods want you to propose. As you can see, I am about ready to attack Mariane. Nevertheless, divine intervention must always be considered. What have you to offer?"

Jon began humbly, "We all realize that ultimately you wish wealth, fame, and respect — the latter, particularly from Mariane and the mariners. Such a deal I have for you. All these are yours for the taking, but it is not through attacking Mariane that such will come. Only death lies upon that path and I am sure that so great and powerful a mage as you have already considered this. However, there is a more certain and much quicker route to achieve all of your goals — not only getting the attention of your enemies but also causing them long term worry."

"That last bit intrigues me. I would have them squirm for eternity. Pray continue," Kagor insisted, pulling on his goatee.

"And so they shall, but only if you play your full hand. You have a trump that I am certain you are not aware of." Jon paused, giving the Mage time to wonder. Then, he continued, "Down in your mines you have it — the black, oily sludge."

"Bah, you jest with me. That stuff is utterly worthless!" shrieked Kagor, feeling that he had just been made a fool.

"Wait!" Jon commanded, raising his hand in protest. "I will tell you only one more word. Then, if you think that I still jest, you may slay us as we sit."

Mandy started to protest, obviously feeling that Jon had gone too far. Kagor seemed amused by her reactions and therefore decided to hear Jon out. He nodded his assent.

"Its true name is Liquid Fire," he spoke softly. He then was silent. Everything hinged upon Kagor realizing the significance of the discovery.

The mage looked thoughtful for a moment. A gleam appeared in his eye. Jon knew that he had him. Jon said, "So you recognize the magnitude of your find? That is excellent. May I continue?"

"Yes! Yes, by all means," Kagor exclaimed excitedly, pondering his potential wealth.

"Too bad that you did not made this discovery thirty years ago. Kalanos, the Great, would have paid a king's ransom for the smallest of quantities. Now he is gone."

Kagor's face fell. Jon hurriedly added, "But there is yet another mage who has had the foresight to not give up hope. He has been diligently searching for over thirty years for liquid fire. He has kept two of the great iron vessels free of rust and ready to sail. He lacks only what you have, liquid fire."

Jon watched as new hope returned to Kagor's face. The man was evil, no discounting that, and he cared for no one but himself. Nevertheless, he was a man and good may yet prevail. Jon refused to judge Kagor for all eternity. Mandy might, but he wouldn't.

Jon explained further, "Now I have personally discussed the possibility of a partnership with the ship owner. He will do most anything for the fuel that he needs. I suspect that you could talk your way into a fifty-fifty partnership with that mage — that is if you are a clever negotiator, which I'm sure you are. And one other detail that you may find useful in bargaining: he does not yet have an army. Don't get me wrong, I am sure that you would not be able to steal his ships from him. Even if you did, only that mage knows how to use them. He sailed with Kalanos himself. He will be a valuable ally. However, as you can see, you will need an army to protect your property from the competitors."

Kagor began laughing. It was one of relief, and it sounded more like a sickly, gleeful cackle. He was as cheerful and as excited as was possible for him. "I must meet this mage at once. When can it be arranged?"

"Soon. Actually, I had to restrain the mage. When he found out that someone actually had his precious liquid fire, he demanded to meet you right then. Unfortunately, I had other more pressing business to attend to at that time. Now the first thing I would do, if I were you, would be to collect a large supply to take along. Certainly, that mage will desire proof. Undoubtedly, he will want to try it out to see if it will work in the iron ships."

"Yes, yes, you are most intuitive. By tomorrow, I will be ready. But I have one question. What do you get out of all of this?"

Jon responded, "My price is a high one. Your payment will be your picture book of portals."

"Ah, your price is a steep one. You drive a hard bargain, Jon Brown. However, if this venture works out as you have said, then I will be wealthy enough to buy a hundred such books," Kagor declared.

"I will ask for payment only if the deal works out," Jon added, reassuringly.

Kagor smiled. "Agreed. As for now, you may stay here as my honored guests. I must see to the collection of that precious gold! Darless, you must hold the war temporarily. And see to it that my guests are made comfortable."

"As you wish, my lord," she replied, her voice cold and icy, just like it was when the trio had first met her. She played her role superbly.

Although they did not like the idea of spending the night in Kagor's tower, good manners and good faith dictated they should. They made the best of it. For the most part, they kept to their rooms. Naturally, Jon avoided saying much at all to Darless. Also, Alison explained that magic users usually have magical devices that permitted them to spy on guests and even overhear their conversations. Thus, they said little as well. Mandy grew quite bored. This intrigue stuff definitely was not to her liking. She preferred a straightforward battle for settling differences. However, she restrained herself and played along.

By morning, Kagor had about sixty gallons of the sludge ready to go. Next came the means of transportation. Neither Alison nor Kagor could transport that much weight with one spell. However, Jon estimated that he had enough energy to do it.

As they were ready to leave, Kagor announced, "Darless, I am leaving you in charge of my army. If I have not returned in say a week's time, you know how to bring me back. Also, launch our attack at Mariane at the same time."

"Yes, my lord," came the cold, emotionless reply.

Jon stepped the girls, Kagor, and the six containers of liquid fire to the outskirts of Kalanos City, as seen from the picture book. Earlier that morning Jon had mentally contacted Caleb to let him know of their arrival. Thus, Kagor saw a welcoming party. There were twenty guards and a number of Caleb's magic user trainees standing at attention. Robes flowing in the dry wind, Caleb eagerly rushed forward.

Jon did the introductions. Caleb ordered his guards to carry the precious kegs, while he graciously escorted the party inside the deserted, ghost city. The two men were like eager children at Christmas time.

For more than thirty years Kalanos City had been abandoned. The great Desolation Desert had slowly reclaimed the city. Everywhere, sands had seeped up the massive walls around the city. Most of the numerous buildings were made of adobe and were now in a sad state of decay. Many had crumbled. The actual palace, however, was constructed of stone. Here, Caleb had made his home. The palace proper had been carefully tended. Most of the original trimmings that had had any value had long ago been stripped away by the deserting population. Caleb had repaired much of the damage. Still, it was not a wealthy looking palace — just comfortable.

Throughout the city, there was much ironwork reminiscent of the "Gay Nineties." Most was heavily rusted. Inside the palace, ironworks were plentiful and in a fairly good state of repair. Jon began to wonder about who Kalanos really was.

The first action Caleb performed was verification that Kagor really brought the precious liquid fire for which Caleb was willing to sell his soul. Painstakingly, he compared a precious vial of his with the contents of one keg. Satisfied, he put a tiny quantity from the keg into a small bowl. He touched it with a burning splinter. It burned with lots of curling black smoke. Tears of joy were in Caleb's eyes. He had at long last found liquid fire. His life had not been in vain.

Kagor had been patiently and curiously watching Caleb. Now he asked, "I see that you are satisfied this is the real thing. I would like the same. Where are the two ships I was told you have? I would like to see one run."

"Yes, by all means," responded Caleb. "This way." He led them out of the palace and down a well-worn street to the docks and sea. It was a fantastic sight. Kalanos City in its prime could have hosted thirty giant iron ships at one time. Now their rusted hulks lined the shores, reddish flakes of a bygone era. It was spooky. The roar of the ocean waves breaking on the beach swelled in their ears. And there, looking fresh out of World War I, sat two steamship cruisers.

Both were shiny and appeared ready to sail. Heavy mooring lines fastened both to the docks. Caleb proudly pointed out their names, "I have saved Lucy and Lucky. Welcome aboard. This is truly a great day in the history of Kalanos City."

Quickly, Caleb's men brought the kegs onboard and emptied them into a huge holding tank. Meanwhile, Caleb took everyone on a guided tour of Lucky. Close up, Jon could see that Lucky had undergone many modifications from the original designs from the war. Most changes were to handle the low-grade sludge that they burned. Also, there were no guns. Jon felt like he was on a history tour, but the girls and Kagor were very impressed and asked numerous questions.

Caleb fired up the engines, but not in the way Jon expected. Rather than starting motors and the like, Caleb cast a spell of flames into the engine. The sludge erupted into flames.

"Most efficient," Jon proclaimed. The others looked at him queerly.

"How else would you start the fires?" queried Caleb wonderingly.

Jon shrugged his shoulders. Alison merely explained to her magic using associates, "He's from another world and they do things differently there."

"When do we sail?" interrupted Kagor, eager to see if this iron ship would actually sail.

"Just as soon as we build up some steam. It should not take more than an hour or two. You see, we usually never shut the engines down because of the long time that it takes to get them going again. Once we have sufficient fuel, we can leave the engines running. Then we can set sail any time we desire."

Time passed swiftly. They examined Lucky more closely. Kagor and Caleb discussed cargo capacities and the like. Then, Caleb blew the whistle. Steam shot skyward, and the shrill blast startled everyone.

The mooring lines were dropped. Caleb's entire staff lined the docks cheering them off. Caught up in the excitement, Jon waved back. He was enjoying this as well. For three hours, they sailed up and down the coast. Once they sighted a wooden ship from Mariane. Caleb let loose a huge blast of the whistle, challenging the mariners. They would have a tale to tell when they docked in Zaire!

At suppertime, Caleb ordered a great feast in honor of the day's events. Colorful green and red banners decorated the room. The long table was covered with an amber cloth. Although not wealthy, Caleb endeavored to show his finest. Golden trays, silver platters, golden candelabra, and platinum eating utensils gave the impression of a formal banquet. (Close scrutiny revealed that the platters were very scratched and dented, and the platinum-ware showed long years of use.) Musicians played on recorders and krumhorns, which Jon enjoyed immensely. Servants brought trays brimming with seven different kinds of seafood. Stewed vegetables were strangely spiced; the mead, warmed. However, the two mages spent most of the meal discussing plans. Jon did not interfere and amused himself by trying a bit of each dish. Secretly he wondered how long the goodwill would last. After all, Kagor was still a greedy, evil orientated man.

By evening, Kagor was ready to return home. So just after dark, Jon stepped the party back to Rhones Tower.

At once Kagor presented Jon with his copy of the picture book of portals, saying, "You have earned this. I have the better deal. This has cost me only one magical book. Yet my partner paid much more dearly. It cost him not only his book but also his soul!" Kagor laughed long and hard.

He explained his deal to the trio and Darless. "I did better than fifty-fifty," he sneered. "We are partners. We will share equally all expenses and all profits. Since Caleb wants to take care of the ships themselves, I get to manage the company and all of its finances!" Jon knew immediately what Kagor had in mind. He smiled.

The mage continued, "Darless, I'm terribly sorry, but the war is off. I hope that you will take this like the lady that you are. I do want revenge, but this is a more profitable way to do it. I know you had your heart set on smashing the mariners in combat, but I will need all of my men and army to protect our company — KC Shipping. You still can have the command of my men, if you will stay on with me. But we can talk about that later, in private," he added, leeringly.

Jon recoiled from the thought of this beast loving Darless. No wonder she hated summoning so passionately. He had an idea, but the time was not right.

The next day, Kagor ordered half of his forces to begin marching south toward Kalanos City. The other half was to be his garrison forces. He needed many more men to begin oil recovery operations. Jon was very pleased to hear that Kagor intended to get the men he needed by dissolving the huge northern armies. It would take several weeks to get this all straightened out, so Jon bid Kagor goodbye.

Nodding to Darless, Jon stepped the trio back to Kalanos City and the one remaining loose end there. They were expected when they arrived and Caleb readily presented Jon with his copy of the picture book of portals. He said, "I am in your debt as well as Dispater's. If you need anything, just let me know. I always repay my debts, so they cannot be used against me."

Jon acknowledged his offer, but Alison asked, "What are you going to do about Dispater? He still has a claim on you. Perhaps if you spoke to His Holiness, the Archdeacon, he could help you."

"Thanks. But my new partner has made some suggestions that I think might work."

Jon smiled and said, "Good luck, Caleb. And one piece of advice: watch out for Kagor. He has an evil streak in him."

"Thanks. That, I already know. But he can be used — if you know how."

Jon waved farewell and stepped them all back to the Church of Ukko, Zaire. When they had finished explaining the situation to Prince Reginald and Bard Wendell, they retired to their rooms.

Jon took Alison into his room. "These are yours." He presented her with the two copies of her family heirloom. Tears came into her eyes. Jon added, "I know how you must feel. It is fantastic to get them back, but it also means two more of your brothers and sisters probably have perished." She said nothing and he held her tightly for some time.

# Chapter 16 Morrigan

A week had passed since the two mages had agreed to form a shipping partnership. For Jon, Alison, and Mandy, there remained but one task — to deliver the special battle painting to the goddess of war, Morrigan. While time passed, Jon did nothing but watch Bard Wendell paint his enormous fresco. At last, Mandy could take the inactivity no longer.

"Jon, when are we going to try to give that painting to Morrigan and get this thing over with?" Mandy demanded impatiently.

"In due time, Mandy. Soon, say in two days," Jon replied casually.

"Why the big delay?" she insisted.

"Yes, why are we waiting?" Alison added. She was curious about his reasoning. Alison knew that Mandy had wanted to make the attempt upon their return from Kalanos City. Because Alison believed that it would certainly be difficult to personally contact a goddess, she had been quiet and patient.

"Timing. That's the key here," Jon offered. "Let me explain. I do not have the slightest idea of how to contact a god or goddess. I'm sure that one just doesn't walk out into the open and command the divine to appear before you. If the god was one that you worshiped, you could pray a lot, I suppose. Since Morrigan is not a god that I would worship, contact is even more difficult. So I figure that I need to first get her attention."

"So how do we get Morrigan's attention?" Mandy asked. She considered that contacting her goddess,

Reylona, was simplicity itself. But a foreign goddess — well, she could see that another approach was needed. And she was certain that one *did* have to get their attention. After all, Reylona had tens of thousands of worshipers, so she couldn't listen to everything each said every minute of the day!

"I see what Jon is doing," exclaimed Alison, as she finally understood the delay. "Morrigan is the goddess of war. She has been moving Trundle into a state of war for several years. Then, we come along and divert all of those men from battle to garrison forces and workers. It will take a little time for Morrigan to realize that her carefully prepared war will not occur — that the men are now doing something else." Then, she gasped, realizing their danger. "Oh, Jon. Is she ever going to be upset with us! When she finds out what we did, she'll be furious!"

"Yes, that is the only problem with my plan. I'm sure that if I were to ask Darless to try to contact Morrigan for us, we would have success — remember, Darless was originally Morrigan's assistant, albeit an enforced servant. I have been delaying just to ensure that Morrigan realizes that there will be no war for her edification. Hopefully, that will increase our chances that she will personally see us. Then I can give the painting to her and we are all done."

"Zagroot zounds! Is she going to be angry with us!" exclaimed Mandy, now that she fully understood. "What if there is divine retribution for meddling with the affairs of the gods? Morrigan might not take too kindly to our spoiling her private war. What if she demands something from us?"

"We'll just have to cross that bridge when we come to it," Jon proclaimed, nobly. Secretly, Jon wondered just how close Mandy had come to the truth.

Would Morrigan demand a price for their interference? He strongly suspected that that would be the case. However, he said nothing to avoid unnecessary worry for the girls.

In two days, Bard Wendell was putting the finishing touches on the fresco on the domed ceiling of the high chapel. Meantime, the trio had made their preparations for their last action delivering the painting to Morrigan. They were ready to go.

All hinged upon Darless and her ability to contact Morrigan. Hence, Jon began by locating the alu-demon. Using his mind, he searched for her. He was getting better with his telepathic abilities, and he had her unique mind and beingness located within a minute.

He remembered his embarrassment the last time he had tried to get in touch with her when he had made contact when she was bathing. She had said that he should somehow announce his coming before just establishing contact. He wondered how he could go about this. He could sense other minds on the room. *I suppose I could just listen in on the general conversation. Then, if everything is acceptable, I could contact her. But then am I guilty of eavesdropping? I have not been asked to listen in.* Now the voices faded away. He knew that he could have listened to what was going on, but had thought better of it. *I have it! Why not have her get the idea that I want to communicate — have her reach ever so slightly for me. I will have been invited.*

Jon was now getting quite good at placing an idea in another's mind. It was exactly like verbal conversation, but without all of the vias. To begin, he must have his attention on Darless, and hers on him, however slight. Then, instead of propelling words across a distance to her ears, he'd just have the idea appear behind her head, saving all of the trouble of her having to hear and then understand. He wondered why others did not find this a more convenient way to communicate. It saved time and reduced the possibility of misunderstanding. His idea was simply, "Jon would like a word with me now."

Darless thought, *Yes, that is a good idea. Jon, if you are aware, why not listen in for a moment.* Then, she continued talking to Kagor Dougal. She felt Jon's presence and a glow of warmth that she was not used to feeling spread over her. She stumbled over her words, but recovered at once. "Kagor — Kagor, you know that I cannot stay. I am serving Morrigan. She — she will want my services elsewhere. There is nothing that you or I can do about that. I have stayed too long as it is," she faltered. *I really despise you, you old bastard! But I dare not tell you that.*

Kagor proclaimed, "I have grown to want you, Darless. I shall find a way! One day, I will steal you away from Morrigan and have you all for myself."

Horrified, Jon realized that this was the closest that Kagor could come to saying "I love you." He had to possess his women, heart, soul, and body. Jon sent to Darless, *He'd probably put you in chains. I think that he is a sadistic bastard.*

Darless replied, *He would and is. He represents much of what I hate in humans. But then, demons are worse, Jon. Really, he is not so bad as my other relatives.* A wave of utter revulsion swept over Jon, but he realized that she was probably not exaggerating.

Jon watched through her eyes as she walked through the corridors of the tower to her room. He could not think of any words with which to comfort the alu-demon, so he said nothing, but watched her. She gathered her few meager belongings and stuffed them into a small pack. She paused by a jewelry box. She sent to Jon, *See, he is not all bad. He gave these to me over the years.* She opened the box to reveal numerous gems, bracelets, and necklaces with which Kagor had attempted to buy her love. There was a small fortune in the box.

*I guess it is some compensation for your aid.* Jon sent. *No, I will leave them all. I want nothing to endear or obligate myself to Kagor.* She shut the box and left it on the dresser. *I'm ready to go. What do you want, Jon?*

*Can we meet — say somewhere on the plains of Trundle, where there aren't any prying eyes?*

She sent him a good mental picture of a small, isolated, pond and marsh. She teleported herself there while Jon, likewise, stepped the trio there. When they arrived, Darless gave Jon an embarrassingly strong kiss of welcome and a hug. Then, she greeted the women. Darless felt obligated to tell her friends what had just happened. Then, Jon explained what they needed her to do.

"Oh no. She is furious with you. I do not think that it is a good idea to summon her just now. If you wait a few months, I'm sure that she will have found another battle to monitor and will have completely forgotten this loss," she explained, trying to save her friends from the horrible wrath of the provoked goddess.

"But we do not have that much time," Alison pleaded. She explained again their pact with Dispater.

"Well, I tried to warn you," Darless proclaimed, as if that would lessen her responsibility in the matter. She knew that it didn't and couldn't. But, Darless felt that she had to at least warn them. "Morrigan is not a magic user type of god. She seems almost immune to spells, although she does have and use all the godlike spells. She can teleport anywhere at will, grant wishes, and so on. She is similar to you in many ways, Mandy. She is a powerful ranger and druid. She fights like a titan. She is physically the strongest being I have ever met! So do not cross her. She is also an assassin by training. Beware, she can and has slain foes with one strike. I have warned you. Now I'll get in touch with her. What do you want me to say?"

Jon thought for a moment. He knew that this was crucial. He had to see her personally. "Tell her that I have an appeasing offering for her."

"As you wish, Jon." Darless closed her eyes. Jon felt her mind expanding, searching, roaming. Suddenly, her mind was closed to him. Someone had powerfully blocked him out. Jon became a bit nervous. There was a blinding flash of magical energies and Morrigan herself floated down to the ground.

Jon's stomach turned. He fought the impulse to vomit. He had left his mind expanded, encompassing all three of the girls. Instantly, he felt their mental and physical reactions as well. It was an overwhelming blur of conflicting emotions and sensations. Jon dropped his expanded awareness rapidly, and now tried to handle his own reactions. He forced himself to swallow to override the sickening feeling that had swelled up.

He now knew why she was the goddess of war. He also knew that she was not evil in nature, just horribly perverted. Morrigan was the ugliest woman that Jon had ever seen. She was well built with a large bosom. Yet, she had a most hideous face. Her welted skin was dark gray and clung tightly to the bone. There was no flesh or muscle tissue under the skin on her face giving her the look of some ghastly skeletal creation.

For an instant, his courage drained completely and he felt like fleeing in utter panic. Both Alison and Mandy had similar reactions. He realized that lesser men would have indeed fled in terror from this goddess. Yet, it passed. While facially, she was unbelievably ugly, her torso and arms were extremely strong. Her muscles rippled. She carried two glowing spears; one had a red tip, the other, a yellow tip. He wondered what the significance was.

Coldly, Darless said, "These are they — the ones who have stopped the war. Jon says that he has an offering for you." She stepped back and out of the way.

"Thank you Darless. By our agreement, you are now freed. You have been most helpful. I will remember that. You may go now." Darless humbly said, "Thank you, your grace." She left and walked up and out of the little valley with the marsh and pond. Once out of sight, she hid in the grass and watched. She had to know what fate befell her new friends.

"So you are the meddlers! How dare you interfere with the plans of the gods! I should slay you all as you stand. But, no. I have given this considerable thought, Jon Brown. Ever since I discovered that you had spoiled a carefully devised war, I have been thinking of my retaliation. Mortals must be taught respect for the gods. When the gods are offered great sacrifices by their worshipers for some service, some aid, and the gods agree to fulfill that request, mortals cannot be allowed to destroy what the gods create. Know you that Lady Ursla, at great sacrifice, requested this war. I cannot let mere mortals defile and belittle her sacrifice. What would other worshipers say? Morrigan may not succeed! A goddess may not succeed! Ha!" She laughed disgustedly. Her anger was steadily rising.

"You see, I cannot let you go unpunished. Certainly not I, Morrigan, the Goddess of War!"

"Wait," Jon interrupted. "There is one thing that you must know. Lady Ursla had changed her mind. That must count. Yes, at one time she desired this war. Later, she had a change of viewpoint. Did she not tell you that she wished the war halted? That lets you off the hook, so to speak."

"Yes, I heard that soft-hearted woman. She does not know her own mind — just became cowardly, that's all. On the field of battle, I usually slay cowards instantly. But lucky for her, she was not. Since she did pray and sacrifice to me for this war, it would not be honorable for me to slay the hand that requested the service in the first place. I have spared her. But you are another matter. I wanted a war. And I will have a fight!" She screamed in anger.

Jon retorted, "I know you. You get your power from battles, from fighting, killing, and slaying. Without war, you are powerless. Other gods get power from the prayers of their worshipers. However, who will pray to you if there is no war about to begin? Peace is your most hated foe. No, we will not fight you. You'll get no power from us. I came only to give you an offering, nothing more."

"You will fight — fight for me!" she shrieked, violently angry.

*Jon! We cannot fight a god!* Mandy worriedly sent him. *She is immune to Alison's spells. If she is as powerful a fighter as Darless said, if I fight her, I may cause a few wounds, but she will surely kill me rapidly. Your mental powers will be useless against a goddess! Reylona help us!*

Jon knew that she was completely correct. He also knew that Alison was thinking the same things.

277

Alison thought, *We are helpless. There is no chance that we could successfully fight Morrigan. None at all, I'm absolutely certain. Every one of my abilities is completely useless. No spell I can cast will affect her. I might hit her once with my staff, but what is a bump on her head compared to my death in return? So if this goddess forces us to battle her, we will all perish. This must be Morrigan's retribution for meddling in her affairs. I have never felt so utterly helpless in my whole — no, just once before, when I was three, when the raiders destroyed my home and slaughtered my family. And now Jon is about to be taken from me. He's the first person that I have ever truly trusted — no Alison, be truthful, the first man that you have loved. All others you have hated and loathed or at best tolerated. I must do something, but what?*

Mandy sent to Jon, *I will fight to the death, Jon. Just say the word.* Then, she thought to herself, *May Reylona protect me and guard my soul. Hum, I wonder what a soul really is?*

"Fight me, Jon Brown, fight!" commanded the enraged Morrigan.

"No way," Jon said softly. "I will not give you power. I do not worship you. I will not make you stronger."

"Fight! I command you!" shrieked the goddess of war. Magic energy flashed with her words.

Jon felt an uncontrollable urge to strike out, to attack this ugly creature. Knowing that it was her command and not his desire, he resisted and the sensation passed.

"Coward! Die then!" She hurled the red tipped spear straight for his heart.

Jon watched the rapidly hurled spear fly at him as though it were in slow motion. He knew that he was not fast enough to dodge out of the way. He knew that the tip would pierce his heart. She had commanded it so. Three things bothered him. Neither was the fact that he was about to die. First was that he did not worship any god or goddess. While he did believe in the Lord himself as the supreme creator, he had no real faith or solid belief that the universe and man's creator even knew he existed or cared. Second was that he had failed in his self-appointed mission. He had failed the girls as well. Then he began to wonder to whom do these gods and goddesses report? Who was the higher authority? He began to lament the fact that he'd never find out.

At the last instant, Alison knew that she had only one thing left that she could give — her life. Without a thought, she threw her body in front of Jon's. The spear pierced her heart. Horrified beyond words, Jon caught and held onto her body as she collapsed. Morrigan pulled back her spear and Alison's life gushed out.

"Alison! Alison!" Jon screamed.

She whispered her last words to him, "Do not fight her," and died in his arms.

"You filthy bitch! Swine! May Satan take you to Hell!" cursed Mandy, drawing her sword.

"Hold! Mandy. Don't do it," Jon begged, tears were blinding his vision, but he heard her steel drawn. "Don't give her power!"

Mandy poised, readied the strike, and then held back. At last, she lowered her weapon. "You filthy pig!" she spat on the ground.

"Fight me! Or do I have to slay your other woman as well? Fight me, Jon Brown!" Morrigan cried out. She could taste the blood. It felt delicious. She craved the odor, the taste, the raw emotions.

Just to Jon's left, there came a flash of magical energy.

A voice sweetly called out, "Did someone call for me?"

An icy chill spread over Jon. He did not need to look to know who had arrived.

Morrigan called out in alarm, "Dispater! What do you want?"

Jon realized that this time he did not have to protect himself from that chill of death. Neither did Mandy. Evidently, Dispater wanted them to have freedom of action.

"I have come. I see that I may now have one of your beautiful women, Jon Brown."

"Never!" chorused Jon and Mandy.

"I see. Are you ready to make a deal? You see that you cannot defeat Morrigan by yourselves. I am here. I can torment her, torture her, make her pay for slaying dear, helpless, Alison here. Wouldn't that make you feel so much better? And didn't I just hear you, Mandy, desire that I take Morrigan to Hell? Or was that your wish, Jon Brown?"

Mandy's face reddened. She mumbled, "Well, I did say that, but I meant it figuratively. I make no bargain with you. Attack her if you like."

"Oh, I'm certain you would like that, Mandy dearest, but then Morrigan would not like that, would you? No, I thought not. So you see, I must be paid. Are you now ready to pay me, Jon Brown?"

Jon had been watching Morrigan's reactions. He saw that she was most concerned. Evidently, she knew Dispater's power and feared it. Or at least she had a healthy respect for it. Jon noticed that her blood lust had evaporated, that she was no longer angry. He replied, "Not just yet, Dispater." To Morrigan, he said, "All that I wanted to do was to give you this painting, nothing more. Will you now take it, Morrigan?" He held the painting out toward her. From her angle of view, she could see that it depicted some kind of battle.

This roused her curiosity. Morrigan reached out for it. Jon waited patiently, one arm holding onto Alison, the other, outstretched with the painting. Mandy, feeling awfully small and weak, laid her hand onto Jon's shoulder.

The instant that Morrigan touched the painting, Jon acted. He immediately recalled the fresco in the Church of Ukko and stepped into it.

There was a flash of magical energies, and Jon found himself in a strange land. The ground was more like soft, billowing clouds. Somehow his feet felt as if they were on solid ground even though clouds pillowed about his feet. The place radiated a tremendous feeling of warmth and goodness. Another time, Jon would have called this place truly inspirational. He felt power flowing through him. A perceptible instant later, he watched Dispater arrive. The devil had no intention of leaving just yet — not when he had a chance to get three prized souls. However, this place actually seemed to cause him great pain. Morrigan looked around in horror. Evidently, she recognized this place. She cringed visibly. This was not at all to her liking.

Jon realized that it was the nature of this realm that was causing Dispater to ache so and Morrigan to be worried. Perhaps there is hope yet, he thought.

Suddenly, twenty air maidens floated down from the cloud filled sky. Graceful wings set them gently on the cloudlike ground. They spoke not a word, nor did they draw their swords. They watched.

Jon said, "Check."

Dispater understood. Morrigan did not, until the Arch-devil sent her a mental picture. She grimaced and sneered. Dispater spoke. "Now what, Jon Brown?"

"It is done. I have fulfilled our bargain. You have no claim on me or my friends. You may go," Jon bravely said. "Morrigan, now if you must, you may slay me. But I will not fight you."

Then a deep, commanding voice rolled through the clouds. "Hold all of you. Dispater, you are not welcome here. Can you not see that you will not get these souls? Morrigan, you have made a grave error. You know, as well as I do, that Alison d'Ambrose has not yet fulfilled her destiny. It is not her time to die. Neither is it time for Jon Brown. You have committed an even more grievous mistake. You have failed to honor the wishes of Lady Ursla in this matter. You have brought a measure of disgrace to all of us. Go now, and make amends."

Morrigan looked more sober than Jon had ever seen. She was clearly very upset. "You are right, of course." And she disappeared in a flash of magical energies.

"There will be another time, Jon Brown. I look forward to our next meeting with great pleasure! Until then," Dispater bowed, even though Jon saw that he was in great pain. Then, he left as Morrigan had done. Jon was left alone with Mandy and the lifeless form of Alison in his hands.

An air maiden came over to Jon and touched Alison's body. The voice spoke, "Arise. Arise Alison d'Ambrose. Arise in the name of Ukko. By your action, you have brought great honor to your father and to me." A blue energy arced over her body. The wound in her chest closed and skin reformed. Her eyelids fluttered and then opened. Tears of joy flowed from both Jon's and Mandy's eyes.

"Am I in heaven? Are we all here together?" asked Alison, weakly.

Between sobs, Jon said, "We're together. We're alive, and you are too." He held her tightly.

The voice of Ukko spoke once more. "Be it known that from this day forth, in the lands of Rochelle, you shall now be called Saint Jon. Go now. The air maidens will lead the way. All has been prepared." Three air maidens floated over to the trio.

"Wait, Ukko," called out Jon. "Am — am I supposed to worship you now? There are many things that I do not understand."

The voice spoke, "I cannot tell you whom you are to worship, my son. As you have so correctly observed, Gods get power from the faith of their worshipers. Faith is not something that can be asked for or given. You must find that faith in yourself. Go now. Seek your destiny. This much I will tell you, I am not that for which you seek. Do not worry; Morrigan will not further bother you. Go now."

An air maiden took each one of them by the hand. As one group, they stepped forward. Yet to Jon, it seemed that they were flying down toward a tiny speck that was Zaire. Now he could see the beautiful irises and statues of the gardens in front of the Church of Ukko far below growing larger now as they descended. Thousands of people were gathered below and all eyes were upon the air maidens and the party. Evidently, Ukko had told them of their arrival.

The air maidens set them down gently beside an iris patch and the awaiting Archdeacon, Prince Reginald. Bard Wendell stood to his right. Tears of joy streamed from their eyes. Into that absolute silence, one air maiden spoke. "We return Saint Jon Brown to you, your Holiness." Then, they rose into the air and were gone.

Amid the cheers of the crowd, the Archdeacon led the trio inside the Church of Ukko. From this day onward, the 14$^{th}$ of July became a day of great and holy celebrations in the land of Zaire.

# Chapter 17 Farewells

Alison was confused. She remembered diving in front of Jon to save his life. She had hoped that it would somehow make a difference. She remembered how great the effort had been for her to whisper, "Do not fight her." The reality of death stunned her. Now somehow she was alive and well once more. Air maidens had brought them back to the Church of Ukko. They were saying something about Jon being a Saint. She did not understand what could possibly have happened. She felt most out of place.

The Archdeacon, Prince Reginald Noxwood, graciously ushered the trio into his gilded audience room. Memories of their first meeting with the Archdeacon in this very room came unbidden into her mind. However, this time they were given places of high importance beside the high priest. The three were seated upon gilded chairs with royal crimson and plush velvet cushions. At once, refreshments were brought, but Alison did not feel like eating. She felt weak, tired, and thirsty, but most of all confused.

Only after every imaginable comfort had been offered to the trio did the questioning begin. By this time, the various subordinate priests had filed into the rear of the audience chamber sitting quietly in the rear of the room. His Holiness sat on his throne with Bard Wendell beside him; the trio was in a semicircle to his left.

Reginald began, "Saint Jon, your Holiness, your humble servants eagerly await your report. Obviously, the simple matter of delivering a painting became more than that. You must know that approximately five minutes before the three air maidens brought you down from the sky, a solitary maiden came unto us saying, 'Prepare yea to receive Saint Jon Brown in the gardens.' Then she rose into the sky. As you are aware, we have not had a visit from the air maidens since the dark ages, forty years ago. Today, four have come. It is a holy day. Tell us so that we may properly honor both the events of the day and yourselves."

"It wasn't much," Jon began softly and humbly, trying to find a way to explain what had happened. He saw Alison was particularly eager to know what had happened. Carefully, Jon described their encounter with Morrigan. Tears flooded into his eyes as he explained how Alison had died protecting him. When he told of Dispater's appearance, there was a reaction of surprise and dismay among the priests. Jon told them how he had transported Morrigan to the realm of Ukko, although he did not say how he did that. Bard Wendell's eyebrows rose. Jon knew that the Bard would probably go there soon, just to check it out. At last, Jon told of the intervention of Ukko.

The round of applause and praise tended to overwhelm Jon. He was unused to praise except for his musical playing. He quickly pointed out that if it had not been for Alison's supreme sacrifice, none of this would have resulted. He would have been dead. Now it was her turn to get the flow of admiration and respect. She could not handle it any better than Jon. At long last, the interview was over and the trio was escorted back to their rooms.

Mandy was exhausted. She gave Jon a kiss of thanks and went to bed at once. Alison was even more tired and fatigued, but she wanted to talk to Jon; and he, her.

"I do not know how to thank you for saving my life," Jon faltered, "I — I can find no words."

"It was the only thing that I could give you, Jon," she meekly replied. "I had to do something. I am so — so — proud of you, Jon — but that's not the right word either. And how do I ever thank you for giving me back my life?"

"You gave me your life, Alison. I somehow managed to give you life back," Jon quietly explained.

"What I mean," broke in Alison softly, "is that I admire you and I respect you — more — more than any other man I have ever met!" Her face flushed. "I love you." Before Jon could reply, she hastily returned to her room. *There. I have said it. I didn't think that I could do it, but it's done. I told him. Do I dare hope?* She was so tired that she just collapsed onto her bed into a deep sleep. She did not know that Jon had followed her into her room. She did not know that he tenderly undressed her and tucked her into bed. She did not hear him softly whisper into her ear.

Morning came. Bright light filtered through the stained glass windows. Alison felt alive — more alive than she had in years. Something had changed, but she did not know what. She discovered that she had been somehow undressed and put to bed, but she could not recall doing it herself. From her appearance, she realized that she had not done it and wondered who had. Her face flushed at the only thought that came. Then she heard the noises of eating from Jon's room. She dressed and joined Mandy and Jon. She was starved.

"Hi," called out a bubbly Mandy. "You look terrific, Alison. The sleep did wonders. Congratulations. We did it. Now we can all go home."

They all ate well and discussed their plans. But somehow, the thought that it was all over, sobered both Alison and Jon.

"There is one unfinished thing that I must do," Jon began.

"Wait. All of the tasks are done," interrupted Mandy. "We've handled Lady Ursla; the two mages are content; the war is over; Morrigan has her painting. What else is there?"

"Darless," said Jon softly. "She has done much for us with no thought of payment or even acknowledgment. I will do yet one thing for her, if I can find her."

Her curiosity roused, Alison asked, "What? Morrigan has released her from the summons."

Humbly, Jon said, "I know who she is. I intend to give her her real name. She shall not be summoned again." He said no more, but both girls wondered what he was talking about. All that they could get out of him was that he knew her last name, and it was not what she had been calling herself.

After breakfast, the Archdeacon came to ask if Jon would consider playing that fantasia for the noon high mass. Jon was delighted with the prospect and the group spent the morning bathing and getting themselves ready to leave Zaire. Jon promised that once the mass was finished, they would leave.

Noon came. The high altar room was jammed with worshipers. Jon knew that this day would be long remembered in Zaire. He had even agreed to don some priestly garments offered by His Holiness. He should look the part, Reginald had insisted. (He wore a long, white, cotton alb underneath a magnificent wide sleeved dalmatic, made of cardinal red velvet with a white ermine lining.) The girls wore their elegant gowns and Jon played.

The room was absolutely silent when he began. His notes echoed and resounded from the domed ceiling far above. When he had finished, tears of joy and happiness flowed from up lifted eyes. Even Bard Wendell was deeply moved. He had painted perhaps his life's best work. He now realized it. Then it was over.

Back in their rooms for the last time, the trio changed into their traveling clothes once more. Bard Wendell came to say farewell.

Alison cornered him. "I have a few questions for you. It's about my family's books that you painted." Jon moved close, for he wanted to hear as well.

"I know that sometimes disasters can befall an area. I know that once a cliff slumped, wiping out one trident. That picture then went black in the book. Are those permanently lost? Jon has suggested that if the tridents are replaced that the pictures will return."

"Yes, time can change the pictures that way. I have no ideas about whether they can be brought back. You seem to have more information on that than I do."

She got out one of her books. "See, at least a quarter of the pages are black." She leafed through the book. Suddenly, she screamed, quite startled. One blank page now was of the high altar room!

"That's my little surprise," Bard Wendell replied. "It's my way of thanking you for all that you did for me."

"I do not understand," broke in Jon. "How did you do that? Did you borrow a book and paint it while we were away?"

"No. When I painted that set, I left a number pages blank but still attuned to my master pages. I can and have added pictures over the years. However, when I learned that Castle d'Ambrose was sacked and your family slain, I stopped doing so. Now I will, from time to time, paint some more additions." She was so pleased that she kissed him in thanks.

"I have one question, Bard, how many pictures are now blacked out?" Jon asked, his interest roused.

Wendell examined the book carefully. Jon told him that they had temporarily blacked out two pictures. The Bard replied that ten other pictures were not there any longer. One of these, Alison knew about. But what were the other nine? Unfortunately, he could not remember just what they were. Too much time had passed.

"By the way, Jon," Bard Wendell said, "I have a hunch about that painting you gave to Morrigan. I have given it considerable thought. I think it is a trap, just like Caleb's paper forest. I think that Dispater is trying to settle an old score with Morrigan."

They could talk no further for His Holiness came in to bid them goodbye. He presented both Alison and Mandy identical, gem encrusted necklaces as a token of his appreciation. Later, they were to discover that each was worth one hundred thousand gold coins!

He presented Jon with a beautiful amulet. "Please accept this as a token of our gratitude. It is a magical device." Jon's eyes opened wide.

"We knew that both Mandy and Alison had magical items appropriate to their fields of endeavor. On the other hand, you are a stranger — you have none. I had my sages research what would best serve your needs. They decided upon this — an amulet of life protection. It will protect you from possession and prevent your mind from being blasted or crushed by other mental opponents. May it serve you well."

Jon thanked him heartily. Then, they said their farewells. Jon did promise to return for a visit. Bard

Wendell told him that he could see his next work at that time — a portrait of Saint Jon and the air maidens. Jon grew embarrassed once more. They left and walked out into the royal gardens.

"Where to now?" wondered Mandy. "Where is Darless?"

Jon mentally searched for her. "She's right where I suspected she would be," Jon replied in a moment.

"Let me guess," put in Alison. After a brief pause, she suggested, "With Lady Ursla?" "You got it. Here we go." Jon stepped them before the cabin in Hollybine Wood.

After a warm reunion, Jon explained all that had happened. Darless had seen them disappear and thought that they had all been captured by Dispater or worse. Thus, both Darless and Lady Ursla were very happy to see them alive and well.

Finally, Jon said, "Now for the real reason for our visit." The two looked intrigued. Jon proclaimed, "Darless, I am going to give you your true name."

"But you and I both know what it is," she replied in confusion. She looked helplessly at Lady Ursla.

The druid asked, "Do you want your friends and I to wait outside? The fewer that know her true name the better. I have grown to love her as the daughter that I never could have. I do not want to see her subjected to any further disgraces!"

"No. I trust my friends with my life and you Lady Ursla are involved. You should know the truth. Darless, no longer must you use only your father's first name. From now on, you can use his last name like the rest of us. It will be known only to the five of us."

The alu-demon held her breath in anticipation. This had never happened to her before. She was about to receive the greatest act of kindness anyone had ever given her.

Jon said, "You are really Darless Thornapple Dogoroth."

Lady Ursla fainted.

Alison caught her and they all helped the older woman to her couch. Darless revived her. She began to cry, beckoning for Darless. Darless hugged the druid closely, but did not understand.

Jon spoke softly, "Darless, Hugo Thornapple was Lady Ursla's husband."

Then Darless began to cry too.

Sometime later, when Lady Ursla had regained her composure as well as Darless, she said, "I never have spoken much of Hugo. We were so much in love. But I could not have children. Then after fifteen of the happiest years of my life, Hugo left, saying that he had to have a child. He promised to return later, but never did. Often, Hugo would tell me that no human could ever bear his child except me. He was so loyal. I felt like I had betrayed him. Yet, I could do nothing about it." And she cried some more.

Darless, sobbing as much as the druid, continued Hugo's tale, telling her about Myleen Dogoroth, the succubus. Both cried when she told how he had died. Lady Ursla was grateful that Darless had slain her mother who had murdered Hugo. Darless then added, "No wonder you are so like the mother I so dearly wanted. You and Hugo are so very much alike." They hugged each other and cried some more.

Lady Ursla begged, "Stay with me always, daughter."

"I will never leave you, mother," replied Darless.

After a moment, Darless gently held Jon's hands in hers. She said softly, "Jon, I can never thank you enough for all that you have done for me. How can I ever repay you?"

Having no ideas at all, Jon shrugged his shoulders rather embarrassedly. However, her touch tingled his body, causing numerous and not unwanted reactions. He flushed.

She sent him mentally, *I should cherish mating with you some day — if you would have me.* Now both flushed. She gazed expectantly into his eyes. Jon was on the spot.

He sent, *I like you very much, Darless. It would be an honor for me, but I am not ready for that just yet. For me, it would mean a lifelong commitment. Perhaps, one day. For now, please be my friend.*

She replied, *I understand.* Tenderly, she kissed him. Jon was no longer red faced. Although both girls were curious about what had passed between Jon and Darless, neither ever spoke of it.

Then, promising to return for a visit, the trio departed. Jon stepped them to the hillside beside the Rothwood Castle, where Jon had hidden the trident to protect the castle.

While Mandy removed the stones covering the trident, Alison kissed Jon on the cheek and said, "That was one the nicest things that I have ever seen anyone do, Jon. You literally gave both of them renewed life! I'm so proud of you!" She kissed him again on the cheek. Jon reddened noticeably. Alison didn't notice. She was a bit self-conscious and was wondering what had passed between Darless and Jon.

"Hey, don't I get a chance?" interrupted Mandy. "That was really nice, Jon. You are one terrific guy." She gave him a most passionate kiss. Jon's face turned beet red. He couldn't speak.

Alison did for him. "Ok. Let's go tell the Lord of Rothwood Castle, Sir Giles Grescham, that all is well." Jon welcomed the idea. They did so and were heartily congratulated.

When they had left the castle, Jon said that the next stop was the village of Brunsway. Jon wanted to replace the chiseled out trident. By afternoon, workers had carved a sufficiently good trident that the picture reappeared in Alison's books. She was quite pleased.

At last, Jon said, "Well, that is everything. I — I guess that you'll be wanting to head home, Mandy." He did not want to part from his two very dear friends.

Mandy said, "I'm ready, but I'm not such a hot shot as you two are. I got here very carefully. The only way I'm certain I can get back is to back out of the picture that I was looking at when I came. It was back at Stilmar Pond."

Jon was relieved. It took them an hour to stroll to Stilmar Pond. They talked incessantly all the way there. Jon told them that one day soon he had to return to visit with Sir Wayne and learn more about his grandfather's deeds. The girls agreed. They talked on. No one really wanted to part. At last they reached the pond and the swans. Mandy had to go.

"Only one problem, Alison," Mandy began, as she got her copy of the book out to return home. "The only way I can return home is with the book. If Reylona wishes me to return it, what do I do? How do I get it to you and get back home?" She was perplexed.

"If Reylona wishes it to be returned, then you keep it for me. I wish you to hang onto it for now. I dearly want to stay in touch with you, Mandy. You have become a very dear friend of mine. Come and visit me often," begged Alison.

"Thanks. And I do so want you both to come and see my castle. You would like it, Jon. Blackthorn Castle is a first rate castle! Come visit when you can."

"Yes, but how do we get to your place," wondered Jon.

Mandy showed them the picture of The Gnarled Oaks Wood that Kagor's men had used to visit her world and desecrate the forest. "Blackthorn Castle is about twenty miles due south of there. Just ask. Everyone knows me and will direct you. But *do* come. I love you two," she energetically proclaimed.

Then she turned to Jon. "You know, don't you, that I really like you. I would cherish going to bed with you any time night or day." Jon's face became the reddest Alison had ever seen it. Mandy added, "But I know that you have some hang-ups. Why don't you just get them solved and then come see me? Or even better, just come see me?"

Jon knew that he could not possibly speak, so he kissed her. Mandy kissed Alison farewell and returned to her own world. "There's goes one fine woman," Jon finally managed to say.

Alison stared at the ground, "Yes. She sure is. You — you know she would be — be good for you, don't you?" There, she said it. Relief came. She had been honest with herself, after all, and she fought hard to hold back a tear that had formed.

"Got a cracker?" appeared in both Alison's and Jon's minds. Startled, they turned around and there were the two swans, begging for food.

"Two leggers not come for long time. Got any crackers?" asked the male.

Both laughed. Their tensions melted. They rummaged in their packs and found something suitable. Together they spent an hour laying in the warm grass and feeding the swans. They did not say much. Jon just held her hand. She treasured the moment and wished that it would never end.

By late afternoon, Alison realized that she must leave as well or she might never be able to do so. "Jon, I want very much for you to have your copy of the book. Hang onto it. Let's keep in touch. I remember your code with the flags."

"Thanks, Alison. But do you have to go just now? Can't — can't we talk more?" he pleaded. She could not move, even if she had wanted to.

After a pause, Jon tried to speak, "Alison — I — I love you." His face reddened once more. He had to tell her now or forget it and he could not forget her. He struggled for words, "I — I've got my problems, hang—ups as Mandy says. I'm just very awkward around you beautiful women. What I mean is — I — no — well, I don't want to leave you. I want to be with you forever. I love you, Alison." They hugged each other for some time.

Pleadingly, Jon looked into her eyes, "Do you think that we've got a chance? There are *so* many problems, I mean. I am not even from this or your world. I do not know where I belong. How can I belong to two worlds at the same time? You have never seen my world — it is so very, very different from anything here. It would be hard for you to live in mine. Magic may not even work there."

"Are you really sure about me?" she dared to ask. "I mean Mandy is so much more beautiful than I am. Darless is so very special — " Jon did not let her finish. He kissed her so passionately that she turned as red as he was.

At last, she said, "I'll try hard, if you'll try hard."

"Let's give it a chance. I've only seen a small part of your world. I should see it all and you should see mine — see if you can manage it somehow. Don't forget, I still have to help you recover the two remaining books. So if we can work things out — if we can, dearest Alison, will you — will you marry me?"

"If things work out, Jon, oh yes!" Her lips touched his, and their arms entwined their bodies.

At sunset, Alison finally departed for her home. Jon had promised to come to see her as soon as he had handled a few errands in his world. He watched her go and wished with all of his heart that he could just forget everything and follow her. Yet, something inside of him called him home. He knew that he had to go back to his home world. Tears of longing were in his eyes as he stepped back into his room in the hot apartment above the Laundromat on Green Street.

The End.

# Other Books by Vic Broquard

The Trident Series: (fantasy)
Volume 1 The Trident and the Book
Volume 2 The Trident and the Scepter
Volume 3 The Trident and the Resurrection

Without Warning (fantasy)

The Adventures of Elizabeth Stanton Series: (science fiction)
Volume 1 The Evolution of the Path
Volume 2 The Great Messiah
Volume 3 Of Kings and Queens and Troubadours
Volume 4 Chaos in the Aftermath
Volume 5 Power Plays
Volume 6 Age of Exploration
Volume 7 Abducted
Volume 8 The Emperor and Empress
Volume 9 A Job Worth Doing
Volume 10 Degradation
Volume 11 The Second Crusade
Volume 12 When Worlds Collide
Volume 13 Dark Ages

The Lindsey Barron Series: (fantasy)
Volume 1 The Rod of the Apocalypse
Volume 2 The Board of Governors
Volume 3 The Crown of Moses
Volume 4 Dominus for President
Volume 5 The National Health Care Program
Volume 6 States Justice
Volume 7 Cross and Double-cross

Zoran Chronicles Series: (fantasy)
    Volume 1 A Dragon in Our Town
    Volume 2 Dragons, Power, Courts, and War

Planet of the Orange-red Sun Series: (science fiction)
    Volume 1 When Kingdoms Fall
    Volume 2 Dark Ages
    Volume 3 Age of the Towers
    Volume 4 Difficillis Exitus
    Volume 5 Age of the Lords
    Volume 6 The Renegade Tower
    Volume 7 Rebellions
    Volume 8 The Aliens Return
    Volume 9 Power Struggles
    Volume 10 Guilds, Genetics, and Gods
    Volume 11 Magi, Witches, Swords, and Superstitions
    Volume 12 The Voyage of the Eagle's Seed
    Volume 13 Justifications
    Volume 14 Responsibilities

The Return of the Wizards: Twelve Companions – The Making of Wizards (fantasy)